"I hope you're not going to apologize for that kiss, because I sure as hell won't."

Oh, he was dangerous. His voice was soft, as much as a caress as his kiss had been. Sunshine gleamed from his spiky black lashes and warmed the startling blue of his eyes with flecks of gold. Hayley wanted to lean forward and lick the moisture that slicked his lips. "I didn't plan any of this."

"Too bad. This̶ e̶ had."

"I didn't mean t̶—"

"That you're a j̶ a̶n̶? Or that you wanted to kiss me?"

"Neither." She struggled to focus her thoughts. "Can we just move on? This isn't why I came to see you today, Cooper. I thought we already established that."

"Yeah, I know." He sighed, rocked back on his heels and rose to his feet. His gaze flicked downward. "But the way you look, you're making it hard to remember."

Dear Reader,

Make way for spring—and room on your shelf for six must-reads from Silhouette Intimate Moments! Justine Davis bursts onto the scene with another page-turner from her miniseries REDSTONE, INCORPORATED. In *Second-Chance Hero*, a struggling single mother finds herself in danger, having to confront past demons and the man who haunts her waking dreams. Gifted storyteller Ingrid Weaver delights us with *The Angel and the Outlaw*, which begins her miniseries PAYBACK. Here, a rifle-wielding heroine does more than seek revenge—she dazzles a hot-blooded hero into joining her on her mission. Don't miss it!

Can the enemy's daughter seduce a sexy and hardened soldier? Find out in Cindy Dees's latest CHARLIE SQUAD romance, *Her Secret Agent Man*. In Frances Housden's *Stranded with a Stranger*, part of her INTERNATIONAL AFFAIRS miniseries, a determined heroine investigates her sister's murder by tackling Mount Everest and its brutal challenges. Will her charismatic guide be the key to solving this gripping mystery?

You'll get swept away by Margaret Carter's *Embracing Darkness*, about a heart-stopping vampire whose torment is falling for a woman he can't have. Will these two forbidden lovers overcome the limits of mortality—not to mention a cold-blooded killer's treachery—to be together? Newcomer Dianna Love Snell pulls no punches in *Worth Every Risk*, which features a DEA agent who discovers a beautiful stowaway on his plane. She could be trouble…or the woman he's been waiting for.

I'm thrilled to bring you six suspenseful and soul-stirring romances from these talented authors. After you enjoy this month's lineup, be sure to return for another month of unforgettable characters that face life's extraordinary odds. Only in Silhouette Intimate Moments!

Happy reading,

Patience Smith
Associate Senior Editor

Please address questions and book requests to:
Silhouette Reader Service
U.S.: 3010 Walden Ave., P.O. Box 1325, Buffalo, NY 14269
Canadian: P.O. Box 609, Fort Erie, Ont. L2A 5X3

The Angel and the Outlaw

INGRID WEAVER

INTIMATE MOMENTS™

Published by Silhouette Books

America's Publisher of Contemporary Romance

To my friend Deb.
Thanks for the ear, the shoulder—
and for just being you.

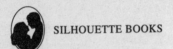 SILHOUETTE BOOKS

ISBN 0-373-27422-X

THE ANGEL AND THE OUTLAW

Copyright © 2005 by Ingrid Caris

Visit Silhouette Books at www.eHarlequin.com

Printed in U.S.A.

INGRID WEAVER

admits to being a sucker for old movies and books that can make her cry. "I write because life is an adventure," Ingrid says. "And the greatest adventure of all is falling in love." Since the publication of her first book in 1994, she has won the Romance Writers of America RITA® Award for Romantic Suspense, as well as the *Romantic Times* Career Achievement Award for Series Romantic Suspense. Ingrid lives with her husband and son and an assortment of shamefully spoiled pets in a pocket of country paradise an afternoon's drive from Toronto. She invites you to visit her Web site at www.ingridweaver.com.

Chapter 1

The woman was lying on her stomach behind the cover of a lilac bush with the butt of a rifle tucked against her shoulder. If it hadn't been for the rain gleaming from the gun barrel, Cooper wouldn't have spotted her. He eased back a step, but she gave no sign that she was aware of his presence. The night and the noise of the storm would have masked his approach. On top of that, he could see that she was entirely focused on her target.

Cooper followed her gaze across the garden to the house on the far side of the lawn. It was three stories high, built of brick and covered with ivy. Light spilled from the first-floor windows, making them sparkle festively through the rain. Figures moved inside, well-dressed people with champagne flutes in their hands. Oliver Sproule was having a party. Of course. He would be celebrating his acquittal.

The woman on the ground shifted, sliding her elbows

along the mud beneath the shrub so she could press her right eye to the scope that was mounted on top of her weapon. The gun barrel inched toward the thin, silver-haired man who had paused at the French doors that led to the terrace.

Even without the aid of a telescopic sight, Cooper recognized Oliver Sproule. He was smiling as he lifted his glass to a cluster of people, oblivious to the threat that lay in the darkness less than thirty yards away. He'd been released this morning. He must be savoring his freedom.

Cooper knew how that felt. Almost four years had passed since he'd been let out, but he remembered that first, sweet breath of free air. Cooper had partied, too, but it sure hadn't been in a mansion with fancy people and champagne.

Thunder growled in the distance. A sudden gust of wind sent needles of rain through the garden. A fragrant burst of lilac blossoms, ghostly pale in the dimness, showered the woman's back.

She didn't appear to notice. She curled her finger around the trigger. "You murdering bastard," she said. Her voice had a throaty edge, sounding as raw as the wind. "How dare you smile?"

Cooper assessed the situation while he gauged his distance to the woman. She'd made it past the electric fence and the guards who patrolled the Sproule estate, but he suspected that was due more to luck than to skill. She wasn't a professional. Pros never got emotional about a hit. And a pro would have been better prepared for the weather. This woman wasn't wearing any rain gear. Apart from her white sneakers, her clothes were dark enough to blend into the shadows, which was good, but they were soaked through, plastered to her body and would provide no protection from the storm.

The real giveaway was the gun. It had no silencer. As soon as she pulled the trigger, she would reveal her position. And Cooper's.

The way he saw it, he had two choices. He could jump her and grab the rifle before she took her shot.

Or he could turn around and walk away.

It would be simpler to walk. It sure as hell would make his task easier. She was aiming at Oliver. With that high-powered weapon from this range, even a novice would be deadly. If Cooper let her follow through, he could consider justice done. His debt would be paid. He could forget about this crazy quest Tony had chosen for him and pick up his life where he'd left off.

Sure, why not leave now? Nothing was stopping him from working his way back to his truck and letting this woman finish her business. What happened to her afterward wasn't his problem. No one would have to know he had been here.

Rain dripped from the rifle, from the woman's hands and the curve of her cheek. The sound of a sob mingled with the noise of the storm.

A woman armed with a gun was dangerous enough. A crying woman was even worse.

Go, Cooper told himself. Turn around now. Let her do what she wants. You don't need this complication. You're not her keeper.

She took her finger from the trigger to wipe the back of her hand over her eyes. A shudder shook her body. Cooper would bet it wasn't due solely to the weather.

The figure framed in the French doors drained his glass.

The woman fitted her eye back to the scope. It wasn't easy. She was sobbing continuously now. Her hands were trembling. The gun barrel wavered.

Aw, hell. What if she missed? Cooper pulled his hands from the pockets of his raincoat, preparing to lunge for her.

Before he could move, she dropped the gun on the ground and pushed to her knees. Her shoulders jerked with a sob. She slammed her fists into the mud. "Damn you!" she cried.

A dog barked from somewhere on the far side of the house. It was answered by a second bark from the direction of the front gates. Cooper glanced around. Terrific. Someone must have set loose the Dobermans.

"I'm sorry." The woman punched the ground again, then sat back on her heels and buried her face in her hands. Her head brushed a branch of the lilac as she rocked back and forth. More blossoms fell on her shoulders and stuck to her wet hair. "I'm sorry. I can't."

The barking grew nearer. Cooper strode forward to snatch the rifle. "Yeah. Too bad you didn't save us both a lot of trouble and figure that out sooner."

The woman staggered to her feet. She spun to face him. She was taller than she'd appeared when she'd been lying down. The top of her head was at a level with his nose. Her soaked clothes clung to long legs and a slender body. Her hair hung across her face in limp, muddy strands. In the dim light that shone through the shrubbery from the house, her features were nothing more than blurred suggestions of planes and shadows, impossible to identify.

Yet Cooper already had a good idea of who she had to be. Plenty of people might want to put a bullet into Oliver Sproule, but only one person would want it this badly.

She held up her palms. Her hands were still shaking. Her gaze darted to the gun.

Cooper emptied the bullets from the magazine, worked the bolt to eject the cartridge that was in the chamber and slipped the rounds into his coat pocket. He slung the strap of the rifle over his shoulder and grabbed her wrist. "Come on. We have to get out of here."

She pulled at his grip. Behind her straggling hair, her eyes were wide, her gaze not completely rational. She shook her head, spattering water droplets and petals.

Through the mud that slicked her arm, Cooper could feel her pulse fluttering against his fingers. Her breath was coming out in shallow puffs. He suspected she was on the verge of breaking down, but there was no time to coax her gently. If he couldn't bluff her into moving, he'd have to carry her. But that might make her scream and jeopardize them both. "Suit yourself." He leaned forward, bringing his face to hers. "If you feel like taking your chances with the dogs and Sproule's guards, go ahead, but I'm not sticking around to watch you bleed."

A healthy dose of alarm flickered over her face. Whether it was the sound of the barking or his harsh words that finally got through to her didn't matter. She shivered, glancing past him.

He let go of her wrist and backed toward the place where he'd scaled the fence. "My truck's over there. I'll give you three seconds and then I'm gone."

She wavered for two seconds, then took a halting step toward him. "Am I…" Her teeth chattered. "Am I under arrest?"

If the circumstances had been different, he might have enjoyed the irony of that. Imagine him, Cooper Webb, being mistaken for a cop. "Seeing as how you're gunning for Oliver Sproule, sweetheart, the cops are the least of your worries."

Hayley opened her eyes with a start. Had she fallen asleep? It seemed incredible. She hadn't been able to sleep for days, not since the jury had gone out.

She lifted her head. She was lying on a couch in a room she didn't recognize. The only illumination came from a gooseneck lamp that sat on an oak desk a few steps away from the couch. On one corner of the desk rested a pair of large cowboy boots, the leather worn to the point of broken-in comfort. Hayley pushed up on one elbow, moving her gaze from the boots to the man who wore them.

He was sitting behind the desk in a green leather chair, his legs stretched out in front of him and crossed at the ankles. His hands cradled a white porcelain mug that he balanced on his flat stomach just above his belt buckle. His chest was broad, straining the fabric of a black T-shirt. Raven-black hair curled past his ears and brushed the sides of his neck. Although the light from the desk lamp left the top half of his face in shadow, Hayley recognized the lines around his mouth and the way his beard stubble darkened the cleft in his chin.

It was the man who had found her at Sproule's. The one who had appeared like a wraith from the storm, his long dark raincoat whipping against his calves, his shoulders squared against the wind, his features slick with rain and hard as stone. The stranger who had seen her reach the absolute rock-bottom point of her life.

Her pulse gave a painful thump. She remembered now. He'd taken her to a black pickup truck in the shadows outside the fence. She had been shivering so he'd draped his coat over her and turned up the heater. As incredible as it seemed, she must have fallen asleep.

She swung her legs off the couch and sat up. A plaid blanket fell from her shoulders to bunch in her lap. The man must have replaced his coat with this blanket when he'd brought her in from his truck, but she couldn't remember walking in. He must have carried her.

It was humiliating to know she'd been so out of it that she'd been helpless and at the mercy of a complete stranger. But it was nothing compared to what he had witnessed…

Good God, had she really tried to kill Oliver Sproule?

She dipped her head, peering through her hair at the mud that smeared her fingers. On some level, she knew she should be horrified by what she'd almost done.

On another, more primitive level, she was ashamed that she had failed.

She drew the blanket aside. Her jeans were stiff with mud but almost dry. So was her blouse. She must have been here a while.

The man behind the desk lifted the mug to his mouth and took a leisurely swallow. The name of a heavy metal band, Metallica, was emblazoned in silver lightning bolts on the front of his T-shirt. He tilted his head toward the gray file cabinet behind him. A coffeemaker sat on top of it. "There's plenty of coffee left if you want some. You look as if you could use it."

His voice was a quiet rumble. His words were mild, yet they carried the same undertone of steel she'd heard him use the last time he'd spoken.

Hayley brushed at the mud on her legs. She didn't want to consider how bad she looked.

But she had almost killed a man tonight. What was a bit of mud compared to the horror of that? How much lower could she sink? How much uglier could she be?

She shoved her hair off her face so she could take a more careful survey of her surroundings. There was a window behind the desk but the blind that covered it was shut tight and blocked the view outside. There was a closed door to her left. Was it locked? She wasn't handcuffed or restrained. Would the man chase her if she made a break for it?

This room appeared to be an office, yet it wasn't like any she'd seen in the Latchford police station. Wait, she remembered he had said something about cops being the least of her worries. She wasn't under arrest. "Where…" She cleared her throat.

"Where's your rifle?" he asked before she could continue. "It's locked in the storage room along with the bullets."

"I meant where are we?"

He drained his mug, pulled his feet from the desk and stood. The room suddenly seemed smaller. He was a tall man, his body lean, his movements projecting a careless sexuality. He took a second mug from the top of the filing cabinet and filled it with coffee. "We're at the Long Shot."

She knew the place. The Long Shot was a bar at the northern edge of the Latchford, Illinois, city limits. The parking lot was usually packed with pickup trucks or cars such as Mustangs and Camaros with tinted windows and oversized tires. Hayley had driven past it many times but had never been inside before. "You're not a cop," she said.

One corner of his mouth twisted upward. "Nope. I'm a bartender, but it's after hours so all I can offer you is coffee. Wouldn't want to break any laws."

"Why did you bring me here?"

"Didn't want to argue with the Sproule guards or the Dobermans."

"I guess I should thank you for getting me off the estate."

"Yeah, you should."

"Thank you."

"No problem." He hooked his chair with one foot, rolled it toward the couch and sat down in front of her. He held out the mug. There was a tattoo of an attacking eagle on his forearm. Its faded blue talons seemed to flex with the shift of his muscles. "You look as if you're feeling better."

She braced her hands on her knees and rocked forward. "Yes. I'll call a cab and—"

"Later. We're not finished yet." He caught her fingers in his before she could stand and wrapped them around the heavy porcelain mug. "Before you go, we need to get a few things straight."

She focused on their joined hands. It was easier than looking at that vicious tattoo or the muscled arm beneath it. "You're not going to turn me in, are you?"

"That depends."

His touch was oddly gentle for a man who looked so…hard. She decided not to struggle. Considering his size, it would be pointless. As it turned out, it was unnecessary—the moment she firmed her grip on the mug, he released her hand. "What does it depend on?" she asked.

"On whether you plan to try shooting Oliver Sproule again."

"I realize how it must have appeared but—"

"Don't lie to me, Hayley. I was there."

He was right. There was no point denying the truth. This man had seen her when her soul was naked.

And he'd said her name, she realized. She wasn't carrying any ID. She hadn't carried anything but the loaded rifle when she'd walked to the Sproule estate. She hadn't thought past pulling the trigger. "How do you know who I am?"

"It doesn't take a rocket scientist to figure out who might want to shoot Sproule. Adam Tavistock had a little sister named Hayley. I read in the paper that she made statements all through the trial about how her brother was murdered and Oliver Sproule should burn in hell. That would be you, right?"

There was no point denying this, either. "Yes, that would be me."

"Better forget the Winchester and stick to talking the man to death."

She inhaled the aroma from the coffee. It was strong enough to make her eyes water. Or at least, that was one way to excuse the spurt of tears. "Oliver Sproule is a criminal. He's guilty of murder. He deserves to be punished."

"He was charged with manslaughter and acquitted."

"The verdict was wrong. He should have been charged with murder. The whole trial was a farce."

"What else did you expect? Sproule owns this town. The only reason he got charged with anything in the first place was because your brother was a cop. That couldn't be covered up, so they went through the motions of a trial."

Hayley blinked. For months it had been only herself and her father. No one else had supported her. Not the police who had been Adam's colleagues and his friends, not the D.A., not even the private detective she'd hired. Oliver Sproule, backed by his wealth and his criminal associates, was just too powerful. To hear this stranger express so easily what she'd fought to prove made her throat close with a lump of emotion.

She'd felt alone for so long. Could she have found an ally?

"Hey, steady there." He took the mug from her hands and set it on the edge of the desk. "You're not going to start crying again, are you?"

She wiped her eyes with her knuckles. Flakes of dried mud fell to her lap. "It wasn't an accident."

"What?"

"Adam's death. It was a clear night and a well-lit street. Oliver Sproule waited outside that nightclub downtown for Adam to walk to his car and then ran him down in cold blood."

"Oh, yeah. That's a given. But if you keep gunning for Sproule, you're liable to meet an accident of your own."

Where was her caution? She was alone with a strange man. Shouldn't she be afraid? Hayley glanced at the door. "Was that supposed to be a threat?"

With a nudge of his heel, the man rolled his chair to the left, placing himself between her and the room's only exit. She would have to climb over him if she wanted to get out. "Relax, Hayley." There was a hint of impatience in his voice. "You were passed out for three hours after I put you on that couch. If I'd wanted to hurt you, I would have already done it."

That was true. He'd had plenty of opportunity to do her harm. For starters, he could have left her in the garden to be mauled by the dogs or caught by the guards. Or he could have taken her to the police. That would have been the ultimate injustice, to be thrown in jail while Oliver Sproule walked free. Instead, he'd brought her out of the rain and covered her with a blanket. He'd let her sleep. For three precious hours. Why?

She returned her gaze to his face. His change of position had put him directly in the cone of light from the lamp on the desk. For the first time she had a clear view of his eyes. They were ice-blue and framed by spiky lashes as black as his hair and the stubble on his chin. His gaze was compelling in the way of something deadly, like the bird of prey that rode his arm.

Awareness tingled down her spine. The way he moved, his voice, his gaze, everything about him was stirring a response in her. Was it recognition? Had she seen eyes like that before? "You know who I am and why I was at the Sproule place," she said. "But you haven't said why you were there."

His gaze didn't waver. And it gave nothing away. "That's my business."

"Do you work for them?"

"If I did, you wouldn't be sitting here. You would already have had one of those handy accidents like the one that killed your brother."

His tone was still mild. Hayley realized that he spoke about evil and the threat of death with the same casualness he displayed when he poured coffee. She wondered once more why she wasn't afraid. "Who are you, anyway?"

"I told you, I'm a bartender."

She made a sharp gesture. "What's your name?"

"Cooper Webb." He continued to watch her. "Mean anything to you?"

Was it a trick of exhaustion, or did that name spark something in her memory, something connected with those startling blue eyes of his? "Should it?"

He lifted one shoulder. He didn't reply.

"Why did you bring me here, Mr. Webb? You didn't really answer my question before."

"Sure I did. I said we have to get some things straight."

"All right. What?"

"I can't let you run around Latchford like some avenging angel. Forget Sproule. He's out of your league. You'll never get him."

"I won't give up. Not about this. I'm going to bring him to justice."

"How? With a bullet?"

Pride made her want to argue. Shame kept her silent. Lord knew, she'd been raised to tell right from wrong.

"The verdict pushed you to your limit, Hayley, and you snapped. I could see that. But you still couldn't pull that trigger. You admitted it yourself when you threw down your gun. You don't have it in you to kill anyone."

"You don't know me."

"Maybe not, but I do know the kind of people who *would* pull that trigger, and you're not one of them. You won't get justice by getting yourself killed."

"While I appreciate your concern and the way you rescued me earlier, I won't—"

"My concern? Rescue?" His mouth quirked in another one of his half smiles. "You've got the wrong idea. I'm no do-gooder. I only made sure you got out of there in one piece because I didn't want you screwing up my plans."

"What plans?"

His smile faded. "Here's the deal. I'm going to keep your gun, but I won't turn you in to the cops or to Sproule as long as you give me your word you'll stay away from him. Let it go. Will you agree to that?"

Hayley hesitated. It would be easy to lie. How would he know?

He regarded her carefully. "You should never play poker, Hayley, because what you're thinking is all over your face. If you lie, I would find out. Trust me, I'm not someone you want to cross."

There was definitely a threat in his words that time. She lifted her chin. "Fine. I won't lie. You're right. I can't kill Oliver. I realize that now. So I can promise I won't try to shoot him again."

"Okay."

"But I can't promise I'll keep away."

"Hayley—"

"One way or another, I'm going to find enough evidence to reopen the case. I'll do whatever it takes to see him in prison for my brother's murder."

"Then back off and let me do the job."

"What?"

"I intend to bring Oliver Sproule to justice myself."

It took a moment for what he said to sink in. When it did, she surged forward and clasped his leg. She'd been right. She had found an ally. Maybe that's why she didn't fear him, and why she found him so…compelling. "Why didn't you tell me that in the first place? We can work together."

His thigh muscles bunched beneath his jeans. He looked at where she touched him. "No."

"Why not? I have my brother's notebook. His last entry showed he was meeting someone at the nightclub who never showed up. Sproule killed him because he was getting too close. The D.A. said I didn't have enough to prove anything in court but if you and I team up we could find more—"

"No."

"Mr. Webb, please." Her grip on his leg tightened. "We both want the same thing."

"Sweetheart, you have no idea what I want." He stood, breaking her hold. He shoved his chair backward. "This isn't some personal vendetta for me. I'm going to see that Sproule ends up behind bars because I have no choice."

"I don't understand."

"You don't need to. All you need to do is keep out of my way."

She got to her feet too quickly. She staggered and grabbed his arm. "We can help each other. I don't have much money left, but I'll give you what I can."

"I don't want your money."

She gave his arm a shake. "Adam was my only brother. Seeing his killer punished is all that my father lives for. I can't quit now. I'll do anything."

"Careful what you promise, Hayley."

"Mr. Webb, please." She moved her grip to his shoulders, lifting herself on her toes so she could look into his face. "We're on the same side."

He regarded her in silence for a minute. A muscle in his cheek twitched as he brought his hand to her hair. He rubbed one mud-encrusted lock between his thumb and fingers until it softened. When he finally spoke, his voice had gentled. "We're not on the same side, Hayley. We could never be."

"Why not?"

He brushed her hair behind her ear, then grasped her wrists and pulled her hands from his shoulders. "If it was up to me, I'd let Oliver party on and enjoy his champagne."

"But he murdered my brother."

"Yeah." Cooper let go of her and stepped back. "And your brother was the son of a bitch who put me in prison."

Chapter 2

Hayley flattened her palms against the tiles, dipped her head and let the spray from the shower sluice down the back of her neck. She didn't know how long she'd been in here. The water was already turning cool. But she was far from feeling clean.

There was a film of grit on the bottom of the tub. Puffs of dirty lather speckled with some kind of flower petals swirled around her ankles. The shampoo bottle she'd emptied bobbed against the drain. It was running slow again. She hoped it wouldn't back up. She wasn't any good at fixing things like that and she couldn't afford to call in a plumber. She shouldn't have used up all the shampoo, either. The brand she preferred didn't go on sale very often, but it was the only kind that didn't leave her hair too brittle to comb.

Oh, God. She dropped her forehead against her arm,

feeling an irrational urge to laugh. She was worrying about a clogged drain and the price of shampoo. Well, it was easier than thinking about how she had gotten dirty.

The storm, the mud, the gun…. It all seemed like a bad dream now, as if it had happened to someone else.

She hadn't held a firearm for years, hadn't wanted to go near one, but the moment she'd felt the weight of her father's old Winchester settle into her palms, the lessons had all come back to her.

Keep your eye on your target. Breathe slow and easy. Concentrate and squeeze.

She had never liked hunting. She hadn't gone since she was thirteen and had thrown up at the sight of her father bringing down a six-point buck. Her squeamishness had disappointed him. Everything about her had been a disappointment to him from the minute she'd been born. It was a mercy neither Adam nor their father had been at Sproule's to witness her failure…

Oh, God. What was she thinking? Her brother was dead. The stroke her father had suffered at the news of Adam's death was killing him one day at a time. That's why they hadn't been there. That's why she had.

But even if she had succeeded, if she had pulled the trigger, she would have failed. Her father would have been devastated if she had sunk to the very level of the murderer she wanted to punish. Both he and Adam had devoted their lives to upholding the law. There was no excuse for what she had attempted. She had been crazy to pick up the gun in the first place.

She twisted the knobs to shut off the water, rattled the shower curtain aside and stepped out of the tub. The storm of the night before was over. A bright-pink dawn was breaking beyond the bathroom window. She wove her way through the piles of laundry that littered the floor, chose a towel that didn't look too bad and began to blot herself dry.

She wasn't crazy.

It was the world that was insane.

Like their father, Adam Tavistock had been a decorated police officer. He'd been almost twelve years older than Hayley and a larger-than-life hero whom she'd worshipped. Throughout his career he'd epitomized courage, honesty and dedication to his duty. He'd always been the apple of Dad's eye, a chip off the old block.

But the very system Adam had sworn to uphold had turned a blind eye to justice and let his murderer go free. Oliver Sproule, with his network of theft, fraud and illegal gambling, had a stranglehold on Latchford. His wealth kept him above the law. Everyone knew it. No one wanted to admit it.

Except one man.

Cooper Webb. She understood why she hadn't recognized him immediately. They had never actually been introduced. Fifteen years ago, he'd been a senior at Latchford High when she had been in her freshman year. Yet it hadn't been only the age difference that had separated them. Cooper had been in with the tough crowd, the boys who hung around under the bleachers and shared cigarettes while they bragged about their cars and their girls. Like many of his friends, he had dropped out before he could graduate. She hadn't seen him since.

If Hayley's mother had been alive then, she probably would have warned her about boys like Cooper. Boys with ice-blue eyes and coal-black hair and that rebel glint in their smiles.

Except for his eyes, Cooper had changed. His smile had distilled to a sardonic twist of his lips. His features had been honed to uncompromising maleness. He no longer had the naughty charm of a teenage bad boy; he had the allure of a dangerous man.

Allure? That was too tame a word. His long, hard body, the lines beside his mouth and the cleft in his chin, the unruly black hair that curled at the nape of his neck, even that awful tattoo…the whole package practically oozed testosterone.

Hayley had been at rock bottom last night, yet she hadn't been so far gone that she'd been oblivious to his appeal. It had been a normal physical reaction. No female, no matter how stressed out, could have failed to notice Cooper Webb.

But his physical appearance alone wasn't what had made such an impact on her. It was the contradictions in his manner that had struck her the most. He had looked hard, yet his touch had been tender; he'd spoken bluntly yet his actions had been tinged with…chivalry.

She shook her head. He was an ex-con who was a bartender at a place she had never worked up the nerve to enter. Who knew what else he did to earn his income? Although her gut feeling told her he wasn't as bad as he seemed, she had to be realistic. There was a possibility he might still be involved in crime to some extent.

A knight in shining armor he wasn't. More like a lone wolf in a Metallica T-shirt.

And she wasn't exactly fair-damsel material.

Hayley wiped the fog from the mirror over the sink with her forearm and stared at her reflection. The mud was gone, but she was still a mess. Not sleeping or eating regularly tended to do that. Over the past seven months she had thrown all her energy into proving Oliver guilty and praying her father lived long enough to see it. Her life had become a blur of vigils at the courthouse and visits to the nursing home. It was no mystery why the verdict had made her go off the deep end.

Cooper had seemed to understand. He hadn't condemned her. He had regarded her attempt on Oliver's life as an inconvenience rather than a sin.

She didn't know how she felt about that. Sure, it was nice not to be judged—Lord knew, she'd been judged all her life and found wanting—but what kind of person could be so casual about something so wrong?

Then again, what did she know about ex-cons? Even less than she knew about the boys who hung around under the bleachers and smoked.

It had still been dark when Cooper had brought her home. The two-story Victorian where she had grown up was at the opposite end of town from his bar, on a street of large houses canopied by hundred-year-old maple trees. It was a safe, well-established neighborhood, yet Cooper had waited at the curb until she'd retrieved her spare key from the planter on the veranda and unlocked the front door. Even after she'd closed it behind her, she had heard the sound of his pickup idling in front of the house. It wasn't until she had turned on the foyer light that she'd heard him drive away.

Considering the tense way their conversation had ended, she had planned to call a taxi, but he'd driven her home anyway. It was the same kind of concern he'd shown earlier, only he had denied it was concern.

He'd called her brother a son of a bitch and yet he claimed he wanted to bring Adam's murderer to justice.

Why?

She tossed aside the towel, picked up a comb and started on her hair.

He'd said he had no choice. It didn't make sense. He'd implied he was being forced to take her side even as he'd insisted that could never happen. He'd told her to back off and trust him to get Oliver.

She had been too shaken to argue last night. He must have taken her silence for agreement.

She was going to have to set the record straight.

"Sorry, ma'am. We don't open until noon. It's only eleven."

"Yes, I know. I'm looking for someone. He said he works here."

At the sound of the woman's voice, Cooper snapped up his head to look across the room. Through the forest of up-ended chair legs he saw Pete Wyzowski, the Long Shot's manager/bouncer, standing at the front entrance. Whoever he was talking to was hidden behind his bulk and the half-open door. He had one foot wedged firmly behind it. Since the door was constructed of oak planks over steel and Pete had a build like a bulldozer, no one smaller than a linebacker could hope to force their way inside.

"Come back in an hour," Pete said.

"Please, it's extremely important. He's a bartender here."

"A bartender?"

"His name is Cooper Webb."

Pete placed one hand on the door frame to bar the narrow gap he'd allowed and twisted to look at Cooper. "A bartender?" he repeated. He lifted his eyebrows.

Cooper tossed his pen on the stack of credit-card receipts he'd been going through and pinched the bridge of his nose. He had hoped to have this paperwork done an hour ago. He hated paperwork. He stunk at math. If his schedule hadn't been so tight, he might have welcomed the interruption.

"If he isn't here yet, just tell me when you expect him."

Pete returned his attention to the woman outside. "That's hard to say, ma'am. Cooper's got a killer commute."

"Then I'll wait."

"Let me give him your phone number and—"

"It's all right, Pete," Cooper said. He might as well get this over with, he thought, as he moved from behind the bar. "I'll take it from here."

Pete stayed where he was until Cooper reached him. "Sure, boss." He let go of the door and gave Cooper a friendly punch in the arm. "But if you don't want her phone number, give it to me."

Cooper had seen the punch coming so he managed not to get knocked sideways. He waited until Pete moved off to begin righting the chairs and setting them on the floor before he looked outside.

He had an instant of confusion. He'd been expecting Hayley to return since he'd driven her home. He'd been certain he'd recognized her voice—Hayley Tavistock had a throaty way of talking that any man would remember—but the woman who stood in front of him didn't look anything like the one he'd left six hours ago.

She was still as blond as she'd been in high school. With all the mud, he hadn't been able to tell before. Rich curls like the kind he'd expect to see on pictures of angels framed her face and tumbled over her shoulders. She was wearing a tailored jacket the color of cream. The matching skirt ended well above her knees, treating him to a good view of her long legs. She looked classy and sexy at the same time.

"Hello, Mr. Webb." She shifted the purse she carried to her left hand and extended her right. "If you're not too busy, I'd like to speak with you for a few minutes."

He glanced at her hand. The mud was gone from that, too. Her skin was pale, her nails clean and buffed to a shine. He remembered how good it had felt when she'd gripped his leg. He wondered how much better it would have felt without the barrier of denim. He enclosed her hand in his.

As soon as he touched her, his confusion dissolved. She might have cleaned up, but she hadn't been able to scrub away the tremor in her fingers.

He moved his gaze to her face. Back in high school she'd been cheerleader-cute. Not his type, yet he couldn't deny he'd noticed. Problem was, she'd been an underage girl from a family of cops so he'd steered clear. Now she was all woman. She had the kind of bone-deep beauty that even mud and matted hair hadn't disguised. Her lips were full and shaped in a feminine bow. Her eyes were hazel and tipped up at the corners, as if she should be on the verge of a smile.

She didn't appear to be a woman who had smiled much lately. The hollows in her cheeks weren't from a trick of makeup. And no amount of makeup could hide the weariness that pinched the edges of her lips or the despair that shadowed her gaze.

Cooper studied her more closely. Her skirt was too loose on her. He realized she didn't quite fill out the jacket, either. Along with the hollows in her cheeks it all pointed to a recent weight loss. He felt a sudden rush of sympathy. And he had a crazy urge to yank her closer and do what he hadn't done last night. He wanted to kiss her until her lips lost their tension and her eyes filled with desire instead of despair.

And he had an even crazier urge to wrap her in a blanket again and carry her someplace safe.

He dropped her hand and hung on to the door. Since

when was he anyone's protector? She might stir his hormones, but she was an inconvenience, a distraction he couldn't afford. "There's not much point talking, Hayley. I already said everything I wanted to say."

"All I ask is that you hear me out."

"I'm busy."

"Tending bar?"

"Not right now. We're closed."

"That man called you boss."

"Yes, he did."

"Are you?"

"Yeah. I own this place. I also work the bar. Is that what you wanted to talk about?"

She shook her head. Her hair rippled in the sunshine. "Why are you going after Oliver Sproule?"

"What difference does it make as long as I get him?"

That made her pause. She pulled her lower lip between her teeth.

Damn, he still wanted to kiss her. He swung the door open and motioned her inside. "You might as well come in before you draw a crowd."

Was it his imagination, or did she hesitate a beat before she lifted her chin and stepped over the threshold? "Thank you, Mr. Webb."

"Call me Cooper." He closed the door and shot the bolt. "I'm expecting a delivery in ten minutes so that's all the time I can give you."

She acknowledged his words with a smile that was too stiff to call real.

There was a clatter of chairs as Pete continued to clear off the tables. Cooper stepped aside and gestured Hayley toward the door at the other end of the room. "We'll talk in my office."

She remained silent as they walked past the bar, her gaze darting everywhere. He had taken her out the rear door when they had left here earlier this morning, so she hadn't seen anything except his office and the back hallway. Cooper looked around, trying to see the place as she would.

Four years ago the building had housed a custom welding shop that had been going out of business. Cooper had liked the location on the outskirts of town since there were few neighbors to complain about noise or traffic. The large, two-story main room had suited him, too. He'd kept the renovations simple, laying down a hardwood floor and installing a rectangular oak bar as an island in the center. He'd also lengthened the existing windows that had been set high under the eaves so he had a view of his surroundings.

Enlarging the windows hadn't been all that practical, since the bar's busiest hours were after dark, but Cooper liked to see outside. It was one of the legacies of the time he'd spent inside.

Each year he'd poured any profit he'd made into added improvements. Now he had pool tables, a big-screen TV and a top-of-the-line sound system. On Pete's suggestion, last winter he'd added a raised stage in the corner beside the front door where local talent had the chance to show what they could do. He liked being able to give them a break.

Cooper was proud of what he'd done with the Long Shot. It wasn't fancy, but it was solid and getting more popular every year. Best of all, it was his.

For now, anyway.

Hayley had asked him why he was going after Oliver Sproule. She was walking through the answer.

Damn Tony and his bargain. It had been four years since he'd made it. It had gone on so long, Cooper had begun to hope that Tony was going to let it slide, but he should have known better. Tony Monaco wasn't the kind of man who forgave anything, especially a debt.

"This is very nice," Hayley said. "It's much bigger than it looks from the outside. I like all the wood."

Her compliment sounded sincere. He tried to keep it in perspective. She wanted something from him, he reminded himself, so she'd say whatever she thought was necessary. "I guess you haven't been here before," he said.

"No. I've been living in Chicago for the past ten years. I only moved back to Latchford last fall. Since then I've been too busy to…socialize."

He pushed open the door that led to the back hall, then stepped to one side so she could go ahead of him. Last fall? Right. That's when her brother had been killed and her father had had his stroke.

But it was more than grief that had kept her out of the Long Shot. Hayley Tavistock didn't strike him as the kind of woman who would normally come to a place like this anyway. She was probably too much of the good girl to let loose and enjoy herself.

She brushed close enough for him to catch her scent. There was soap and shampoo, but there was still a trace of earthiness. Maybe he was wrong about her not letting loose. Just because she was a Tavistock and dressed with class didn't mean there wasn't passion beneath the surface. He'd already seen some of it.

They reached his office in silence. Hayley stopped in front of his desk and looked out the window. The shade was up, so she had a good view of the orchard on the far side of the parking lot. The trees had come into bloom the week before. The blossoms were pretty well finished now. Last night's rain had knocked down of most of them but there were a few still stubbornly clinging to the boughs.

Again, Cooper caught himself wondering what she thought. Before Sproule had set up business here, much of Latchford's economy had depended on the surrounding farms. Only a few pockets were left, like this overgrown apple orchard. Although this window also overlooked the loading ramp at the back of the building, a practical feature which allowed Cooper to keep track of delivery trucks when they arrived, the trees were the main reason he'd chosen this room for his office.

The bargain he'd made with Tony was what allowed him to have this. It could also make him lose it all.

He closed the door behind him more forcefully than he'd intended.

Hayley gave a nervous start and turned to face him.

He felt like a jerk for making her jump. "I'm sorry about your troubles, Hayley," he said.

"Everyone's sorry. No one except you wants to do anything about it."

He wanted to pull her into his arms. He shoved his hands into the pockets of his jeans instead. "That's right," he said. "I mean to do something about it. I plan to see that Oliver pays for his crime. If you want that to happen, the best thing you could do is keep out of it. You shouldn't have come here."

She chewed her lip again, as if restraining herself from asking the same question as before. "While I do appreciate your help last night, I'm afraid you might have gotten the wrong impression about me."

"Oh, yeah? What part?"

"I'm not always that…" She paused, as if searching for the right word.

"Passionate?" he supplied.

"Irrational." She straightened the cuffs of her jacket. "As

you mentioned, I was pushed to my limit. I snapped. I wasn't myself."

"Sure, you were. No one can fake feelings that strong."

"Yes, well, I feel much better now."

"Did you sleep?"

"Excuse me?"

"After I took you home. How much sleep did you get?"

She brushed at a wrinkle in her skirt. "That really isn't relevant."

She was right; he wasn't her keeper. But that didn't stop him from wanting to kiss the weariness from her expression. He locked his elbows to keep his hands in his pockets.

"I came here to assure you that you don't need to fear I would hinder your plans if we worked together," she said.

"Soap and clothes won't change who a person is, Hayley."

"That's my point. You got the wrong impression."

"Not about one thing. There's no mistaking the fact that you're a Tavistock," he said bluntly.

Color flared in her cheeks. "I won't apologize for my brother. He was a dedicated policeman."

"Right. I know. Just like your father. You come from a long line of cops."

"What does my father have to do with this? Adam's the one you're holding a grudge against."

"I was locked in a cage for three years of my life and your brother was the one who put me there. Saying I hold a grudge doesn't cover it."

"What were you arrested for?"

"Hijacking a truckload of computer chips."

She studied him for a moment. "Were you innocent?"

He kept his gaze steady on hers. She would probably feel more comfortable if he lied, but he wouldn't deny what he used to do any more than she would apologize for her brother. They both were what they were, and there was no changing that. "I was guilty as sin, Hayley."

"Then how can you resent Adam? He was only doing his job."

"Yeah, I know. But do you have much luck telling yourself how you should feel?"

Her gaze wavered. The color in her cheeks deepened. "No, but sometimes to get what we want, we have to put our feelings aside. That's why we should work together, no matter how much you dislike me because of my brother."

"Dislike you?" He moved to where she stood, unable to restrain himself from touching her any longer. He pulled his hands from his pockets and tipped up her chin with his index finger. "Where did you get that idea?"

"You said you don't want to work together."

"I don't. That doesn't mean I'm blind." He stroked his thumb along the edge of her jaw. This was another one of those times he didn't have much luck telling himself how to feel. Sure, she was a distraction he couldn't afford, but his body wasn't listening. "You're an attractive woman, Hayley. I could see that even when you were wearing half of Sproule's garden."

She didn't pull away from his caress. He'd expected her to. Then again, she did want something from him. She might think accepting his touch was as necessary as making a compliment about his bar.

He fingered a curl that rested against her neck. The way it sprang back against his hand made him smile. Her hair was soft but stubborn, sort of like her. "You cleaned up real good, too."

Beneath the classy jacket her breasts rose as she inhaled unsteadily. The pulse beneath her ear beat hard against his fingertips.

She wasn't much good at hiding her feelings, Cooper decided. He could see her awareness, just as he could see her distress over it. She didn't want to be attracted to him any more than he wanted to be attracted to her. He should let this go, but some demon inside him wanted to push. Last night she'd said she'd do anything, hadn't she? He leaned closer. "How about it, Hayley?"

Her lips parted. "What?"

"Aren't you curious? I know I am." He traced his fingertip down her throat to the V of her jacket neckline and tapped her breastbone. "What other passions do you keep inside here?"

Her gaze sparked with an unmistakable response. It was anger. She pushed his hand aside and stepped back. She didn't get far. She was stopped when the back of her legs hit the edge of his desk. "Don't think you're going to scare me off with some fake come-on, Cooper. That's just too obvious and it won't get rid of me."

He exhaled hard. Would he scare her off if he told her there had been nothing fake about his interest?

"Could we get back to business, please?"

He raked his hand through his hair, then rubbed the back of his neck. "We don't have business together. Even if I wanted a partner, it wouldn't be you."

"What Adam did to you is history. Surely you can put your grudge aside and—"

"Hey, Coop!" It was Pete's voice, coming from the hallway outside the office. The door rattled with a hard knock. "You better get out here."

Cooper hadn't heard him approach. That jarred him. Even through a closed door, Pete's tread was always heavy enough to hear. Cooper must have been too focused on Hayley to notice. He stepped away from her and opened the door. "What's going on?"

Pete looked worried. "Sorry to interrupt, boss, but your two o'clock appointment got here early."

"My appointment? What the…" It took him a second to change gears. "Aw, hell. Where is he?"

"Still in his car out front. He sent four of his men to check the place out first."

Cooper turned to look at Hayley. "Where did you park?"

She looked at him blankly. "I don't understand. Why—"

"Just answer the question. Where's your car?"

"I don't have one. It was repossessed last month. I took a taxi here."

He flicked his gaze to the window behind Hayley. He could see a man in sunglasses and a dark suit walking across the parking lot toward the loading ramp. Cooper hadn't noticed him before, either. "It's too late to get you out the back way," he said. "They'll see you."

She twisted her head to follow his gaze. "Who? What are you talking about?"

He snatched her purse from the desk and shoved it into her hands, then grabbed her arm and tugged her toward the door. "Come with me. You'll have to wait upstairs until they leave."

Her heels slid across the floor. She hooked her purse strap over her shoulder and caught the door frame with her free hand before he could pull her through. "No. We're not finished. I'm not going anywhere."

He moved his grip to her upper arms and brought his face to hers. "Hayley, this isn't the time to argue. You can't be seen here."

"Why not?"

"Because everyone in Latchford knows how you feel about Oliver Sproule."

"Well, yes, but—"

"That's why we can't work together. It's why you have to get out of sight now. If Oliver suspects that we teamed up, I don't have a hope in hell of getting close to him."

She shook her head. "You're not making sense."

He glanced past her to the window and muttered a curse. The man by the loading ramp had taken a gun from beneath his suit coat.

"Boss," Pete warned. "He's carrying."

"Yeah, I saw it," Cooper said. There was no time left for finesse. He pulled Hayley's hand from the door frame, leaned down to wrap his arms around her thighs and tossed her over his shoulder. "Pete, call Ken. Tell him the game's on."

"Sure thing, Coop," he said, digging his cell phone out of his pants pocket.

Hayley thumped her fist into Cooper's back. "Put me down! What are you doing?"

"Saving your pretty little butt. Again." He clamped his hand over her bottom to hold her steady, then jogged down the hallway to the door that was set halfway between his office and the barroom.

Pete called after him, "What do you want me to do after I phone Ken, Coop?"

"Give me five minutes to get Hayley out of sight," he replied, raising his voice over her continued protests. "Then unlock the back door and bring Sproule to my office."

Chapter 3

"Sproule?" Hayley braced her palm against Cooper's back to lift her head. Her heart was pounding, her palms wet. Had she heard him right? "Oliver's here?" she asked.

"Yeah."

She clenched her jaw, fighting a wave of light-headedness as Cooper opened a door and made a sudden turn to his right. By the time she got it under control he was halfway up a staircase. The lighting was dim. Combined with the jostling from Cooper's pace, it was disorienting.

Hayley stopped struggling and anchored her fingers in his shirt. She didn't want to send them both tumbling down the stairs. "Why is he here?"

"Because I invited him."

"Why?"

"I don't have enough breath to explain and carry you at the same time."

Hayley knew that wasn't true. He was taking the stairs two at a time and wasn't even breathing hard. She could feel the strength in his hands and in the corded muscles along his arms and shoulders. "Put me down," she said. "I want answers."

He didn't comply until they reached the landing at the top of the stairs. He bent his knees and let her slide off his shoulder until her feet touched the floor.

There was a varnished wood door in front of them that looked identical to the one at the front of the building. A lock with a numbered keypad was set into the wood below the knob. Hayley had barely registered these facts when Cooper punched a combination into the lock and swung the door open. He grabbed her hand and pulled her inside with him.

After the dim staircase, the brightness of the room they entered made her squint. The place was big, appearing to stretch away from her the entire width of the building. She glimpsed a large unmade bed on a low platform in the far corner, some overstuffed couches and a leather recliner in the center of the room and the gleam of stainless-steel kitchen appliances set into a U-shaped counter to her right. Dominating everything was a long wall with three multi-paned warehouse-style windows that overlooked the same overgrown orchard she had seen from Cooper's office.

But she had no chance to take in more detail. Cooper grasped her cheeks and turned her face to his. "Hayley, you have to stay here," he said. "Keep away from the windows. Don't open the door to anyone except me."

Out of principle she didn't like taking orders any more than she allowed anyone to manhandle her, but she could see the anxiety on Cooper's face was genuine. "What's going on?"

"I didn't want you involved in this. I warned you that you're out of your league. You should have stayed away."

"Cooper—"

"I'll explain later." He dropped his hands and returned to the door. "I've got to go."

She ran after him. "Cooper, wait!"

He paused in the doorway, his body hard with tension. He looked at her over his shoulder. "I can't, Hayley. It's already been set into motion."

"But what are you doing?"

"Applying for a job."

"With Oliver? I thought you wanted to see him punished."

Cooper's gaze was like ice as it bored into hers. "I'm an ex-thief with a criminal record and a public grudge against the man Oliver murdered. Those credentials will get me places that you and the law could never go."

She stopped before she reached him. She tried to think, but it was hard. Too much was happening too fast. "I still don't understand."

"You're a bright woman, Hayley." He turned away. "I'm sure you'll figure it out."

Oliver Sproule sat completely still, his hands folded neatly on his crossed legs. Two of his men stood behind him, their bulk a marked contrast to Oliver's greyhound-slender frame. Against the dark backdrop of their suits, his hair shone like platinum.

He hadn't moved since he'd taken the chair Cooper had offered. Not one fidget of his manicured fingers, not one rustle of his silk suit, not even a scuff of his hand-stitched shoes. He was as composed as a corpse.

Cooper didn't like it. He'd never met anyone who was so difficult to read.

Yet by his very composure, Oliver revealed something basic about his character. He was a control freak. That's why he'd shown up three hours early. It was also why he'd elected to have their meeting in the barroom at a table of his choice rather than in Cooper's office.

The fact that he'd chosen to meet in Cooper's territory instead of his own had provided yet another opportunity for one-upmanship. A second car had arrived while Cooper had been busy with Hayley. In addition to the two goons at the back of Oliver's chair, there were several more at each exit and another four in the parking lot. Oliver's men outnumbered Cooper's by more than four to one. He'd essentially turned Cooper's turf into his own.

Cooper couldn't let him see how much that part of it bothered him. The Long Shot was his.

"While I'm flattered that you would like to do business with me, Mr. Webb," Oliver said, "I'm curious to know why."

Cooper hooked his thumbs in his belt loops and leaned back in his chair, endeavoring to keep his body language casual. "Money. Why else?"

Oliver arched one platinum eyebrow. "Indeed."

"I figure you could be interested in some extra cash flow now that you fixed your legal problems."

One corner of Oliver's upper lip lifted in a barely suppressed sneer. The first chink he'd allowed. "Go on."

"Congratulations, by the way," Cooper said. "Nice piece of work on that verdict."

"I fully support the justice system in this great country of ours."

"Yeah, I bet. I would have popped Tavistock myself if I'd had the chance."

"It was an unfortunate accident."

"Sure. Whatever. The thing is, I've been wanting to get some action going but I need a way to move the merchandise. My former associate who used to handle that for me is doing twenty to life."

"I don't run a van line, Mr. Webb."

"I thought you would know the trucks are my specialty, Ollie."

The nickname brought on an eyelid twitch. Oliver regained control and regarded him stonily.

Cooper decided it was time to get to the point. "Okay, here's the deal. Say I bring you some TVs. You find a buyer, you take ten percent of the proceeds."

"Sixty."

"Twenty, and you provide storage until the merchandise can be moved."

Oliver snapped his fingers. The men behind him stepped forward and drew back his chair as he stood. "Forty percent and secure space in my warehouse where you can unload."

Cooper got to his feet. "You've got a deal."

"Agreed."

Cooper nodded and held out his hand. "Great. I'll be in touch."

Oliver slid his palm against Cooper's and gave him a token squeeze. He moved toward the exit, his bodyguards falling into step behind him.

Cooper waited until he saw the cars pull out of the parking lot, then carefully wiped his right hand on his pants. The groundwork had been laid. He'd established an angle that would get him into the organization, just as he'd planned.

That didn't stop him from feeling dirty.

It had been seven years since his last job. Four years since he'd made his promise to Tony. He'd become accustomed to feeling…clean.

Soap and clothes won't change who a person is.

That's what he'd told Hayley. Had she realized he hadn't only been talking about her?

He helped Pete finish the preparations for the day, then left him to manage the bar while he headed upstairs. There was no sound coming from the other side when he reached the door to the loft. He didn't think Hayley could have gotten out—he'd instructed Pete to keep an eye on the staircase during the meeting with Oliver to make sure she remained out of sight. But Cooper had made no attempt to mask the noise of his boots on the steps. He'd expected her to meet him with more questions and demands.

As soon as he unlocked the door, the reason for her silence became obvious. She had fallen asleep in his chair.

Cooper eased the door closed behind him and set the lock, then crossed the floor to Hayley. For a minute he indulged himself and simply looked at her. She had discarded her shoes and was curled on her side like a kitten, her bare feet drawn up on the seat and her cheek pillowed on the chair arm. Her hair hung over the side in a tangle of curls. In the daylight that poured through the windows, the hollows in her cheeks and the lines of strain around her eyes were more obvious than ever.

Was the woman trying to self-destruct? Didn't she realize she had to start taking better care of herself? When was the last time she'd had anything to eat or had a full night's sleep? This was probably the only rest she'd gotten since she'd slept on his office couch.

She looked so defenseless, it was hard to believe that she had taken on Oliver Sproule alone. Saying she was out of her league was an understatement. Yet even though her presence was turning into a complication he didn't need, Cooper couldn't help feeling a twinge of admiration for her. She had guts, he'd give her that. Despite his attempts to get rid of her, she didn't scare off easy.

On the other hand, he hadn't tried all that hard yet, had he? He had to stop thinking with his libido.

He knelt at the side of the chair and picked up a lock of her hair, letting the curls twine through his fingers. His gaze moved to her mouth. Her lips were parted and completely relaxed. It would be a shame to wake her up. If he had the time, he'd let her sleep her fill the way he had before, but they had to straighten this out. For her own safety, he had to convince her to back off.

Besides, he had too much riding on this to allow anyone, including her, to get in his way. "Hayley?"

A frown line appeared between her eyebrows. She sighed, moistened her lips and snuggled her cheek against the chair arm.

Cooper released her hair and leaned closer. "Hayley, wake up."

Her lashes fluttered. Her lips moved into the ghost of a smile. "Cooper?"

"Yeah."

He never saw it coming. Later, he would wonder how different things might have turned out if he had. As it was, any good intentions that might have lurked somewhere inside him were swept away when her hand stole around the back of his neck and she tugged his head to hers.

The kiss she gave him was sweet and sleepy. It was the kiss of a woman who wasn't completely conscious, who didn't know what she was doing. It didn't mean a thing. She was probably dreaming, reacting instinctively, reaching for comfort the same way she would reach for a blanket.

Cooper didn't give a damn. He tilted his head and gave her a kiss that brought her completely awake.

* * *

As soon as she felt Cooper's tongue slide over her lips, Hayley realized it wasn't a dream. No dream could be this vivid.

Cooper kissed the same way he moved, with a careless sexuality, as warm as the sunlight that poured through the wall of windows beside her, as supple as the leather of the chair that cradled her, as bold as the hair that curled around her fingers where she held the back of his neck.

Yet beneath the sexuality there was tenderness. She could feel it in the way he coaxed her response instead of demanding it. He tilted his head, testing angles until his lips fit perfectly over hers. The pressure was gentle, a sweet exploration, giving more than he took. This wasn't the brusque-mannered bar owner who had carried her out of his office, this was the protector who had rescued her from the Sproule estate and had seen her safely home.

And for a crazy instant Hayley wanted to pretend she was still asleep. It was so tempting. It would give her an excuse to let the pleasure last a few moments longer.

But this was a man her brother had put in prison. How could she be kissing him? She knew what she wanted from him, and her own needs weren't high on the list. She let go of his neck, pulled back and opened her eyes.

He was kneeling on the floor, one hand braced on the chair arm, the other on the seat beside her ankles. The sleeves of his chambray shirt were rolled above his elbows. His forearms—and the eagle—flexed. "If I'd realized you woke up like that," he murmured, "I never would have let you sleep last night."

Oh, he was dangerous. His voice was soft, as much a caress as his kiss had been. Sunshine gleamed from his spiky black lashes and warmed the startling blue of his eyes with flecks of gold. She wanted to lean forward and lick the moisture that slicked his lips.

What was the matter with her? How could she let him affect her like this? Even worse, how could she have relaxed her guard enough to fall asleep again? Maybe she really was going crazy. She pushed herself upright. "I can't believe I dozed off."

"I can. I saw you were still strung out when you got here."

"But I didn't intend…" She cleared her throat, uncertain what to say. *I didn't intend to dream about you. Or to enjoy the reality more than the dream.*

He stroked his thumb along her foot to her calf. "I hope you're not going to apologize about that kiss, Hayley, because I sure as hell won't."

That was exactly what she should do, but she wasn't certain where to start. "I didn't plan any of this."

"Too bad. This was the first good idea you've had."

"I didn't mean to give you the impression that—"

"That you're a passionate woman? Or that you wanted to kiss me?"

"Neither." She pressed further back in the chair. The recliner was large so she was able to draw away from Cooper's touch. Yet she still felt the imprint of his thumb on her leg. And his tongue in her mouth. She struggled to focus her thoughts. "Can we just move on? This isn't why I came to see you today, Cooper. I thought we already established that."

"Yeah, I know." He sighed, rocked back on his heels and rose to his feet. His gaze flicked downward. His cheek twitched. "But the way you look, you're making it hard to remember."

She glanced at her lap. Like most of her wardrobe, her skirt was too loose on her—she hadn't realized it had ridden up almost to her hips. She hurriedly tugged it into place over her thighs. "I'm here because of my brother. I want to talk about Oliver Sproule."

"There's nothing more to talk about, Hayley. You need to back off. Leave Sproule to me."

She thought about the last thing Cooper had said before he'd gone downstairs. He'd claimed he wanted a job with Oliver.

He'd also claimed he wanted Oliver brought to justice.

It hadn't been that difficult to connect the dots. The hard part was concentrating on them when he was still close enough for her to catch his scent. His aftershave was spicy, his soap smelled of pine, and his mouth had tasted warm and sexy and pure male—

Focus, she reminded herself. "You're planning to gather evidence against Oliver from the inside, aren't you?"

"I see you figured it out."

"Some of it. If you're going to pretend to work with Oliver, I can understand why you wouldn't want to be seen with me."

"There won't be any pretense about it, Hayley." He backed up a few steps, then walked to the window in the center of the wall. He angled himself to the side of the window frame and scanned the area below. "I'll be right in the middle of the Sproule organization."

"That's going to be dangerous."

"Bingo. That's why you have to keep out of it."

She looked around for her shoes, slipped them on and followed him. Mindful of his earlier warning about keeping away from the windows, she was careful to stay behind him so she wouldn't be visible from outside. She shifted her gaze to his back. Sunlight filtered through his shirt, silhouetting his broad shoulders and long, lean torso.

She did her best to ignore the view. "Why are you taking this risk in the first place?" she asked. "You're not working with any law-enforcement agency, are you?"

He snorted. "Nope. I trust them about as much as I trust Oliver."

"And you made it clear you don't have any affection for Adam, so you're not doing this for his sake."

"No, I'm doing this for me."

"Why?"

"What difference does it make?"

He'd asked that before. She'd thought about her answer while he'd been gone. "Unless I get an answer I'm satisfied with," she said, "I have no reason to believe that you'll do as you say."

He fisted his hand on the window frame. His rolled-up sleeve tightened across his biceps. "We don't have time to go around with this again. We've got to get you out of here before Oliver decides to send some of his guys back to keep an eye on me. He doesn't trust me yet, either."

"Then you'd better answer my question, because I'm not leaving until you do."

Swearing under his breath, he grasped the cord that hung beside the window and gave it a sharp tug. A Venetian blind clattered downward over the glass, the slats diffusing the sunshine. He moved to the other two windows and did the same, then leaned one shoulder against the frame of the center window. Shifting his weight to one foot, he propped the toe of his other boot against the floor. He studied her for a minute, as if deciding how much to reveal. "Ever hear of a man named Tony Monaco?"

"No, I don't think so."

"His family used to run an organization that would make Oliver and his friends look like Boy Scouts."

An organization, she thought, as in organized crime. And *worse* than Oliver? She swallowed. "Used to run?"

"Tony got out of the business ten years ago, but he's still not a man you would want to mess with." He paused. "To cut to the chase, Tony financed the Long Shot. Unless I bring Oliver Sproule to justice, he's going to call in the loan and I'll lose my bar."

"I don't see the connection. Did Oliver do something to this Tony Monaco? Is that why Tony wants you to go after him?"

"That's beside the point. You said you were interested in my reasons, not Tony's."

"It sounds like a strange way to repay a loan."

"Tony isn't a banker. If he was, he wouldn't have given me any money in the first place. Ex-cons aren't real high on a banker's preferred-client list."

She couldn't disagree. Anyone with a criminal background would be considered a bad credit risk. As unfair as it might be, there would be few, well, conventional financing options open to someone like Cooper. "It seems as if your business is doing well. Every time I've gone by, the parking lot is crowded."

"It didn't happen overnight. Tony gave me the loan when I got out of prison. I've spent every day of the four years since then building the Long Shot into what it is now. Going straight has been damn hard work."

"Going straight?"

"Surprised, sweetheart?"

She realized she was. Not by his claim that he'd gone straight—although she was glad to hear him say it, all along her instincts had told her he wasn't as bad as he seemed, despite his gruff manner. What surprised her was the flicker of hurt in his gaze at her thoughtless response.

But what did he expect? He'd been throwing his criminal past in her face since they had met, as if he were trying to shock her, as if he *wanted* her to assume the worst about him.

Then again, she had already decided he was full of contradictions. Like his primitively sexy yet ultra-sensitive kiss…

She jerked her thoughts back on track. "I'm sorry, Cooper. I didn't mean to offend you. It's admirable that you, uh…"

"Don't get carried away. I'm not due for a halo anytime soon. Keeping my nose clean was one of the conditions of Tony's loan."

There had to be more to the story, she decided. From the sound of this, Tony was a former mob boss. Why would he care whether or not Cooper went straight…unless he didn't want Cooper's activities to compromise his investment. Yes, that was probably it.

But as Cooper had already said, she should be concentrating on his reasons, not Tony's. "Regardless of why, you should be proud of what you've accomplished."

He lifted his shoulders in a stiff shrug. "The funny thing about earning something honestly is you don't want to lose it. The Long Shot is mine. I plan to do whatever it takes to keep it."

"Including putting your life at risk to infiltrate the Sproule organization?"

"Whatever it takes," he repeated. "Like I said, Tony Monaco isn't a man you would want to mess with. I owe him. I intend to pay him back." He pushed away from the window and folded his arms over his chest. "Satisfied now?"

"What?"

"I've answered your question. You know why I'm going after Oliver. Anything else you have to say, you can say it in the truck." He nodded toward the door. "Let's go."

She had never met anyone as single-minded as Cooper. This man would be a formidable enemy. She had to convince him that he wasn't hers. She crossed her arms, mirroring his posture, and stayed where she was. "You haven't told me anything to change my mind. It still makes sense to team up."

"Hayley, haven't you listened to anything I've said?"

"No one has to know, Cooper. Now that you've explained why we can't be seen together, we'll both be careful not to let that happen. But that's no reason why we can't help each other."

"How?"

"The evidence I told you about yesterday, the information in Adam's notebook, is only part of what I have. I've been gathering material on Oliver and his business since last October. I'll share it with you. It would give you an advantage before you go into the Sproule organization if you have a framework of knowledge to start from."

His expression sharpened, his gaze suddenly alert.

Something clicked in Hayley's mind. "*That's* why you were at the Sproule estate last night."

"What was?"

"You were planning on getting into the house to do some investigating of your own while everyone was distracted with Oliver's party."

He hesitated a beat. "Could be."

"Of course! If you had been there to apply for a job, you wouldn't have hidden your truck or climbed the fence, you would have used the front gate. You wouldn't have worried about being caught there."

"All right. So what?"

"Then that's even more reason to take advantage of the help I'm offering. Your plans were interrupted because of me, so it's only fair to let me make it up to you."

He regarded her in silence for a while. He still wasn't agreeing, but at least he wasn't moving toward the door.

"Think about it, Cooper. You said you can go where I can't. Well, that works both ways. I have connections, too. I can use them to check out whatever lead you discover."

"If you mean your connections with the Latchford police," he said, "then forget it. Oliver has to have people on the inside there."

It pained her to admit it, but she was beginning to suspect that much herself. Her father had become so agitated at the idea the one time she'd mentioned it to him that she hadn't brought it up again, yet she had to be realistic. Whatever the reason, the police hadn't helped her so far. They would be even less likely to help her now that the trial was over.

She shook her head. "No, I meant the connections I have in the financial world. I worked as a forensic accountant in Chicago so I have a lot of experience following money trails. I can follow Oliver's."

"What good would that do?"

"We could get solid evidence of Oliver's motive to kill Adam, which would prove my brother's death wasn't an accident. We might even be able to prove Oliver bribed his way to an acquittal."

He raked his fingers through his hair. "This is sounding complicated."

"It doesn't have to be. Would Tony object if you worked with a partner?" she asked.

"Tony Monaco's never been real particular about methods. He's more interested in results."

"Then there isn't any good reason why we shouldn't team up. You did say you would do whatever it takes to keep your bar."

He turned back to the window and lifted a blind slat to look outside. "Yeah, I did say that."

"Why can't that include working with a Tavistock?"

He shook his head, muttering something under his breath.

"Well?"

The silence lasted longer this time. Finally, he left the window and strode directly to where she stood. He took her by the shoulders. "If I agree to this, you'll keep your distance from Sproule, right?"

Her heart began to pound. She wanted to think it was from what he was saying, but she knew it was more from his touch. "I'll stay away as long as you don't shut me out of what you're doing."

"Hayley—"

"I mean it, Cooper. Don't shut me out. I want you to keep me up to date on your progress."

He moved his palms along her shoulders to her neck. "I'll do more than that. Once I bring you in with me, you'll be all the way in."

"That's how I want it."

"Don't be so fast to agree, Hayley, seeing as how you cleaned up so good and all." He touched his fingertip to the pulse at the base of her throat. "The kind of dirt you'll be getting into now won't be so easy to wash off."

Chapter 4

Cooper heard the distinctive rumble of the split carburetor well before he saw the bike's headlight sweep past the chain-link fence to the broken gate. Nathan Beliveau was right on time, which wasn't surprising, considering his business—he was the president of the largest courier company in the midwest. He would know about keeping schedules. But his choice of transportation was…unexpected. Cooper leaned back against the front fender of his truck and waited as the Harley Davidson coasted down the ramp into the abandoned gravel pit and slowed to a stop beside him.

The echoes of the bike's engine faded gradually, replaced by the ticking of cooling metal. A cloud of dust tainted with exhaust floated through the headlight briefly before the beam was extinguished. The meeting place they'd agreed on was five miles out of Latchford and half a mile from the highway. The floodlight that had been mounted near the entrance when the pit had been in operation was long gone, but it was a clear night and the moon was almost full, so there was enough light to see what he needed to.

The man astride the motorcycle stretched his long legs on either side to balance the machine but made no move to get off. He could probably afford to travel by chauffeured limo, but he appeared completely at ease on the powerful bike. "You're Webb?" he asked.

"Yeah." Cooper made no attempt to hide his scrutiny—it would be expected. "Nice hog, Beliveau."

"She's a beauty, all right." He slipped off his helmet and rested it on the gas tank in front of him. "It sure beats riding a desk."

Cooper shifted his scrutiny from the bike to the man on it. Moonlight gleamed from his straight black hair and the sharp ridges of his cheekbones, revealing the stamp of native heritage. He would probably look just as comfortable riding bareback on an Appaloosa.

Wind rustled through the weeds that ringed the pit, muffling the distant whine of tires on the highway. Nathan lifted his face, as if testing the breeze. "Tony said you wanted televisions."

"Know of any?"

"How about a trailer load of sixty-two-inch plasma screens?"

Cooper whistled. "That'll do."

"They're at an electronics manufacturing company in Hammond where they're scheduled for an overnight shipment to Kansas City. The pickup's slated for ten-thirty tomorrow night. That means you should be out of there by ten."

"Sounds good."

"Can you handle a big rig?"

"No problem. Have you got one with a sleeper compartment?"

"There's one at the Chicago terminal. I'll arrange to have it parked in a rest area off the Interstate. You'll have until seven in the morning before I'll have to report it missing."

Cooper calculated the time it would take him to get the truck to Hammond, do the pickup and drive back to Latchford. It would be cutting things close, especially since he would be taking detours onto secondary routes to get around the weigh stations. "I'll have it back by then."

"Try to keep the damage to the rig to a minimum. My insurance rates are already killing me."

"Except for the wires, it won't have a scratch."

Nathan turned his head toward Cooper. His eyes were too deep-set for the moonlight to touch, making his expression inscrutable. "You better be as good as Tony said you were. I heard it's been a few years since you did a job like this."

"Some things you don't forget."

Nathan studied him. "That's right. Some things you don't forget."

Cooper couldn't help being curious about Nathan's connection to Tony, but he knew better than to ask. The fact that he was here said enough. Nathan was indebted to Tony Monaco, just like Cooper, just like all the members of the Payback network.

And he was probably as eager as Cooper was to settle his debt and get on with his life.

Leather creaked as Nathan slipped his hand inside his riding jacket. He withdrew a folded sheet of paper and held it out to Cooper. "Here are the rest of the details about the load. It should be all the information you'll need."

"Thanks." Cooper pushed away from the fender of the

truck, took the paper and shoved it into the pocket of his jeans. "If there's anything I can do for you, let me know."

"Count on it."

"About those TVs…"

"What about them?"

"Who's covering the loss?"

"Nobody. The guy who runs the electronics company in Hammond owes Tony a favor." Nathan switched on the ignition, gripped the throttle and kicked the bike back to life. "I heard he decided not to pay it back."

One hour later, concealed by the overhanging boughs of the maple at the back of the Tavistock yard, Cooper grasped two of the wrought-iron arrowheads that ran across the top of the fence and vaulted to the other side. He paused to look around, but there was little chance of his arrival being witnessed—the houses on this side of the street backed onto a park, which was not only picturesque, it could prove to be a useful setup. Hayley had probably cut through the park when she had carried the rifle to the Sproule estate.

He turned his attention to the house. When he'd brought Hayley home last week, he'd noticed that the front of the house had a big veranda decorated with gingerbread trim. There was no porch in the back, nothing to use to climb to the second story, and the rear door was solid wood with a deadbolt. But the ground-floor windows were the sliding-sash kind and had conveniently wide ledges.

No dog. No alarm. A yard with overgrown trees that blocked the view of the next-door neighbors. For a family of cops, they should have paid more attention to making their house secure. Cooper used the gas meter that stuck out from the wall for a foothold and hoisted himself onto the nearest window ledge. He scowled as he let himself in. He'd have to tell Hayley to get better locks.

Right. Otherwise, someone like him might get inside.

He waited for his eyes to adjust to the darkness, then scanned the room he had entered. A long oval table sat in the center, surrounded by chairs with curving wooden backs. Teardrop prisms of a large chandelier glinted above the table and the flat glass front of a china cabinet gleamed next to the wall on his left. It looked like more than a cop, even a police commissioner, could have afforded, but Cooper had heard that Hayley's mother had come from money.

The archway across from him led to a center hall. It was dark, but a sliver of light showed beneath a door to his right. Keeping his weight on the balls of his feet to minimize the noise of his footsteps on the hardwood floor, he moved to the door and eased it open.

The room was lined with bookshelves. The light came from a green-shaded banker's lamp that rested on the top of an old fashioned roll-top desk. Hayley was sitting on a swivel chair in front of it, the kind with oak slats in the back and casters on the feet. She had her back to him, her fingers clicking at the keyboard of the laptop computer in the center of the desk. She lifted her hand to rub her eyes, then reached for a water glass that sat on a stack of file folders beside her elbow and downed the contents in one gulp.

Cooper's scowl deepened as he studied her. It was two in the morning, but she didn't look as if she had been to bed. She was dressed in jeans and an oversize gray sweatshirt, her hair tied haphazardly at the nape of her neck with a scarf. Her feet were bare, her toes curled against the chair casters. She looked lonely, vulnerable and too damn approachable.

So far, she had kept her word—in the four days since

he'd agreed to her deal, she hadn't gone near Oliver. Instead, she had spent most of her time at the nursing home with her father. Cooper had been pleased that she'd been smart enough to stay away from the Long Shot, yet it was as if she had been there anyway. Echoes of her presence lingered. He kept picturing her on the couch in his office, or curled into the chair in his loft.

He kept remembering the taste of her mouth.

But he was here because she could be useful to him, that's all. She had been right—she had connections and skills that he didn't. They could help each other. He couldn't afford to let it get more complicated than that. She had been intruding into his thoughts too much as it was.

She wasn't his type, no matter how alluring she looked right now. One glance at the kind of place she lived in told him that. So did the room she was sitting in. Scattered among the books on those bookshelves there were framed photographs of men in uniform. Police uniforms. What looked like certificates hung on the wall behind the desk. Those were probably two generations worth of official commendations. He moved his gaze along the frames.

Which one of them was the commendation Adam had received when he'd arrested Cooper?

He gave the door a push to swing it the rest of the way open and stepped over the threshold. "Hello, Hayley."

She reacted instantly, her head snapping up. She spun the chair to face him. "Cooper! How did—"

Her words cut off at the sound of a crash as the empty glass that had been beside her elbow shattered against the floor.

"Aw, hell," Cooper muttered, striding across the room.

Hayley shoved herself out of the chair. It rolled sideways and thudded into the front of the desk.

"Stay where you are!" he ordered.

She glanced around quickly, her eyes wide. "What? Is something wrong?"

"Don't move or you'll cut your feet." He went past her and took the top file folder from the stack on the desk, then squatted down and used its edge to sweep the shards of glass into a pile.

She pressed her hand to her chest and drew in a shaky breath. "You don't have to do that."

"I have boots, you don't."

"You shouldn't have startled me."

"Couldn't be helped." He checked the floor for the glint of stray pieces. When he was satisfied it was clear, he scooped the remnants of the glass onto the folder, then straightened up and looked around. There was a small wicker basket half filled with crumpled paper beside the desk. He dumped the glass into it. "I wanted to make sure you were alone."

"Of course, I'm alone. It's the middle of the night."

He slapped the folder on his leg. The loose neckline of her sweatshirt had slid down when she'd jumped out of her chair, baring her shoulder. There was no sign of a bra strap. Cooper tried hard to keep his gaze on her face. "For a woman who kisses like you do, that's not something I'd take for granted."

Color seeped into her cheeks. She grabbed the back of her chair. He wasn't sure whether it was for balance, or to have something on hand to shove between them. "You could have called first."

"Yeah, but then I wouldn't get to see that pulse in your neck. I like seeing you excited."

"Cooper—"

"You need better locks on your back windows."

"Is that how you got in? Why didn't you simply knock?"

"Force of habit, I guess."

She paused. "I don't believe that. You were deliberately trying to shock me."

"Maybe I wanted to see what you wear to bed."

"I don't believe that, either. You didn't risk coming here just so you could flirt with me."

Flirt? It sounded so innocent, the kind of stuff kids like Hayley would have done in high school. He smiled. "Are you naked under that sweatshirt?"

The blush on her cheeks spread to her neck, to the place where a vein fluttered beneath her delicate skin. It was true, he did like seeing her excited. He enjoyed watching the spark in her eyes chase away the worry. Too bad she hadn't been asleep when he'd gotten here. He would have liked to wake her up with a kiss the way he had the last time. He'd meant what he'd said—a woman who kissed the way she did shouldn't be alone at night.

But she wasn't alone, was she? He was here.

So what was he going to do about it?

His smile fading, he lowered his gaze. The gray fleece that covered her breasts was thick, but not thick enough to hide the reaction of her body. He could clearly see the outline of her nipples. They were hard.

And just like that, his own body responded. Blood surged into his groin so fast his mouth went dry. He imagined slipping his hands under that loose shirt, sliding his palms to her breasts, stroking his thumbs across those tight little nubs…

What the hell was he thinking? He could control himself better than this, couldn't he? He backed up to hitch one leg over the corner of the desk and strategically positioned the folder he still held across his lap.

She yanked the neck of her sweatshirt into place to

cover her shoulder. "That's not the kind of information I offered to share, Cooper."

"Right."

"We might be partners, but what I wear or don't wear is none of your business."

"Fine."

"If you got the wrong idea about the nature of our relationship because of the incident last week—"

"The what?"

"The kiss. It wasn't intentional. It didn't mean anything."

"Yeah, you made that pretty clear."

"Good. I don't want things to get, uh…"

"Hot?"

"Awkward."

Awkward didn't come close to describing what would happen if he did what he wanted to do to that drooping sweatshirt of hers with a roomful of cops looking on.

He moved his gaze to the largest of the photographs that sat beside the lamp on the ledge at the back of the desk. It was Adam Tavistock. Judging by his crisp new uniform and the proud smile on his face, the picture must have been taken at least twenty years ago, shortly after he had joined the Latchford force. Adam was looking straight at the camera, so it seemed as if he was staring right at Cooper.

That did the trick better than a cold shower.

Cooper blew out a slow breath as the pressure in his jeans subsided. He used the folder to gesture toward the photograph. "Except for the blond hair, your brother didn't look much like you."

There was a silence before she spoke. Her voice was strained. "I resemble our mother. He took after our father."

Cooper shifted his gaze to another photograph. Adam was in a football uniform this time. He stood in front of a set of bleachers that looked a lot like the ones behind Latchford High. An older man stood beside him, his arm around Adam's shoulders. They were the same height, both had the same pale, slightly down-turned eyes and their long chins were almost identical.

It was an old picture too, yet Ernie Tavistock was easy to recognize, even without his uniform. He'd been a high-profile police commissioner before his retirement. Rumor had it that Sproule had exerted pressure on his friends in the mayor's office to force the senior Tavistock out so he could replace him with a cop he could buy.

It wasn't going to be easy to bring Oliver Sproule down. Cooper was going to need all the help he could get. It would be plain stupid to let his libido alienate Hayley when they had barely gotten started.

Cooper returned his gaze to Hayley. She was staring past him to the picture of her brother and father.

Usually he found her easy to read, but for once, he couldn't identify her expression. It wasn't exactly grief. It was closer to longing.

It struck him then. There were no pictures of Hayley in the room. There were only pictures of cops like her father and Adam. Adam in high school. Adam at his graduation. Adam who would have been one hell of a tough act to follow.

Hayley's feelings for her family had to run deep—she was wearing herself out trying to avenge her brother's murder—yet from the look of things, the Tavistock men hadn't found time to take a snapshot of her.

Damn, that had to hurt.

Cooper had a sudden urge to pull her into his arms. It wasn't from anything as simple as lust. It would have been easier if it was.

She rubbed her palms briskly over her sleeves and

looked away from the picture. "Most of what I've gathered is in the boxes on the floor."

He wrenched his gaze away from her and glanced down. Cardboard file boxes were lined up in a row in front of the nearest bookshelf.

"The boxes are labeled by date," she said. "There are newspaper clippings, a transcript of the trial and the notes I made of my conversations with the D.A. There's also the report from the private detective I hired, but it doesn't contain anything that I don't already have."

He was impressed by the amount of work that must have gone into assembling the material. It was a lot of information by anyone's standards. No wonder she didn't sleep much.

"You're welcome to look through everything, but I'd prefer it if you leave the files here. I've taken seven months to put them together and they would be difficult to replace."

"Sure."

"Same with Adam's notebook. It's the only useful thing I found when I cleaned out his apartment. Aside from that, he didn't bring his work home." Hayley moved her chair aside and reached out to close the lid on her laptop. Although Cooper sat on the desk beside the computer, she was careful not to brush against him. "The file you're holding contains some of the information I have on Latchford Marine."

Her scent distracted him. So did the lock of hair that had slid loose from her scarf and swung against her cheek. His hand itched to smooth the hair back, to feel it twine around his fingers....

He flipped open the folder and scanned the first few pages.

Latchford Marine was the town's principal employer. It was an outboard motor assembly plant, run by Sproule as a money-laundering front for his more profitable businesses. Cooper already knew that much, but Hayley had added details to back it up. He couldn't make much sense of the numbers, though.

"They shut down one of the production lines last summer," she continued as she repositioned her chair a yard away from the desk and sat down. She stacked her bare feet on one of the casters and tucked her fingertips under the outside of her thighs.

He looked at her defensive posture. Was it because of him, or because of this room? "I remember. The layoffs hit the town hard. Business at the Long Shot was down twelve percent in August compared to the year before."

"Despite that, Sproule built a new warehouse on the Latchford Marine property."

"That's right."

"They're currently bringing in parts from overseas so they can restart the line."

He frowned. "That's news to me."

"It doesn't make sense from an economic viewpoint. I did a rough projection that showed the added transportation costs will mean they'll be running at a serious deficit. I think this might be connected to what Adam uncovered. He circled the dates of the layoffs and the beginning of the warehouse construction in his notebook."

"I'll have access to the new warehouse tomorrow night. It would be a good time to nose around a bit and see what's going on."

"Tomorrow?"

"That's when I officially start working with Oliver."

"What will you be doing?"

He considered not telling her. It wasn't a matter of trust—she had nothing to gain by double-crossing him. It couldn't be a matter of conscience since he'd given her fair warning that things would get dirty.

It was because of the expression he'd seen when she'd looked at that photo. That longing. That hopeless yearning to belong. It stirred something protective inside him...

"Cooper?"

Aw, hell. If he didn't tell her, she might try something on her own again that would screw this up for both of them. He closed the folder, replaced it on the pile on the desk and got to his feet. "I'm going to steal a truck and hijack a shipment of TVs. Want to come?"

Chapter 5

Through the small, rain-streaked windows that flanked the bunk at the back of the truck cab, Hayley couldn't see anything except one gray brick wall of the Hammond electronics plant, a chain-link fence at the edge of the floodlit yard and asphalt shining with puddles. Yet with her senses enhanced by anxiety, she was excruciatingly aware of everything that was taking place in the trailer behind her. Each scraping clank, each muffled thump, every whine of the electric forklift and thudding vibration of work boots on the metal floor meant another pallet of televisions was being loaded into the truck.

Hayley backed away from the window, inching across the mattress until she reached the darkest corner of the bunk. Drawing her knees to her chest, she wrapped her arms around her legs. Trying to calm her nerves, she focused on the sound of the rain on the cab roof instead of the noise from the trailer. Yet as the minutes dragged past, her worry grew.

Any second now they would be found out. Someone on the loading bay would realize they were impostors and raise the alarm. Cooper would be caught. She would be discovered. Both of them would be arrested.

If her brother was still alive and had worked in Hammond instead of Latchford, he could be the one to snap on the handcuffs. And if her father ever heard what she'd done, the shock could very well kill him.

Why on earth had she agreed to this?

She bit her lip, pressing her forehead to her knees. She knew very well why she had agreed. This was the first step in Cooper's plan. It had seemed logical when he'd explained it to her yesterday. He'd claimed it would be simple, that there was zero risk of violence and no one would get hurt.

She had insisted on being included. After all, she had said she would do anything to bring her brother's murderer to justice, hadn't she?

This truckload of stolen goods would be Cooper's passport into the Sproule organization. In addition, the sleeper compartment of this truck would provide the perfect means to smuggle her into the warehouse where she should be able to access one of the Latchford Marine computers. With any luck, in a matter of minutes she would be able to find out more than she had accomplished in months. That was too good an opportunity for her to pass up.

There was a prolonged rattling clank from the back of the trailer, followed by two metallic thuds. Hayley shuddered and hugged her legs tighter. She had dressed in black jeans and a black cotton sweater. Cooper had said dark clothes would help her blend into the shadows once she got into the warehouse office—but her hands were shaking so badly now, she doubted whether she would be capable of working a keyboard even if she did make it that far.

Footsteps approached the driver's side of the truck. The cab rocked as the door opened. Hayley lifted her head in time to see the short curtain that separated the sleeping compartment from the front of the cab swing outward, letting in a gust of cold, damp air. Light showed at the edge of the fabric. The driver's seat creaked.

She held her breath and concentrated on remaining motionless. Oh, no. No. *Please don't look back here. Please*—

The door slammed shut, the light went out. An instant later, a familiar voice sliced through the darkness. "Hayley? Are you okay?"

It was Cooper. Hayley exhaled on a rush of emotion. There was relief, but it was sharp and fast, only temporary—she knew this night was far from over. Yet tangled up with the relief, there was a quick stab of awareness, an involuntary surge of warmth at the sound of her name spoken in Cooper's deep, rich tone.

Awareness? Oh, Lord. Not now. Not *him*. "I'm fine," she said, uncurling from her crouch. On her hands and knees she moved forward. "Is it done?"

"So far, so good." The engine turned over a few times, then caught with a deep rumble. "Better stay out of sight until we clear the yard."

The exhaust stacks on either side of the cab vibrated against their clamps. There was a hiss, a slight jar, and the truck started to roll forward. Hayley grasped the edge of the mattress to hold herself steady. The wheels splashed through the puddles, moving them toward the exit with agonizing slowness. Through one of the side windows she glimpsed two men walking toward a pair of parked cars.

One man lifted his hand toward the truck. "Oh, no," she said. "Cooper, what do you think he wants—"

Before she could finish the question, two quick blasts of an air horn boomed through the truck.

"He was saying thanks," Cooper said. "I just told him 'you're welcome.'"

Hayley craned her neck to watch as the yard fell behind them. The men got into their cars. Headlights blinked on. "He's *thanking* you for stealing these televisions?"

"They don't know that. These guys are glad I got here early so they can go home. This was their last shipment of the day. Hang on, there's a sharp right turn coming up."

Hayley braced herself as the truck swung onto the street that ran in front of the plant. She watched another long gray building slide past, a chemical plant, then another parking lot. They were traveling through an area of small and mid-size factories, the majority closed for the night. Hayley waited until they had turned a second corner and started to pick up speed before she parted the curtain and dipped her head to look out the front windshield.

In a sense, the scene was eerily familiar. The steady beat of the wipers and the flaring circles of streetlights on the glass reminded Hayley of the night she had met Cooper. So did the kernel of hysteria in her stomach that she was trying her best to suppress.

Only this time Cooper wasn't driving his shiny black pickup, he was driving an eighteen-wheeler that bore the distinctive gray-and-white silhouetted wolf logo of the Pack Leader Express courier company.

"This should be far enough," Cooper said. "You can join me up front, unless you want to have a nap while you're back there."

"I don't always fall asleep, Cooper." She swung her

legs off the mattress, climbed down the steps from the sleeping compartment and dropped into her seat. Hunching her shoulders, she tucked her fingers under her thighs.

Cooper brushed his hand down her arm. "Hey, relax. This was the easy part."

Beneath her light sweater, her skin tingled at his brief caress. The interior of the truck cab was big, yet she was vividly aware of Cooper's presence. His scent. The way his thighs flexed as he moved his long legs to work the pedals…

The awareness had to be partly due to anxiety—*all* her senses were enhanced—yet she knew his presence could make her heart race, no matter what they were doing. He was just that type of man. She leaned away from his touch. "I can't believe they're letting us drive away like this."

"Why wouldn't they?" He returned his hand to the gearshift. "As far as the guys on the loading dock know, they were only doing their jobs."

She looked at him. He was wearing a ball cap pulled low over his eyes and a rain-spattered dark-gray jacket, both of which bore a patch with the Pack Leader Express wolf logo just like the truck.

She'd had doubts that the ruse would work. It had seemed too simple. The load of televisions had been scheduled for pickup tonight—all Cooper had done was to show up in a courier truck half an hour early. "What's going to happen when the real driver shows up looking for his load?" she asked.

"By the time he gets there, the place will be locked up for the night. He'll probably figure someone at the plant got the times mixed up."

She rocked forward so she could see the mirror that was mounted outside the passenger door. The curb stretched into darkness behind them. The only lights she saw were streetlights, not the flashing red of a police car. "But when the theft does get noticed, it's going to be reported."

"No, it won't, Hayley."

"Why not? There must be close to a quarter million dollars worth of goods in this truck."

"The owner isn't going to go to the police. I guarantee it."

She returned her gaze to his face. In the sliding bars of light from the street lamps, his expression was difficult to distinguish. "I don't understand this, Cooper. How can you be so sure?"

He shifted gears, lining the truck up for the ramp that would take them to the Interstate. He didn't look at her. His attention appeared to be completely focused on the task of keeping the heavy vehicle steady on the rain-slick pavement. It wasn't until he had brought the truck up to speed and merged into the traffic that he finally replied. "The main thing to keep in mind is that as far as Oliver is concerned, this truck and everything it's carrying are stolen."

"What do you mean, 'as far as he's concerned'?"

Cooper pulled off his ball cap and dropped it between the seats, then raked his hand through his hair. For the first time tonight, he looked distinctly uncomfortable. "Technically, I haven't really stolen anything."

Hayley looked pointedly at the telltale wires that hung under the dashboard. "How can you say that? I saw you break into this truck. I watched you twist those wires together to start it."

"I'm borrowing this truck."

"But—"

"I hot-wired it to make it look like a theft so the man in the courier company who arranged to leave it at the rest stop where we picked it up won't be held liable if something goes wrong, but he knows he'll get it back when I'm through. He won't report it stolen unless I don't return it by the morning."

Hayley leaned forward to look in the rearview mirror again. She focused on the trailer rumbling behind them. "What about the televisions?"

"I'm collecting them as payment on a loan."

"A loan? What kind of banker would…" Her words trailed off. She remembered what Cooper had said about bankers last week. She twisted on her seat to study him more closely. "Does this have something to do with that mobster you told me about who financed the Long Shot? Tony Monaco?"

He gave her a sideways glance. The lines beside his mouth deepened. "Tony wouldn't appreciate being called that. I told you, he got out of the business. He's strictly legit now." He hesitated. "Well, mostly."

She pulled her lower lip between her teeth. With everything else that had been happening, she had managed to put Cooper's connection to that mob—no, *former* mob boss— to the back of her mind. Oh, God. What exactly was she mixed up in? She made a gesture with her hand for Cooper to continue.

"The owner of the plant where we picked up the TVs won't call the police to report the loss. Right about now he'll be getting a phone call from Tony advising him not to."

"And Tony?"

"The goods rightfully belong to him. He knows I have them and he's letting me use them. That's why technically they're not stolen, either."

She tried to sort through what he had said. Someone in the courier company was letting them borrow the truck. They were taking the televisions the same way her car had been repossessed when she couldn't repay her loan.

Was stress muddling her brain, or did this make a strange kind of sense?

Not that this convoluted scheme they were playing out could be considered completely legal, but from one point of view...

"Cooper, are you telling me that everything we've done so far is some kind of charade?"

"It's real enough for our purposes."

"But it was all a setup."

"The best jobs usually are."

"That's why you were so sure it would work."

"Uh-huh."

"There was never any real risk of being caught by the police."

"Not much."

"Why didn't you tell me sooner?"

"Why are you sounding so pissed? Are you disappointed we didn't really steal anything?"

"We're partners, Cooper. You should have trusted me enough to tell me the truth."

"That's what I'm doing now, isn't it?"

"Why now? Why tell me at all?"

"So you'll quit checking the mirrors for cops every two minutes. So you'll stop chewing your lip. So for once I can see your eyes without that haze of worry that tightens the lines at the corners and so maybe you can sleep tonight." He flicked on the turn signal and accelerated to pass a slow-moving station wagon. The truck cab filled with the roar of the engine.

She let her head fall back against the seat, struck silent by his outburst. He sounded as if he was admitting that he cared about her feelings. He definitely hadn't sounded pleased that he did.

Yet that's how it was between them. He was quick to flirt with her, but he was even quicker to deny any suggestion of decency in his motives. This was a man who was more comfortable having her believe he was committing a crime than having her suspect he had scruples.

Cooper checked his speed, muttered a curse and brought it back to within the limit. "You're a smart woman. I knew you would start asking questions so I thought I'd keep you in the dark because it was less complicated that way."

She realized that was as much of an apology as she would get.

She wasn't sure how she felt about this. She was annoyed that Cooper had kept her in the dark, but at the same time she was relieved. Of course, she was relieved. *Technically* neither of them had yet committed a crime.

But now she had a whole new issue to worry about. "Tony seems like a powerful man."

"He is."

"If he has something against Oliver, then why doesn't he, well, take out a contract on him or something?"

"I told you. Tony got out of the business. He might bend the law but he doesn't break it."

"But if he has the connections to set up this pseudo theft, why doesn't he go after Oliver himself?"

"Because he asked me to."

"Why?"

He remained silent.

"Don't shut me out again, Cooper. I've kept my half of our deal. I've been willing to share everything I have. Just by being here I've proven that I'm committed to our partnership. The least you could do is tell me exactly what it is that I'm involved in. You said Tony financed the Long Shot, so why doesn't he want you to pay him back in cash?"

"Because it was more than cash that he gave me."

"I don't understand."

He squeezed his jaw. Beard stubble rasped against his palm. He raked his hand through his hair again and rubbed the back of his neck.

"It's another two hours back to Latchford," she said. "I'm not letting this go."

"Geez, you could talk a man to death."

"So I've heard."

The wheels sloshed along the blacktop. The wipers thumped rhythmically. It was a full minute before he finally spoke. "The real thing that Tony gave me was a chance, Hayley. He gave me a break when no one else would. His loan made it possible for me to turn my life around. That's what he does. He finds people on the wrong side of the law and helps them move to the right side."

This was the last thing she expected. She had been thinking of Tony in terms of some type of loan shark, not a…benefactor. "People? There are more?"

"Tony's been at it for ten years, so there must be a hundred people in the network by now."

"Is this a charity?"

"It's no charity, Hayley. Tony hasn't changed that much. Every person who joins the Payback network knows going in that Tony Monaco's no saint. If they don't pay up when he asks, he'll make sure they lose everything he helped them build. He puts them right back where they were when they started."

"Payback. Is that what he calls it?"

"That's what it's all about. He gives people like me the chance to choose the straight road. In return he expects us to even things up. We have to promise to pay back the favor by righting one wrong in the future."

"What does that mean?"

"Sometimes the law isn't that good at bringing the guilty to justice."

"The guilty. Like Oliver Sproule?"

"Oliver's had a free ride in Latchford for years. The law hasn't been able to touch him. Even when he killed your brother, he was acquitted of the crime. Like you told me, that verdict was wrong."

At last, the connection clicked. "Oliver's acquittal is the wrong that you have to set right."

"That's the task Tony chose for me. Once I do it, my debt to him will be paid in full."

"And Payback's been going on for ten years? Do the authorities know about it?"

Cooper moved his head in a slow negative. "In his early days Tony made a lot of enemies on both sides of the law, so he needs to keep a low profile. Most of the time, he gets Payback members to do his work for him." He tipped his head toward the back of the truck. "That's why we have those TVs."

"You're collecting on a loan that wasn't repaid."

"Right. If I don't pay up, he'll make sure someone else from Payback pays a visit to my bar. One way or another, he'll put me out of business."

"That sounds like extortion."

"It's no worse than bankers who work with a pen. The end result is the same."

He had a point, she realized. Still, she was torn between admiration for what Tony was doing and revulsion over the way he did it.

Tony Monaco's never been real particular about methods. He's more interested in results.

She pulled her heels onto the seat, hugging her legs to

her chest as she mulled over what she had learned. She didn't know what to say. If Cooper was to be believed, he was part of a clandestine network established by a former criminal in order to rehabilitate other criminals and ensure that justice was done, even if it meant they operated outside the law.

It was all so unbelievable.

Yet she didn't doubt for one second that Cooper was telling the truth. As strange as it seemed, it fit. It explained why he was so determined to bring Oliver to justice even though he acted as if he had little respect for the law. It was as contradictory as everything else about this complex man.

She leaned her chin on her knees as she looked at him. His jaw was clenched so firmly a muscle in his cheek twitched. His gaze was fixed straight ahead on the road, yet she had the impression that he was conscious of every breath she took, as if he were waiting for her reaction…although he would never admit that it mattered to him.

Did he realize how much he had just revealed about himself? Tony's network was unorthodox, but its aims were honorable. Cooper had made a conscious decision to join it. That had to mean he was honorable, too.

But she had suspected that much from the start. It was all rolled up in that odd chivalry she had sensed in him. "Can I ask you a personal question?"

Without taking his gaze off the road, he drew off the gray Pack Leader Express jacket one arm at a time, then hung it from a hook behind his seat. He wore a black sweatshirt beneath. He pushed the sleeves to his elbows. "I'll save you the trouble. I sleep in the nude."

An image of the large unmade bed that she had seen in Cooper's loft flashed into her mind. She couldn't help picturing how he would look with his black hair tousled against the pillow and his long, lean body sprawled boldly across the sheets...his ice-blue eyes with those sinfully thick, spiky lashes crinkling into a smile of invitation....

"Anything else?"

She realized he had effectively distracted her. This wasn't the first time he'd tried to throw her off balance with a suggestive comment. "You know perfectly well I didn't mean a question about your personal habits. I meant a question about you."

"Damn, it's going to be a long two hours," he muttered.

"Where did you learn to hot-wire a truck?"

He glanced at her sideways. "Why?"

"I'm curious. You seem...skilled."

"It's not that difficult if you know which wires to cross," he said. His tone was matter-of-fact. It seemed this was one topic he wasn't uncomfortable discussing. "Cars, trucks, vans, they all run on the same basic principle."

"I imagine they do."

"Same with the door locks. All you need is a flat piece of metal and ten seconds of privacy and you can pop most factory locks without any problem."

"Did you figure it out on your own?"

"Nope. My old man taught me."

That surprised her. She had assumed he might have fallen in with a bad crowd or chosen the wrong friends, but his *father?* "How old were you?"

"He showed me on the day I turned fifteen."

"Do you remember what happened?"

"Oh, yeah." He lifted one eyebrow as he looked at her. "Everyone remembers their first time."

"Well?"

"We were living in an apartment over a 7-Eleven in the north end of town then. My mother had taken off for good by that time and Donny was between girlfriends, so it was just the two of us. Some kid who worked at the store had parked this brand new red Mustang in the alley. It was Donny's idea of a birthday present."

"Donny?"

"I never called him Dad."

"Oh."

"It was a real sweet little car. Too bad I hadn't learned how to drive yet. I went through the guard rail where the highway crosses Latchford Creek." He shook his head. "Rolled twice before I hit the water. Totalled the Mustang."

Her stomach turned over. "You could have been killed, Cooper."

"I wasn't."

She thought of the tough kids under the bleachers. Had Cooper bragged to his friends about his reckless joyride with that red Mustang? Then she thought about her fifteenth birthday. Adam had given her a new CD player and a pair of in-line skates, her father had given her a book on the history of Latchford, and they had gone out for sundaes at the Dairy Queen.

The life that Cooper had sketched with his brief description was completely foreign to Hayley. The only thing they had in common was the lack of a mother's presence, but other than that, his childhood couldn't have been more different from hers.

It made the fact that he'd accepted Tony's deal and had turned his life around all the more admirable. "What happened after you, uh…"

"Stole my first car?"

"Yes," she said. "What happened then?"

"I learned to steal other things."

"Oh."

The rain eased to a drizzle. Cooper adjusted the wiper speed and checked the dashboard clock. He leaned over to reach between the seats and picked up the ball cap he'd dropped. "Here. Take this."

She took it from his hand. "What for?"

"You better tuck your hair inside it. Even in the dark a man would have to be blind not to notice you."

She gave him a smile. "Thanks, Cooper."

"Hayley..." He hesitated. "There was another reason I didn't tell you this job was fixed."

"You mean besides not wanting to explain about Payback?"

"Yeah. Besides that. I wanted you to have a taste of what being scared felt like."

"Why? Did you enjoy seeing me terrified?"

"No, I already told you that I didn't."

"Then why?"

"So far this has been a dry run for you. When I drive this rig through the door of Sproule's warehouse, it's going to be the real thing." He tapped the rim of the steering wheel with his fist. "I wanted you to know what to expect so you can decide whether or not to go through with it."

"I already told you I would."

"That was before. It's not too late to bail."

"I'm not going to fall apart the way I did when I tried to shoot Oliver. I've already explained to you that I wasn't thinking clearly then. I wasn't myself. I'll do better this time."

"I'm not trying to make out that you can't do this, Hayley. You've got guts and you're stubborn. I'm just trying to give you an option."

"Don't you want my help getting into the Sproule computer system?"

"Sure, I do. I don't know anything about that stuff, but

I want you to understand that if you don't feel like going any further, we'll find some other way to get what we need."

She wound her hair into a twist and fitted the hat on top of it. "If I didn't know better, I would think that you're trying to be noble, Cooper."

He snorted. "Noble?" He looked at her upraised arms, then boldly dropped his gaze to where her sweater stretched across her breasts. "It's a damn good thing you do know better, Hayley."

Chapter 6

Cooper hated being wrong. The Latchford Marine warehouse should have been dark and practically deserted at this time of night. Okay, Sproule might have put on a few extra people as a show of power because this was Cooper's first job with him, but at most, there should have been maybe three or four men. They wouldn't have been too much to handle. He could have cleared out some of the guys with free handouts of the merchandise and diverted the attention of the others while he unloaded.

Yet the instant the overhead door rolled up and Cooper eased the rig inside, he knew he had miscalculated big time. He never should have brought Hayley with him. No way was anyone going to move around here unnoticed. The place was lit up like Christmas and crawling with guards.

It was too late to get her out. Through his side mirror, he could see one of the men who stood by the control box hit the button to lower the door as soon as the back of the trailer had cleared it. Another man walked in front of the truck, swinging his arm to guide Cooper toward an empty space near the left wall. Like the others, he had an Uzi slung over his shoulder.

The warehouse was bigger than it looked from the outside, with more space than Cooper thought that an outboard-motor plant would need. Most of the floor was covered with stacks of cartons. Some were cardboard and bound together with shrink wrap, others were printed with pictures of motors. It was a pile of wooden crates near the back wall that seemed to be drawing most of the attention. He counted six men working on them with crowbars.

Damn, he wasn't just a little wrong. He was up to his ears in some serious trouble. No one needed armed guards to unpack outboard-motor parts.

Cooper dug into his jeans pocket for a stick of chewing gum, unwrapped it and folded it into his mouth. "We've got a problem, Hayley." He pitched his voice as low as he could and timed his words to the rhythm of his chewing for the benefit of anyone who was watching him through the windshield. "Your job is off. Don't move. Don't make a sound. Don't look out the windows."

Her whispered reply was barely audible above the rumble of the engine. "Why is it so bright in here?"

"Something major's going on." His palm slipped on the knob of the gear shift. He realized it was slick with sweat. He eased the truck to a stop. "Get under a blanket and keep your head down. Whatever happens, don't come out."

"Cooper?"

He set the brakes and killed the engine. "Not for anything, you hear that? You're going to have to trust me on this. I got you into it, I'll get you out."

There was a soft rustling from behind him, then silence. "Okay."

He unwrapped another stick of gum, popped it into his mouth and reached for the door handle. "I won't be nosing around tonight. I'll just get rid of this load and—"

The door was wrenched open. "Hey, Webb!"

Cooper felt his pulse spike. Using every ounce of his control, he managed to restrain the impulse to glance behind him to check if the curtain over the bunk was closed. He turned to his left.

A square-built man with a shaved head stood in the angle of the open door, one foot propped on the bottom step and the other hand on the stock of his Uzi. He looked familiar, but it took a second for Cooper to place him—he'd had a full head of brown hair the last time Cooper had seen him. It was Isaac Pressman, a small-time numbers runner. They had been on the same cell block during his last year in Joliet.

"Dammit, Izzy. Don't point that thing at me." Cooper swiveled on the seat and swung his legs out of the cab. "You'd be better off shooting whoever gave you that haircut."

Izzy grunted a laugh as he ran a palm over his scalp. "You should try it yourself, Webb. The chicks love it."

"Yeah, right." Cooper caught the grab bar and hopped to the warehouse floor. He landed so that Izzy had to step back. "So, how long have you been out?"

"One month, three days. I been meaning to look you up."

Cooper was glad he hadn't. He'd never trusted Izzy. "You working for Sproule now?"

"It's the only game in town."

"That's what I heard. Sure looks busy in here."

"The hours suck, but the pay's good. I told Sproule you were okay. You thinking of getting in on it?"

"Maybe." Cooper went into a leisurely stretch, flexing his arms until his back cracked. He finished up by casually closing the door. "Right now I've got other business. Oliver said he'd move some TVs for me."

"Yeah. He wants them over by that wall."

Cooper turned toward the trailer. "I've got to ditch this rig before daylight but I'm beat. Give me a hand unloading, will you?"

Izzy was still looking at the cab. His gaze moved over the window in the upper side. "That's one big mother. What you got in there?"

A bead of sweat worked its way down Cooper's temple. He angled his head so Izzy wouldn't see it. "A sexy blonde who's got the hots for me." He snapped his gum with his tongue. "That's why I'm beat."

Izzy hesitated a second, then guffawed, punched his arm, and followed him to the back of the trailer.

Hayley set the carton of orange juice and two glasses on the table and sank onto the bench of the breakfast nook, automatically sliding to the spot beside the window that had been hers as a child. Sunlight was filtering through the maples at the back of the yard, spreading a mottled pattern of gold across the table. It looked wonderfully ordinary and normal. It was just what she needed. She flattened her palms in the middle of it.

She remembered eating her cereal here before school. She used to love the kind with marshmallow bits but her father only bought granola. Until he moved out, Adam would regularly sneak a box of the marshmallow kind into the cupboard. Sometimes at night, her brother would play cards with her at this table. He had tried to teach her poker, but she hadn't been much good at it. She was incapable of bluffing.

Funny, Cooper had figured that out on the night they had met.

"Forget the orange juice." Cooper strode across the kitchen, yanked open the refrigerator and looked inside. "We could use some beer."

"Sorry, I don't have any."

"I can see that. You don't have much of anything in here except rabbit food." He squatted to peer into the bottom shelves. His jeans tightened, outlining the long muscles in his thighs and the taut curves of his buttocks.

Hayley was exhausted, yet at the same time she was strangely charged, as if the nervous energy that had been humming through her body for the past ten hours was floating around loose with nothing to focus on. She should try not to focus on Cooper. She jerked her gaze away from his butt and leaned forward, sliding her hands through the patch of sunshine. "There's some white wine on the door. Help yourself."

"Do you want some?"

"It's eight o'clock in the morning."

"So? Live dangerously."

She dropped her head between her extended arms, feeling a mad urge to laugh. "I think I've had about all the excitement I can take for one night, Cooper."

"Don't sell yourself short. You handled the whole thing pretty good for an amateur."

"I didn't do anything."

"Sure, you did. You kept your head. That's why we got out of there in one piece." The refrigerator door whooshed shut. Cooper's footsteps thudded against the tile floor. "You're still too wound up, Hayley. If you're not going to have any wine, do some deep breathing. You've got to relax and let this go."

She closed her eyes, not wanting to remember those endless hours in the warehouse. Or at least, it had felt like hours. In reality, it could only have been minutes—Cooper had emptied the trailer in less than a third the time it had taken to fill it. "I thought everyone in that warehouse would have heard my teeth chattering."

The bench across from her creaked as he sat. His knee bumped hers under the table. "That's why I chewed gum, so no one would notice mine."

"You were as cool as ice, Cooper. I can't believe you had the nerve to joke with that man who wanted to know what was in the cab."

"You mean Izzy?"

"Yes. I heard the whole thing."

"Who was joking? You're blond and you have a bad case of the hots for me, don't you?"

Another laugh threatened, but her throat was too tight to let it through. "What if he'd looked into the cab anyway?"

He touched her knuckle with his fingertip. "Before I let it go that far, there would have been skid marks on the warehouse floor and a hole in the overhead door the size of that semi."

The resolve in Cooper's voice warmed her as much as his touch. He sounded protective, yet if she mentioned it, he would probably claim his main concern had been not blowing his cover. She lifted her head, pulling her hand away from his to shove her hair from her eyes.

He leaned back and draped his arm along the top of the bench. The tattoo on his forearm stood out starkly in the daylight, rippling over the contours of his muscles. His sweatshirt pulled snugly across his shoulders. The night's growth of beard stubble shadowed his jaw. His hair bore the grooves of his fingers. Against the homey backdrop of the sunlit kitchen, he looked barely civilized. And outrageously masculine.

She tried to focus on business. "At least the first part of your plan worked. You started your association with Oliver."

"We did more than that, Hayley. We saw that you were on the right track. Oliver's got some major action going on from that warehouse."

"What do we do now?"

"I'll wait for him to sell those TVs before I talk to him again, but I'll probably meet up with Izzy before that. I'll see what he knows about those crates by the back wall that everyone was so interested in."

"The wooden crates?"

"Yeah."

"They were from Russia."

"How do you know that?"

"My college roommate grew up in Moscow and used to read newspapers from home. The label on the top crate was written in Russian. I recognized the alphabet and a few of the words."

"You shouldn't have seen anything. You should have kept your head down."

"I did. I only saw the top of the stack."

He drummed his fingers on the back of the seat, then reached for the carton of orange juice, poured a glass and pushed it toward her. "You said Sproule was bringing parts in from overseas. Any from Russia?"

She picked up the glass and sipped. "There was one company that was based in Vladivostok."

"Can you can get some names to go with that company?"

"I'll try."

"We need to find out what kind of goods these people are known for."

"Goods. Do you think they're smuggling something into the country in those crates?"

"It's the only thing that explains all the security."

"Drugs?"

"There are plenty of things he could be into, but that would be my first guess. There's a big profit margin in drugs."

"If that's what Adam found out, Oliver would have kept him from telling anyone. If we can prove Oliver is involved in smuggling, we can connect this with Adam's notebook and establish a solid motive for murder."

Cooper jiggled the orange juice carton—from the sound of it there wasn't much left. He held it out to her. When she shook her head, he lifted the carton to his mouth and drained it. "It would be less complicated to concentrate only on the smuggling."

"Instead of Adam's notes?"

"No, as a crime. It would be easier to prove than murder, and we could take it to the feds so we wouldn't have to go through the Latchford police and run the risk of having the case covered up. Depending on what's in those crates, Sproule could be facing some hard time for trafficking."

"But he's guilty of murder. I thought you had to right the wrong of his acquittal."

"He's guilty of a lot of things. As long as Sproule ends up in jail, does it matter how he gets there?"

Her first impulse was to protest. She wanted Adam's killer convicted for his murder. She wanted public acknowledgment that Oliver was guilty. She had spent the last seven months working toward that goal. She had promised her father that Oliver would be punished and she hadn't wanted to settle for less.

Yet the idea of compromise was no longer as unthinkable as it had been only yesterday. She had already compromised her principles. Charade or not, the theft she and Cooper had acted out had felt real, and she had been a willing accomplice. And she couldn't forget what she had almost done a week ago.

No, principles didn't seem as black-and-white as they used to.

Cooper's approach had merit. Now that he had established a working connection with Sproule, he could learn details of a significant portion of his criminal dealings. It would probably be easier to gather evidence of crimes that were ongoing rather than one that was seven months old…

The realization struck her all at once. Of course. Cooper would have known that it would be difficult to find concrete evidence proving Adam's death wasn't accidental. That wasn't the reason he had gone undercover. "You never planned to get Sproule for murder," she said. "You were intending to find evidence of some other crime all along."

He nodded. There was no apology in his gaze. "That's right. After all this time, there's not much chance of proving murder."

"You could have told me."

"I warned you that we didn't want the same thing."

"Yes, you did, but I had assumed you meant in spirit."

"That, too. I told you it wasn't a personal vendetta for me. You know how I feel about your brother, and I'm not out to avenge his death. I'm doing this to keep my bar."

"What about Tony? Will having Oliver arrested on something other than murder satisfy him?"

"All he's interested in is justice. How I do it is up to me."

"Is there anything else you haven't bothered to tell me, Cooper?"

"Why are you sounding so pissed again? I thought you would be happy that we're making progress."

"I am, but I don't like the way you dole out bits of the truth to me. You're always doing that. I've been completely honest with you."

"Bull."

"What's that supposed to mean?"

He stood, walked to her side of the breakfast nook and braced his knee on the bench beside her hip. Gripping the edge of the table with one hand and the top of the seat with the other, he caged her between his arms. "You haven't been honest with me about one thing, Hayley."

"What?"

His gaze dropped to her mouth. "That kiss last week wasn't meaningless."

Just when she'd thought she was getting the attraction under control, he was close enough for her to catch a whiff of pine from his soap and the unique, musky scent of a man who had been awake all night. She was helpless to stop the sudden jump of her pulse. "You're trying to change the subject and it won't work. I'm not going to be sidetracked."

He put his finger on the dip at the base of her throat. "We were talking about honesty."

"Cooper…"

"So I'm going to be honest. You're still on a high from the job. That's why you're so edgy. You don't really want to argue with me, you're just searching for a way to get rid of all that tension."

"Of course, I'm tense. Why wouldn't I be? I've never ridden a truckload of extorted televisions into a warehouse full of armed men before."

"Are you still scared?"

"No."

"Do you want to call off our partnership?"

"No!"

He hooked his thumb into the neck band of her sweater and tugged her toward him. "Do you want me to stop?"

God, no, she thought. But this was crazy. She knew her priorities. "Cooper…"

"You're no good at hiding your feelings, Hayley, and the way you've been looking at me since we got here is driving me nuts."

"I'm sorry if I gave you the wrong idea, but—"

"There's nothing wrong with this idea." He dragged his knuckle along her collarbone. "We've both been thinking about it for a week."

She could have moved away. Averted her head. Pressed further into the corner by the window. She could have grabbed his wrist and taken his hand away from her sweater. Simplest of all, she could have told him to stop.

She didn't. Whether this was an aftereffect of anxiety or a consequence of fatigue didn't seem to matter because it was precisely what she had needed since he had brought her home. So why shouldn't she allow herself this one indulgence?

Any further thought was impossible. He lowered his head and kissed her.

He tasted of orange juice. On his lips, it seemed exotic, turning a flavor she had grown up with into something different, dark and exciting. He didn't need to test for the best angle this time. He fitted his mouth to hers with the confidence of a long-time lover.

Delight flowed through her, loosening the lingering anxiety from the night. Each change in pressure, every shift of his lips was a renewed exploration, building on the kiss before. He made her feel as if this was all there was, all that mattered. How could she help but kiss him back?

At her response, he slid his knuckles from her neckline to the upper slope of her breast. The caress was light—he'd looked at her more boldly than he was touching her—yet the sensations that followed warmed her to her core. Passion mixed with comfort and…rightness.

She arched her back, lifting herself more firmly into his hand.

He crowded closer on the bench beside her and spread his fingers, cupping her breast with swift possessiveness. His touch was no longer light. Heat tightened her stomach and streaked to her thighs so fast she shuddered. She opened her mouth. His tongue plunged inside. The kiss turned carnal, a sensual, frank exchange of pleasure.

It was more than she could have imagined. His breath on her cheek, the scent of his skin, the press of his thigh against hers…she felt engulfed by his presence. He slipped his hands beneath her sweater and deftly unhooked her bra. She gasped at the pleasure. He knew just where to stroke, just how to squeeze, using his fingers and his palms in a way that made her quiver.

She lifted her arms to his neck, leaning into him, hanging on as her senses spun. The more he touched her, the more she wanted. Her nipples were so tight, they stung. Pressure built to an ache between her thighs. Their mouths mimicked what her body craved. It was reckless and exhilarating, escalating so rapidly within minutes they were both on the thin edge of control.

He caught her arms and slid backward, tugging her off the bench with him. As soon as she was clear from the table, he splayed his fingers over her hips and pulled her against the front of his body.

She could feel his erection against her stomach, and she knew that's what he'd intended. It was a declaration. A question. And oh, she couldn't stop her tremor of response. She had never been this totally aroused. He was incredibly, blatantly…male.

He ran the point of his tongue down the side of her neck. "Hayley?"

No sweet words. No promises. She understood what he was offering. Sex. Simple and straightforward, with no pretenses that it was anything else. After the kiss they had just shared, that's what any man would expect.

You're still on a high from the job.

Some of the heat ebbed. Was that all this was, just a mindless physical reaction? Probably. It was an outlet for their adrenaline. A natural result of the excitement of the night.

He must have sensed her hesitation. He raised his head. His nostrils were flared. His gaze bore into hers as his thumbs dug into her waist.

There was no tenderness in his expression, no hint of the sensitivity she had glimpsed before. He wanted sex. He didn't want intimacy.

It's a damn good thing you do know better, Hayley.

Finally, her brain kicked into gear. Indulging in a kiss with a man like Cooper was one thing, but anything else would be asking for heartache. She placed her palm on his chest. "This isn't what I want."

He trailed the pad of his thumb across her lower lip, rubbed the moisture against his fingertips and held them up to her. "No?"

She took a step away. Her legs were unsteady. She grabbed the back of the bench. "All right. I admit it. I enjoyed the kiss. It wasn't meaningless, but that's as far as it goes."

"Why?"

"We have to work together. This wasn't part of the deal."

He covered her hand where it gripped the bench. "How long has it been?"

"What?"

"Since you ate a good meal? Since you slept the night?" He stroked her hair from her cheek and tucked it behind her ear. "Since you slept with a man?"

"Are you asking me that only because you want me to sleep with you, or because you actually care about me, Cooper?"

He didn't reply. He looked as uncomfortable as he had after his outburst in the truck when he'd behaved as if he'd been concerned about her feelings.

Reality returned with a thump. The rest of the pleasure dissipated. She felt a sharp prickle behind her eyes as another thought occurred to her. "Or are you doing this because I'm Adam Tavistock's little sister?"

His gaze shuttered, as if a door had slammed somewhere inside him, but not before there was a flash of pain. "Is that what you think of me?" His voice was carefully controlled, as cold and distant as stones dropping into a well. "Do you believe that I would want to have sex with you as some sick scheme to get back at your brother?"

Hayley pressed her fingers to her mouth. Her instincts were screaming at her that he hadn't deserved her accusation, but now that the words had been spoken, they stood like a wall between them.

Yet wasn't that why she had said them? To push him away before either of them could get closer?

He yanked her hand away from her mouth. Grasping the back of her neck, he held her in place and gave her a hard kiss. His lips were firm and unyielding. He kept his eyes open, his blue gaze snapping with anger. It wasn't so much a kiss as a challenge.

He released her and walked to the door. He spoke without looking back. "It's the other way around, Hayley," he said. "I don't want to sleep with you because you're Adam's sister. I want to sleep with you in spite of it."

When he'd been alive, Adam had loomed large in Hayley's life. It seemed as if his death hadn't changed that. He still cast a shadow she couldn't escape. One way or another, his presence continued to tinge every relationship and each aspect of her world.

"Is Adam coming today?"

Hayley took a steadying breath, then picked up her father's hand and gently chaffed his fingers between hers. His skin felt loose over his bones. "No, Dad. He won't be coming."

Ernie Tavistock dropped his head against the pillows, as if he'd spent all his energy lifting his head to look toward the door. His left lid drooped, as did the corner of his mouth. Through his thinning layer of white hair, his scalp looked as fragile as water-stained paper.

He had been such a powerful figure throughout Hayley's childhood, she couldn't get used to seeing him like this. Even a year ago, at seventy-one, he'd been exceptionally fit for his age. The stroke he had suffered last fall had devastated him physically, but it was the emotional blow of Adam's death that had hit him the hardest. It was difficult for him to accept something so wrong.

There was no gray in Ernie Tavistock's world, only black and white. Right and wrong, law and order, crime and punishment—he believed vehemently in all those clichés. His beliefs had propelled him to a distinguished career in public service. He had been a man everyone had looked up to.

Adam had followed in his footsteps every step of the

way. He'd been the perfect son. He'd made Ernie proud with everything he'd done.

Hayley squeezed her father's hand. As long as she could remember, she had wished she could make him proud of her, too. "It's a lovely day. Let's go outside."

"Adam might call."

"I'm sorry, Dad, but Adam's gone."

His chin trembled. He drew his hand away from hers. "I know, Hayley. Sometimes…I forget."

She left the bed and moved to the wheelchair. She refolded the mohair throw that she had draped over the back. "The lilies beside the front entrance are blooming. We can go past there and then head toward the lake."

"I remember now. The trial's over."

"Yes."

He thumped his hand onto the mattress. "Sproule is free."

"I'm sorry, Dad. He—"

"My son is dead and Sproule is walking around free. It's a…travesty. It's—" His words dissolved into a fit of coughing.

Hayley quickly took the pitcher from the bedside table, poured a cup of water and held it to his lips. "Please don't upset yourself, Dad. You know that isn't good for you."

He swallowed a few mouthfuls and closed his eyes. He waved the rest of the water away.

She replaced the cup beside the pitcher, taking care that it didn't block the picture of Adam that was propped there. "Dr. Byers is pleased with the progress you're making. She wants to expand your therapy."

He didn't respond. He usually ignored any talk of his condition. Like Adam's death, it didn't fit with his view of the world.

Voices sounded in the corridor as two of the nurses

went by. Hayley listened to the brisk squeak of their shoes on the tile as she lifted her gaze to the window on the other side of the bed.

The Applewood Manor nursing home was one of the top-rated long-term-care facilities in the state. Along with access to the best medical facilities and rehabilitation programs, it provided a healing environment, nestled into ten acres of well-tended grounds near the small lake that had given the town of Latchford its name. Her father's insurance paid only part of the fees, her dwindling savings paid the rest.

Yet she knew in her heart that money wouldn't buy what her father needed. If he was ever going to recover, he needed to get over his grief. He needed closure. He needed Oliver Sproule behind bars where he belonged.

Oh, how she wanted to give that to him.

"Talk to the D.A.," he said. "Get him to appeal the verdict."

"He refused. He said there wasn't enough evidence."

"I'll ask the new commissioner. Johnson. Jim's a good man. He came yesterday."

"Jim can't help, either. Dad, I—"

"Judge Mercer. We went fishing together. I'll call him. He wouldn't let my son's murderer go free."

He already did, she thought. They all did. She and her father had had variations of this conversation every day for the past week. It always ended the same way, with her father fading into himself just a little more.

She wasn't sure when she had decided that Cooper had been right, but he was. It didn't matter how Oliver ended up in prison as long as he did. It might not be the black-and-white justice Ernie wanted, but at least it would give him something to hope for.

Hayley pulled a chair closer to the bed and sat. She took her father's hand again. "Dad, he won't be free for long."

He opened his eyes and looked at her.

"I'm not giving up." She leaned closer and lowered her voice. "I'm gathering evidence of Oliver Sproule's other crimes. He's going to face justice."

"How?"

She saw a spark of hope in his gaze. She went on eagerly. "It's too soon to tell anyone else yet, Dad, but I'm going to finish what Adam started. He discovered Sproule was using Latchford Marine to smuggle something into the country. I'm working on learning more. Sproule will be punished. I promise you."

A flash of vitality tightened the slack muscles of his face. For an instant, he was the father she used to know, indestructible and invincible.

Hayley smiled. "It'll work, Dad. You'll see."

And then you'll let yourself heal.

And maybe then you'll look at me the way you used to look at Adam.

And maybe, just maybe, you'll love me back.

Chapter 7

From the corner of his eye Cooper saw Izzy weave his way through the crowd near the pool tables, his shaved head gleaming like a cue ball. He had his arm draped around the shoulders of a short brunette in a bright-pink tank top and his hand was already working its way under one strap. There was no danger of the top slipping down, though—it was stretched so tight across the woman's bust it could have been spray-painted on.

Several heads turned to follow her display as she and Izzy approached the bar, but Cooper's wasn't one of them. He was remembering how classy Hayley had looked in her cream-colored suit the day she had come to the Long Shot. Then he thought about how good the weight of her breast had felt in his palm yesterday morning.

The towel squeaked so hard across the glass he was drying he felt the vibrations in his wrist. He set the glass down carefully. He'd already broken three tonight.

Why was she getting to him? He'd made a pass, she'd said no. End of story. He knew it was for the best. She was a passionate woman, but he didn't need the complications that came along with her.

Damn, if he'd been smart, he would have walked away when he'd seen her on her belly in the rain.

The hell of it was, he couldn't walk away now. She was proving to be more of a help than he'd anticipated. She was clever, and she was persistent. He still needed her.

And he still wished he could ease the loneliness he saw on her face, wrap her up and protect her, watch her sleep, make her smile, hear her laugh...

He braced the heels of his hands against the edge of the varnished pine slab in front of him. This bar was what he cared about. His business, his new life, the chance that Tony had given him, those were his priorities. Looking out for number one was how he'd survived until now. There was no room for weakness in his world.

Instead of being frustrated, he should be thankful Hayley had reminded him of that.

"Hey Webb!" Izzy stopped in front of the bar and grinned. His fingertips were no more than an inch above his girlfriend's left nipple. "Nice place you got here."

Cooper took a second to fix a bland expression on his face, then lifted his shoulders in a careless shrug. He rolled the sleeves of his shirt above his elbows. "The hours suck but the pay's good," he said, echoing what Izzy had said to him. "Depending on the tips."

Izzy laughed. With his free hand, he dug into the pocket of his pants and brought out a thick wad of bills. He nimbly thumbed off the one on the outside and slapped it on the bar. It was a fifty. "Give us a pair of tequilas. You can keep the change."

Cooper picked up the bill and held it under the counter-feit scanner he kept out of sight beneath the bar. It was real. That ruled out one possibility about what Sproule was into. He snapped it between his fingers and handed it back. "Your drinks are on the house."

Izzy stuffed the money back in his pocket. "What'd I tell you, Nina?" he said to the woman. "Cooper's all right."

She looked at Cooper and gave him a smile. Dark circles of mascara ringed her eyes. Two large gold hoops swung from her ears and a smaller one pierced her right nostril. Her mouth was covered with bright-red lipstick—hooker's lipstick, Cooper thought—but her skin was smooth and plump as a baby's.

His gaze sharpened. He took a closer look at her features and realized she couldn't be more than sixteen. Cooper set only one glass on the bar and reached for the tequila bottle. "You got any ID with you, Nina?"

The girl's smile wavered. She looked at Izzy.

He tapped his fingers against her breast. "Come on, Webb. Does she look like a kid?"

The man was a pig. If Cooper didn't want information from him, he'd throw him out. He poured a shot into the glass and pushed it toward him. "Ditch the jailbait, Izzy. Then we'll talk."

"Dammit, Cooper, I don't care how old she is. I only been out one month and four days." He snatched the shot glass and drained it in one gulp. He slammed it back on the bar. "Don't you remember how it was?"

Cooper remembered, all right. When he had finished his prison term, it had been tough to control his physical drives after being celibate for so long. It had made him irritable, antsy and spoiling for a fight. But those urges had been unfocused. The ones he felt now were centered on only one woman.

Hell, couldn't he get through two minutes without thinking about Hayley?

Under the makeup, Nina's baby cheeks had turned as pink as her tank top at Izzy's remark. Any doubts about her age were impossible after that blush. Cooper glanced around the barroom. He spotted Pete Wyzowski near the platform where the band was setting up and whistled through his teeth to get his attention. When Pete looked at him inquiringly, Cooper pointed at Nina, then cocked his thumb toward the door.

Izzy sputtered, but as soon as he saw Pete's size, he stopped arguing. Pete had that effect on people. Cooper refilled Izzy's glass and watched Nina leave. He trusted Pete to see that the girl got home safely. Whether she liked it or not, he would probably give her a free lecture along the way—Pete had raised four rebellious sisters of his own.

"Don't get excited, Izzy," Cooper said. "I just don't want to lose my licence for serving a minor."

"Damn." He knocked back the second tequila as quickly as the first. "I already wasted more than fifteen bucks feeding her."

Cooper braced his hands against the bar again, trying to remember why he shouldn't throw Izzy out anyway. "Yeah, that's some wad you're carrying. What does Sproule have you doing for that?"

Izzy glanced around, then leaned one elbow on the bar and motioned Cooper closer. "I'll show you." He dipped his hand into his back pocket and pulled out a brown leather wallet. It was flat—the cash was in his other pocket—but it wasn't empty. He slipped out a small, square packet and held it pinched between his first two fingers. "I was saving this for Nina."

At first glance it looked like a condom. Cooper felt a wave of disgust. Then he noticed that the packet wasn't the opaque foil of a condom wrapper, it had the gleam of plastic. There was some kind of white powder inside.

"Horse is easier to move than TVs," Izzy said, waggling the packet between his fingers. "You got a good setup at this place. With the business you do here, in one night you could distribute—"

Cooper grabbed Izzy's wrist and smashed his hand on the bar. "The Long Shot is clean."

"Hey, man!"

"The only thing I sell here is liquor."

Izzy tried to yank back his arm. "Take it easy. I'm trying to do you a favor."

Cooper could feel the grind of bones beneath his fingers and realized he was a split second away from breaking Izzy's wrist. Somehow he managed to restrain himself. "Does Sproule know you're helping yourself to the merchandise?"

Izzy clawed at Cooper's fingers with his other hand. "There's lots more where this came from. He won't miss it."

"You stupid son of a bitch. When Sproule finds out what you're doing, you're dead."

"Back off, Webb. And let go of my arm."

"Is there some trouble here, Cooper?"

Cooper looked around. Ken Martinez, the Long Shot's regular bartender, moved into the rectangle formed by the bar, a case of beer balanced on his shoulder. Ken swung the case to the floor one-handed and stood poised on the balls of his feet, his arms held in the deceptively relaxed readiness of a martial arts expert. Theresa, Ken's wife, set down a tray of glasses on the other side of the bar and reached past them to put her hand on the phone.

"No problem," Cooper said. "I'm just taking out the garbage."

Ken and Theresa both nodded, yet they remained watchful. Cooper returned his gaze to Izzy. He no longer bothered to hide the revulsion he felt for the man. He released Izzy's wrist and wiped his hand on his pants. "I'm only going to say this once, so pay attention. If you try pushing that stuff on a kid or bringing it anywhere near my bar, you better hope it's Sproule who catches up with you first and not me."

"It's heroin." Cooper stepped around the file boxes that were piled on the floor of the study and paced past the bookshelves, his big body moving with the fluid grace of a stalking predator. He looked edgy, dangerous and barely restrained.

Hayley swivelled the chair away from the computer to keep him in sight. "How do you know?"

"Izzy showed me a sample tonight." He pivoted and walked to the window. He gave the curtain a yank to close it more securely. "It wasn't pure white so it was already cut. He probably mixed it himself."

While they had both guessed that it was likely drugs that were being smuggled, she still felt sick at the idea. Heroin. It was one of the worst, the drug of hard-core addicts. This was far more abhorrent than the theft and gambling that Oliver was already involved in. "What did you do?"

"I threw him out and flushed his junk down the toilet."

"But I thought you wanted to work with him."

"Not now. He's skimming off Sproule's profits. I don't want anything to do with him."

"You still have your connection to Sproule. I guess you didn't really need Izzy."

He folded his arms over his chest. "He brought that garbage to the Long Shot, Hayley. To my turf. He thought I would distribute it."

Hayley had glimpsed his anger yesterday morning. It had been deep and cold. That had been mild compared to what she saw now. Tension flowed off him in waves. His fists were clenched. Beneath the rolled-up cuffs of his shirt, the veins stood out in his arms.

She had a pretty good idea what his foul mood was about. Izzy's assumption that Cooper would deal drugs had insulted his honor.

Just as she had insulted his honor when she had suggested he wanted to sleep with her to get even with Adam.

Not for the first time, she wanted to apologize. The distance she had put between them yesterday was still there. They had kept their conversation limited to business since he had arrived at the house. He hadn't flirted, he hadn't touched her, he had scarcely made eye contact. Logically, she knew it was better that way—getting romantically involved with Cooper was the last thing she needed—but she missed the camaraderie they had developed in the truck.

Yet the situation was already volatile enough. It was after midnight, she was dead tired and it was difficult to keep her mind on business when his emotions *weren't* stirred up. When he was like this, with his hair endearingly tousled by his fingers, the lines beside his mouth deepened by the shadows and his body heat sending delicate shudders tickling across her skin each time he walked past....

No. This was for the best. She wasn't going to let her emotions cloud her thinking. She had her priorities straight. She swallowed her apology and swiveled back to the computer. "Did you find out anything else?"

He did another circuit of the room, then halted at the

side of the desk. "That's it, besides the fact that Izzy's a pig, but I knew that already. What about you?"

Although she stopped herself from looking at him, she could see him on the edge of her vision, a tall, dark form still dominating her senses. She focused on the screen of the laptop. "I researched the company from Vladivostok that's supplying parts to Latchford Marine."

He hitched one hip on the desk. "Any luck?"

"As a matter of fact, yes, but it took me a day to unravel. It was a shell company nestled inside a whole series of shell companies." She called up her e-mail program and scrolled through the messages. "I contacted a friend of mine in New York who works the overseas markets and asked if he could help me out."

He leaned his shoulder toward her and twisted to see the screen. His shirt tightened, sending folds slanting down his torso. "Did he?"

She opened a message and pointed to the type halfway down the page. "Yes. That's the name of the owner of the company. A Russian national named Stephan Volski. He divides his time between Chicago and Novosibirsk."

"Volski? You're certain?"

"Completely. Once I knew what to look for, I found a large amount of material on him. He's a very wealthy man."

"I've heard of him."

"Really? What did you hear?"

"He's Russian mob. Real bad news."

She chewed her lip for a moment. Her hand hovered over the keys. "Stephan Volski owns several manufacturing plants both in Russia and in America, an import-export business in Moscow, a chain of dry cleaners in Chicago and a race track in Kentucky."

"And he's bringing heroin into the country in Oliver Sproule's outboard-motor parts."

She dropped her hands to her lap. "It looks that way, but it's still only speculation."

"It fits."

"We don't have enough to take to the FBI or the DEA. If we just give them a tip, there's no guarantee they'll be able to arrest Oliver. We need more."

"Izzy didn't find that packet he showed me under his pillow, Hayley."

"I realize that, Cooper. You don't have to be sarcastic."

"Who's being sarcastic? I thought you liked honesty."

"Look, I know you're frustrated because Izzy brought those drugs to the Long Shot, but—"

"That's not the main reason I'm frustrated." He slid off the desk and stood in front of her. "Do you have any idea what it does to me when you nibble on your lip like that?"

Heat sizzled through the room. What had been under the surface since he had arrived had burst into the open. She rolled her chair backward and got to her feet.

He didn't move closer. He didn't make a motion to touch her. All he did was look at her mouth. It was a bold gaze, filled with knowledge as well as promise.

The memory of their kiss tingled on her tongue. The scent of soap and his skin filled her lungs. Her pulse skipped. She was achingly conscious of the late hour, how he stood only one step away, how his hands looked so large and steady and how right his hands had felt on her body. She was tempted, oh, so tempted, to forget about being sensible and close the distance she had put between them…

She curled her nails into her palms to resist the urge to reach out to him. "We were talking about Sproule and the drugs, Cooper."

He looked past her, his gaze skimming over the bookshelves. He raked his fingers through his hair, rubbed the back of his neck, then shoved his hands into the pockets of his jeans. He turned his head toward the desk and looked straight at the graduation picture of Adam. "Right."

"Cooper…"

"Your father should have put up a picture of you."

The comment was so unexpected, his tone was so fierce, it took her a moment to register what he had said. He had obviously noticed the other photographs of Adam that were scattered around the room. He must have realized there were no photographs of her.

She was amazed to feel a sudden lump in her throat. After a lifetime of slights from her father, she took them for granted. To have Cooper not only notice but sound indignant on her behalf moved her more than she liked.

Still, this was one place she didn't like to go. The roots of this pain went too deep, all the way back to her birth. She tried to deflect the topic. "My dad was very happy when Adam followed in his footsteps, so it's natural that he'd want to put up his pictures. Same with all the awards Adam received. That's why Adam gave them to him. Dad enjoyed displaying them alongside his own."

"You're doing a better job of getting evidence against Sproule than the cops ever did." He walked past her and squatted in front of the file boxes. He bent his head to read the labels, then flipped off one of the lids and looked inside. "Not that they tried all that hard."

"Adam tried."

He pulled out a folder and spread it open on top of the box.

"Our dad was very proud of him," she said.

"Donny used to be real proud of me, too." He turned over the first page in the folder. "Kind of ironic, isn't it?"

Hayley thought about that. Adam had gone into police work because of their father just as Cooper had been introduced to crime because of his.

It *was* ironic. Sad, too. Underneath all the toughness, Cooper was an intelligent—and at times uncomfortably perceptive—man. How different might his life have turned out if he'd had a better start? What if his father had been a law-abiding citizen with a steady job and he'd had a stable family life?

Then again, Hayley's life would have been different, too, if her mother had lived and her father could have loved her.

She looked at Cooper's back, at the too-long, rebellious hair that curled over his collar, then went to peer past his shoulder at the file. It was the one on Latchford Marine that he had looked through the other day. "Where—" She cleared her throat. "Where's your father now?"

He ran his finger down a column of numbers. For a while it seemed as if he wouldn't answer. When he did, his voice was guarded. "He died five years ago. Lung cancer."

"I'm sorry."

"The doctors warned him it was killing him, but he wouldn't quit smoking. I quit when I was a teenager, but he'd done it all his life so he was hooked bad."

She knelt at his side. "That must have been difficult for you, not to be able to stop him."

"I couldn't have done anything for Donny at the end. I was in prison when he died."

And Adam had been the one to put him there. Although neither of them voiced the fact, it was as clear as if it had been spoken.

Yet another reason for Cooper to resent Adam. It wasn't

a logical reason—Cooper had readily admitted that he hadn't been innocent of the crime he was imprisoned for—but feelings seldom were logical.

She watched him leaf through the papers, his forehead furrowing as he concentrated. She should probably let the subject drop, but she felt compelled to defend her brother. "I am sorry you couldn't be there with your father, Cooper, but Adam was only doing his job."

"Arresting me got him a commendation. That's why he got promoted to detective."

"I didn't know that."

"It's probably on the wall here someplace."

She glanced at the commendations and plaques in the study. "It wasn't personal, Cooper. Adam was very good at what he did."

He flipped over another page and paused to read it before he spoke again. "Adam wasn't that good, Hayley. He wouldn't have gotten me without my help."

"What do you mean?"

"You're not the first Tavistock I struck a deal with."

"I don't understand. Did Adam get you a plea bargain?"

"Something like that. I made it easy for him. I confessed to hijacking that truckload of computer chips."

She sat back on her heels. "You confessed? Why?"

He splayed his hand over the paper he'd been reading. The edges crumpled beneath the pressure of his fingertips. "With Donny going downhill, I didn't want to risk a long prison term. Your brother guaranteed that I would get a reduced sentence by cooperating and that I would be out in less than a year. It seemed like the best option at the time, so I pleaded guilty."

"What happened?"

"Things didn't work out the way Adam promised. I

served a full three years. By the time I got released, Donny was dead."

She didn't know what to say. Her brother wasn't to blame for the sentence—the length of time to be served would have been up to the judge and the D.A.—yet she could understand Cooper's resentment. Yes, Cooper had been guilty and needed to pay for what he had done, but Adam shouldn't have promised anything he couldn't deliver.

Right and wrong had once seemed so clear, but nothing about this was pure black and white, was it? She touched her fingers to the tattooed eagle on his arm. "Cooper, I'm sorry it turned out the way it did."

He looked at her. "I'm not angling for sympathy. I was a sucker for taking the deal."

"You couldn't have known what would happen."

"No, but I never should have trusted a cop. My old man taught me better that that." He studied her for a minute, then picked up the paper he'd been reading, folded it into quarters and slipped it into the breast pocket of his shirt.

Her thoughts were still muddled from what he had revealed. It took her a moment to realize what he'd done. She frowned. "What was that? What did you take?"

"The schedule for the parts shipments."

"What are you going to do with it?"

"You were right. We need more proof if we're going to go to the feds. The best way would be to set things up so they catch Sproule the next time he gets a shipment of heroin. Anything less and he'd be able to lawyer his way out of the charges."

He had returned to the topic of Sproule and the drugs, just as she had asked him to. She held out her hand. "Let me make a copy of that schedule first. It took me weeks to verify."

"No, I'll handle it from here."

"What does that mean?"

"Like I said, Sproule's new pal Volski is Russian mob. That's bad news. Things could get ugly." He rose to his feet. "I don't want you involved in this anymore, Hayley. It would be safest for you if you backed off."

"Don't you dare start that again." She stood and reached for his shirt pocket. "I'm not quitting."

He caught her wrist before she could grasp the paper. "You will if you want me to get Sproule."

"You still need my help."

"I'll get by." He lowered her hand to her side. "And I'll get Sproule. You can count on it. I want you out now, before you get in any deeper."

"You wouldn't have known that Oliver was involved with Volski if it wasn't for me."

"That's true. Thanks."

"This isn't fair." She went for his pocket with her other hand. "You have no right—"

He grabbed her arm, then pushed both of her hands behind her back, crossed her wrists and circled them with his fingers. "I don't give a damn about what's fair as long as I get what I want. You should know that by now."

Her pulse tripped at the way he restrained her. With her hands held behind her, her shoulders were thrust back. Each breath she took squeezed her breasts against his chest. She tried to ignore the intimacy of the position. "Then why are you worried about my safety at all?"

"Because I hate being wrong." He pulled her closer. "I shouldn't have agreed to our partnership, Hayley. I knew you didn't belong in my world the first time I looked around this room."

Hayley's breathing grew ragged. "Cooper—"

"And I knew it for sure when I saw those drugs in Izzy's hand tonight."

"Was that what changed your mind?"

"The Long Shot is clean. It's the first decent thing I've had in my life and it's going to stay that way."

"I understand that, but—"

"I don't want the ugliness to touch you, either." His gaze moved over her face. "You're a good woman, Hayley. We never should have teamed up."

"If you're trying to get rid of me just because your deal with Adam didn't work—"

"Dammit, you keep throwing your brother between us, but this has never been about you or about Adam for me—it's about keeping my bar. That's it. That's all. The Long Shot, nothing else."

"Then why can't we continue as we have been? As long as no one knows what we're doing, the risk isn't any worse than before."

"The stakes are too high now. With Volski and his drugs involved, Sproule is more dangerous than ever. Our partnership is over."

"I can't quit. I'm going to finish what Adam was working on."

"Then back off and let me do the job."

"This is where we started a week ago."

"Looks like this is where we end."

She blinked, trying to stem a wave of frustrated tears. Her heart was pounding so hard, she could hear her pulse. It was from what he was saying. It was from the way he was holding her, the familiar strength of his body.

And oh, God, it was from the look in his eyes, that intense spark in the ice blue that had nothing to do with Adam or Oliver or any of the ugliness.

Focus! she told herself. Think of your priorities. "I'm not giving up," she said. "Whatever happens, I can handle it."

"Hayley—"

"Go ahead and keep that schedule you took. It's not going to stop me. I'll put together another one." She broke free from his grasp and stepped back. She inhaled shakily.

And caught a whiff of something foul. She twisted her head toward the study doorway. It was an odor like…rotten eggs.

Cooper grabbed her elbow. "I smell gas."

She jerked away. "I must have left the stove on. I'd better shut it off—"

"Hayley, no!"

A blast of air from the doorway hit her face like a fist. A split second later, a ball of flame erupted from the dark hall and knocked her backward into Cooper's chest.

Chapter 8

There wasn't enough time to blink. Cooper curled himself around Hayley as they were flung across her father's study. He tried to shelter her, but his muscles wouldn't move fast enough. The flames roared over their heads, singeing his hair and sucking the air from his lungs.

He landed on his back in the center of the file boxes. The boxes crushed beneath their combined weight, turning into a slippery mass of paper and cardboard. A second wave of fire licked past the doorframe on the heels of the blast. The hall beyond it was already an inferno.

Cooper had smelled the gas mere seconds before the explosion. If a gas line was open, it would be feeding the fire like a blow torch, so there was no hope of stopping it. Their only hope was to get out.

Hayley's elbow cracked his nose as she tried to scramble off him.

Cooper clamped his arms around her and rolled toward the desk. This was an old frame house. Whatever hadn't been ignited by the initial explosion was going to go up in a matter of minutes.

But where was the gas leak? What had ignited it?

Not what. Who. Hayley hadn't left anything on by mistake. This couldn't be an accident. Cooper was certain of that. Someone must have ruptured the main line.

But he would worry about who and why later. Right now, he had to get her out. He ran his hands along her arms and over her back. "Are you okay? Can you move?"

She nodded. He felt it more than saw it.

"Stay low!" he ordered, dragging her with him as he crawled across the floor. Smoke was billowing into the room more quickly than they could cross it. The explosion had blown out the window. The fresh air pouring in from outside was accelerating the spread of the flames. "We can't get through the door. We'll use the window."

Her body convulsed with another cough. "The files! I can't leave them."

"Hayley, no!"

She twisted away from his arm and lunged backward.

He made a grab for her, catching her by the ankle. She fell face-down, her arms outstretched. Without breaking his grip, he reached up with his other arm and caught the bottom of the curtain that was fluttering in front of the shattered window. He gave it a sharp tug to rip it down.

Hayley rolled to her side and jerked her foot. "Let go, Cooper!"

He didn't have any choice, not if he wanted to get them through the window. His throat stung from the smoke. He had to shout over the roaring from the hall. "Stay put. I'll have you out in a second."

"Okay!"

He released her ankle and got to his feet. Squinting through the smoke, he wrapped the curtain fabric around his hand to knock out the shards of glass that clung to the frame, then reached back for Hayley.

She wasn't there.

Damn! Cooper looked behind him. Flames were already licking up the side of the bookshelf that was closest to the door and curling against the ceiling. One of the frames on the wall ignited in a burst of yellow, then fell to the floor. In the midst of it all, Hayley was on her hands and knees, tearing through the smashed file boxes.

"Hayley!" He ran back and grabbed her by the waist. "Come on!"

"Adam's notebook!" she gasped. She spun on her knees toward the desk. "My computer. We need them."

He picked her up, flipped her over his shoulder and started back across the room. Another frame ignited and smashed to the floor.

She coughed, her palms sliding down his back as she tried to lift her head. "Cooper, no!"

He reached the window and tossed her outside, then grabbed the top of the frame, pulled up his feet and swung himself through. He landed on the grass beside Hayley just as a crackling whoosh sounded behind them. The fire must have reached the paper on the floor, he realized. One glance back confirmed the entire room was ablaze.

He scooped Hayley into his arms. Chances were that whoever had caused the explosion would be long gone, but he took the time to scan the area anyway. When he didn't see movement or the glint of a weapon, he held her to his chest and jogged toward the front of the house.

She scissored her legs and pounded his shoulder with her fist. "Let me go! I need to go back."

He didn't slow down until he reached the curb. Through the trees that canopied the street, he could see lights coming on in the neighboring houses. The blast had probably been felt blocks away. Someone would have called 911 by now.

"Cooper, please! Those files." She choked on a sob. Her breath wheezed. "All my papers."

"They're gone, Hayley."

"No. They can't be. I have to—"

"Hayley." He turned so that she faced the house. "It's too late."

She trembled from her head to her feet, one cold, tight shudder. Then she went completely still.

The fire was spreading with incredible speed. Flames shot out from every window, blackening the clapboard siding. Shards of blown-out glass glinted orange on the lawn and the floor of the front veranda. Smoke poured from the roof, lit from below by roiling billows of fire. Boards split and nails swelled and popped from the heat—the house groaned as if it were alive and knew it was dying.

Hayley clutched his shirt. "No. I can't lose this, too. Oh, God."

He set her on her feet and folded her into a hard embrace. It had been close. Too close. One more minute and Hayley could have been caught in there. She could have gone up with those files. He buried his nose against the top of her head. The acrid bite of smoke masked the scent of her hair, yet he inhaled anyway. He needed to fill his lungs with her as he was filling his arms. He had to reassure himself that she was still here, that he hadn't lost her.

The strength of his need shook him. This was more than a need for her body. He was starting to care about her. He didn't want to. He'd been taught better than that. People came and went and only a fool let himself care.

Go, he told himself. Leave now while you still can. It's not too late. No one has to know you were here.

That would be the smart thing to do. Sproule had to be behind the explosion. Somehow, he must have figured out that Hayley wasn't going to leave him alone. He might even have discovered she was asking around about Volski. With drug profits on the line, Sproule wouldn't take any chances.

Hayley's knees gave out. Cooper caught her before she collapsed, sat down on the curb and cradled her on his lap. He heard a siren in the distance. People were starting to appear on the street: a gray-haired woman in a long green dressing gown and a short, plump man hobbling with a cane, a middle-aged man with striped pyjamas beneath an overcoat and two teenage boys on bicycles. These were her neighbors. Someone here would make sure she saw a doctor. They would see to her. He didn't need to stay.

Cooper was fairly sure that Hayley had been the sole target. He'd been too careful to keep their association secret, and he was positive that no one could have seen him arrive or could have known he was there. If he left now, he might still be able to salvage his plan to work from the inside.

She turned her face to his neck. He felt her tears on his skin.

And he knew damn well that he wasn't going anywhere.

Hayley cradled the mug in her hands, anchoring her mind on the details. The same plaid blanket that Cooper had covered her with when she had slept on his couch the night they had met was draped around her shoulders, but she wasn't on the couch in his office, she was on one of the overstuffed sofas in his loft. Like the big leather recliner, it was angled to face the wall of windows. The slats of the blinds were tilted open, allowing a view of the overgrown orchard in the field behind the Long Shot. The tops of the apple trees were tinted gold with the first rays of sunrise.

With disbelief, she realized it was already morning.

The deep murmur of Cooper's voice as he spoke on the phone came from the corner of the loft that made up the kitchen. A minute later, he finished the call, set the phone down on the counter and crossed the room. The sofa cushion dipped as he sat beside her. His warm thigh brushed against hers.

The contact steadied her, as it had throughout the horror of the night. He'd given her a solid shoulder to lean on while the fire trucks had lined the street. His arms had sheltered her from the backwash of the spray as the firemen wrestled hoses across the lawn. The only time he'd let go of her was when he had insisted that she get checked out by the paramedics. Aside from some scrapes and bruises, she was uninjured. Neither of them had needed any treatment for the smoke they had inhaled, thanks to the way Cooper had gotten them out so quickly.

Everything had seemed to go by on Fast Forward. In a way, she was thankful that the night was a blur. She didn't really want to remember watching her childhood home go up in flames. Who would have guessed that a one-hundred-and-twenty-year-old house could be destroyed in a matter of minutes?

The debris was still smoldering when they had left. The stately old Victorian had been reduced to a jumbled mass of charred beams and twisted pipes. Between the explosion and the fire, the devastation was near total. There was little hope of salvaging anything.

"I asked Theresa to stop by the mall when it opens and

pick up some clothes to tide you over until you can get to a store," Cooper said. "I guessed at the sizes you would need. I thought you might feel like getting cleaned up."

She glanced down at herself. Her blouse and slacks were covered with black-ringed holes where sparks had fallen on her clothes. "Theresa?"

"Martinez. She waitresses here. Her husband, Ken, is my bartender."

"That's very nice of both of you, but I can change when I…" She stopped. She had been about to say when she got home, but she didn't have a home. She didn't even have any clothes except the ones she was wearing. "It's going to take a while to sink in."

Cooper wiped his thumb across her cheek. "That house meant a lot to you."

"It was my mother's house. Her great-grandfather built it when Latchford was founded. Adam and I grew up there. It's been in the family for five generations."

He dried her other cheek. "It was insured, wasn't it?"

"I let the policy lapse. My mother's money went to my dad when she died, but there's barely enough left now to cover the taxes and the upkeep. I never dreamed… Oh, God! I can't believe it's all gone. Every piece of furniture had a history. My grandmother's china, my grandfather's books, even if there was insurance, they could never be replaced. I should have saved them."

"You couldn't do anything, Hayley."

She felt an echo of the helpless grief that had shaken her during the night. She lifted the mug to her mouth. The rim clunked against her teeth. Cooper closed his hand over hers to steady her as she took a sip.

Hot chocolate, heavily laced with something alcoholic, trickled down her throat. It burned at first, then left behind a comforting dullness, soothing the soreness that lingered there. She glanced at the sunlit treetops. It was too early in the day to be drinking, but as Cooper had once said, why not live dangerously?

She hiccupped on a sob and downed the rest of the liquid in the mug. Warmth spread down her chest to her stomach. Dangerous? How could she be worrying about the house or the furniture or even those files she had tried to save? She and Cooper could have been killed.

The firemen had said it looked as if the gas line behind the house had been tampered with where it entered the back wall. There had been scrape marks from some kind of tool on the metal pipe. They weren't calling the explosion deliberate yet—the investigation into the cause wouldn't start in earnest until the wreckage had cooled down—but they weren't calling it accidental, either.

Cooper was taking it for granted that Sproule had been behind it.

She turned to look at him.

Stiff, frizzled ends of singed hair stuck straight up along his hairline. He had used a damp towel to clean his face, but a streak of soot remained on his forehead. More soot had settled in the lines that fanned out from the corners of his eyes.

He had saved her life. It wasn't the first time.

Except this time, he had done it publicly. She belatedly realized what should have been obvious hours ago. "Cooper, you gave the police and the firemen your name."

"They had to know where to reach you, and you needed someplace safe to go."

"But what if Sproule finds out I'm here? That's going to ruin your plan to work from the inside."

He took the empty mug from her hand and rose to his

feet. "You need to rest," he said, walking toward the sink. "We'll talk about it later."

She shrugged off the blanket and pushed herself off the sofa. The room tilted for a second. She waited until it steadied, then followed him across the floor. "No, we should talk about it now. I can't stay here. It's going to get back to Sproule."

He rinsed the mug in the sink. "It probably already has."

"But what if it hasn't?" She turned toward the door. "I should go someplace else."

He caught up to her and grasped her by the arms before she had taken two steps. "Hayley, you can't go anyplace right now. Sproule tried to have you killed. That explosion wasn't an accident any more than Adam's death was."

She looked around. She spotted his phone on the counter. "I'll call the police. I'll explain I need protection…" She stopped. She exhaled hard. "They won't be able to help without any proof."

"If whoever you talk to is on Sproule's payroll, proof won't make any difference."

Her head was spinning. The scope of the disaster was continuing to expand. She whipped her gaze back to Cooper. "Why would he try to kill me?"

Cooper trailed his fingers down her arm and took her hand. He led her to one of the wooden stools that rested beneath the side of the counter that defined the kitchen. He hooked a rung of the stool with his foot to pull it toward her and eased her to sit. "It looks like he knew you were still after him."

"That's impossible. I've kept away from him since you and I made our deal."

"He might have found out you were investigating Volski."

"I don't see how. Besides my friend in New York, we're

the only two people who knew I was tracing the ownership of that parts company…" She drew in her breath.

"What?"

"No, that's not possible. He wouldn't have said anything."

"Who? Who did you tell?"

She bit down on her lip. She felt sick.

Cooper squeezed her hand. "Hayley, did you tell your father?"

She nodded, stricken. "Two days ago. He's been so despondent. I wanted to give him hope so I told him I was going to finish what Adam started. I told him Oliver was smuggling something, but I didn't know about Volski or the heroin then… Damn, I didn't think. Someone must have overheard. I never close the door of his room when I visit."

"Or your father could have told someone."

"I asked him not to but lately he forgets. He gets confused. I wanted to ease his mind so he could heal and—" And so he would love me.

Oh, God. She had probably brought this on herself. She had known her father still spoke with his old colleagues, she was aware Sproule might have informants on the police force, but she couldn't believe that would include one of her father's friends.

That would be hitting too close to home.

"It doesn't really matter how Sproule found out, it's done, Hayley."

She touched her fingertips to the singed hair at the edge of his forehead. "This is my fault. Cooper, I'm sorry."

"Regrets don't change a thing, so don't beat yourself up over this."

"But if Oliver knows that I'm investigating the smuggling, he'll be on his guard. It's going to be more difficult than ever to find evidence against him."

He took a folded paper from his shirt pocket and spun it onto the counter. It slid to a stop against the phone. "He'll probably change his schedule, too, so this won't do us any good."

She looked at the paper blankly before she realized it was the one he had taken from her files.

Cooper had wanted to end their partnership. He was going to cut her out of their plan.

The argument was pointless now. The information she had gathered and offered to share with him was gone. In all likelihood, any chance of Cooper working undercover was gone, too.

She swiveled on the stool to prop her elbows on the counter and dropped her face into her hands. "This just keeps getting worse."

"We're still breathing, so it's not that bad." He cupped her shoulder. "The way I see it, Hayley, you have two options."

"What?"

"You could forget about avenging your brother and go back to Chicago."

"No." She twisted to look at him. "Absolutely not. I'm not giving up until I see this through."

He moved his hand to her back, rubbing gently. "At least think about it."

"I don't need to. I have nothing to go back to. I quit my job when I came home. I gave up the lease on my apartment. I put everything I had into getting justice for Adam."

"You could get another job in Chicago."

"When my money runs out, I'll get a job in Latchford. I'll stay at the Y. Whatever I need to do. I'm not leaving until this is over."

"Leaving is the safest choice."

"Do you really expect me to take it?"

One corner of his mouth lifted. It was the first hint of a smile he had allowed all night. "No, but I thought it was worth a shot."

"What was the other option?"

"You stay here with me until Sproule's in jail."

She stared at him. "Stay here? You mean in your apartment?"

"The people who work for me know what's going on. They're not going to let Sproule or any of his men near the Long Shot."

"I'm not going to hide in here with the blinds drawn again the way I did when you met downstairs with Oliver. That would be as bad as running back to Chicago."

"You won't have to hide. Your presence here won't be a secret, so we don't have to sneak around anymore. When you go out, I'll go with you. Sproule's going to know you're under my protection."

He did sound protective, almost…possessive. She felt a surge of warmth. She didn't even bother trying to tell herself it was only because he was still willing to work with her. She did feel safe with him. She always had. Considering the circumstances, his suggestion was a sensible one.

And yet, if she accepted it, she would be opening herself up to a different danger. The more time she spent with him, the more she learned about him, the more compelling she found him. How could she share his home with him and hope to maintain her distance?

She glanced around the room. "The last I heard, you wanted to dissolve our partnership."

"It's too late now, Hayley."

"You seemed pretty definite before."

"The fire changed that." He paused. "It changed a lot of things."

"But—"

"If you won't leave town, then I want you to stay where I can keep you safe."

"Your loft is only one room, Cooper."

"It's a big room."

"There's only one bed."

"Plus two sofas and a chair you've already slept in. It's your choice where you bunk down."

Despite the turmoil of the night—or perhaps because of it—her heart began to pound. "Just so there's no misunderstanding…"

"When I said the choice is yours, I meant it. Like you told me, sleeping with me was never part of our deal." He touched his thumb to the skin below her ear. "Not unless you want it to be," he added.

She was sure he could feel her pulse race. She could see the knowledge in the gleam that lit his eyes.

For a mad instant, she wanted to tell him she would choose his bed. He had been by her side throughout the past night. What would it be like to spend a night in his arms, in his bed, to feel his large body move over hers, to give in to the mindless physical attraction that even now was making her sway into his touch?

Why not? she thought recklessly. She had lost everything else, hadn't she? In the space of a few hours, she had lost all her belongings, her family home, seven months of painstaking research and her best hope of bringing her brother's killer to justice. Why not go all the way and lose her heart?

Her heart? Oh, God. Was that what was happening? She jerked back from his hand and slipped off the stool. "I'll take the sofa."

"Are you sure that's what you want?"

"Yes, it is."

He hesitated, then reached out, caught her chin and touched his mouth to hers.

It was a mere brush of his lips, as gentle as his grip on her jaw, but her emotions were so raw, it jolted her down to her toes. The tang of smoke mixed with the scent of Cooper. Images of flames, of loss, spun through her mind. She wanted to drive them out.

His hand shook against her chin.

She clutched the front of his shirt to lift herself into him, sealing their mouths more firmly.

He groaned, stepped closer and tunneled his fingers into her hair. Gripping her head, he pushed his tongue between her lips.

She couldn't help but respond. She sank into the kiss, closing her eyes, absorbing the familiar taste and texture of this man. Her chin tingled at the rasp of his morning beard stubble. Her nipples tightened at the contact with his chest. She brought her hands to his shirt buttons, fumbling to open them, needing to get closer.

He moved his mouth to her neck. "Hayley?"

Her fingers were trembling. She couldn't open his buttons so she slid her hands to his belt. A sob scraped her throat.

He caught her wrists and curled them against his chest. He rubbed his teeth over her earlobe. "Tell me you changed your mind."

"I didn't. I just need… Oh, Cooper."

For an endless moment, he didn't move. His fingers spasmed around her wrists. Finally, he pressed his face to the crook of her neck, his breath hot and fast across her skin. "It's okay, Hayley," he murmured. "I know what you need." He brought his mouth back to hers.

He kissed her again. More gently this time. She could feel tension ripple through his arms, his chest, his legs, yet he kept his touch light. He lifted her hands to his face and breathed a kiss into each palm.

The tenderness was too much. Her knees buckled.

He caught her in his arms. How many times had he done that tonight? She felt his body shift against hers as he carried her across the room, his strides long and steady. He nuzzled her ear, then leaned down to lay her on her back.

Not on the bed, on the sofa. The cushion dipped beneath his knee, the warmth of his chest grazed her breasts, but he held his weight off her. He braced his hands beside her head and brushed his lips along her cheek. She hadn't realized she was crying again until she felt him kiss a tear. When they ran out, he brought his mouth to hers in a slow, heart-stopping caress.

Then Cooper did something that touched her heart more than passion ever could.

He covered her with the plaid blanket, pressed a kiss to her forehead and walked away.

Cooper took a final look at the locked door at the top of the stairs, then sat sideways on the bottom step, propped one boot in front of him and banged the back of his head against the wall of the stairwell.

Why the hell had he done that? He could have been wrong. Maybe he'd misread the fatigue on Hayley's face. She might have wanted more than comfort. She might not have been as upset as he'd thought. There was always the possibility that she had changed her mind about him and had known what she was doing.

Yeah, right. If he was going to start pretending, he could hope there was always the possibility that Sproule was going to decide to walk into the police station and make a full confession.

But he'd never been big on make-believe. If he had pushed Hayley, he would have been taking advantage of her. She was vulnerable right now. She had also downed a double shot of whiskey with her cocoa. He'd wanted her to relax so she could get some rest. He hadn't planned to get her drunk and seduce her with that kiss. He'd just needed to kiss her.

Cooper banged his head against the wall again.

"You okay, boss?"

Cooper glanced up. Pete stood in the doorway to the back hall, his face creased with concern. "Yeah, never been better," Cooper replied.

"You look like hell. Is the shower in the loft broken?"

He poked at a soot-ringed hole on the knee of his jeans. "Hayley's upstairs. She needs to rest." And she wouldn't get much of that if either of them had an excuse to get naked. "I'll finish cleaning myself up down here."

Pete hunkered down, bracing the knuckles of one hand between his knees as if he were taking his position on a line of scrimmage. "What do you want Ken and me to do?"

"Just keep the place locked up."

"For how long?"

Cooper thought about that. He couldn't close down the Long Shot indefinitely. Not only couldn't he afford it, he knew there were too many other people depending on the place for their livelihood. "Today at least. I need time to figure things out."

"We're all behind you, Coop. Whatever you decide."

"Thanks, Pete. That's good to know." He rubbed his jaw. Beard stubble rasped under his palm. It surprised him to realize it was only one night's growth. Somehow the time that had passed seemed longer. "How did things go with that kid yesterday?"

"You mean Nina?"

"Uh-huh. Did you get her home okay?"

"I checked it out before I dropped her off. Her parents had thought she was at the library studying for an exam. They seemed genuine."

"What's your take on it?"

"They look like solid people. Nina was scrubbing her face like crazy trying to get rid of the makeup when we pulled into the driveway. I think she's a good kid, but she's in too much of a hurry to grow up and got in over her head." His mouth thinned. "That cue ball she was with knew damn well she was underage."

"Have you seen any sign of Izzy?"

"Who?"

"The cue ball."

"No."

"Watch out for him. He was always mean when he got crossed."

"Will do."

"On second thought, there is something you can do for me, Pete."

"Name it."

"If we're going to open the Long Shot tomorrow, we'll need some more security. I want people we can trust."

"You thinking of getting the guys back together?"

Cooper nodded. "Spread the word. I can't pay up front but they'll know I'm good for it."

Pete pushed off from the floor and straightened to his full height. "They'll come, Coop. After what you did for them, they owe you."

"Thanks."

"Anything else?"

"Yeah." Cooper glanced up the stairs, then thudded the back of his head against the wall again. "Keep me away from that damn door."

Chapter 9

Darkness had fallen by the time Hayley awoke. She had slept almost twelve hours straight. For a few, luxurious minutes she lay where she was and marveled at that. In the seven and a half months since her brother had been killed, she hadn't slept for more than a few hours at a time before she would startle awake with her heart pounding and her stomach in a knot. She napped when her body reached exhaustion, but the sleep was never deep or restful. Here in Cooper's apartment, she felt restored. Strengthened. Safe.

She sat up, pushing her hair off her face as she looked around. A dim glow came from the kitchen—the light over the stove was on—but the rest of the loft was lit only by the moonlight that streamed through the slats of the blinds. She saw at a glance that she was alone, yet Cooper's presence still surrounded her. The macho furniture, the big windows, the clean gleam of the hardwood floor, the hint of his scent that clung to the blanket, all of it was like an embrace.

She picked up the blanket and hugged it to her chest, pressing her face into the folds. She caught a whiff of smoke from her clothes and braced herself for the rush of loss.

Yet it wasn't as bad as she'd thought it would be. Cooper's presence was in her memories, too. He had given her the comfort that she had needed, his support had blunted the nightmare, and his kiss…

Oh, Lord. That kiss. She didn't know how that had happened. It was a good thing he had stopped before it had gone any further. He must have realized she wasn't thinking straight, that she wasn't herself.

Sure, you were. No one can fake feelings that strong.

That's what he had said after she had tried to shoot Oliver. He had seen her at her worst then, and he had stuck with her. He'd done it again last night. She pushed to her feet. For once, no dizziness accompanied the sudden movement. It had to be because of all the sleep.

How long has it been…since you ate a good meal…slept the night…slept with a man…?

It had been noble of Cooper to stay with her after the fire, just as it had been chivalrous of him to walk away and let her rest. There was a good character underneath his tough shell. He would deny it, of course, but his actions continued to prove otherwise.

Yet she couldn't let herself read more into this situation than there was. She was here because she and Cooper had a common goal, that was all. Yes, there was a strong physical attraction between them, but it was irrelevant. Once Sproule was in jail, their alliance would be over. She exhaled hard and headed for the shower.

Forty minutes later, she pushed open the swinging door

at the back of the Long Shot's main room. The lights at the front of the room were dim. The square bar in the center of the floor was deserted and the chairs stacked upside down on the tables. The only illumination came from an oblong metal-shaded lamp that hung from two chains above the middle of the three pool tables.

Cooper was bending over the table, his left arm extended in front of him and his fingers braced on the cloth to guide the end of his cue. Against the backdrop of the darkened room, his tall, rangy body was dramatically outlined.

He looked up as she entered, but he didn't change his position. He studied her carefully, his gaze missing nothing. "You're looking good, Hayley."

She brushed self-consciously at a fold of her dress. She had found it on a hanger in the bathroom, the sales tag still attached to the label. The fabric was soft, cream-colored knit jersey cut in a simple short-sleeved style that skimmed her hips and ended in a flare above her knees. It was a size smaller than the rest of her too-large wardrobe, so it fit perfectly. So did the bra and panties that had been hooked on the hanger with it.

Cooper had guessed her size with disconcerting accuracy, right down to her cup size. It shouldn't surprise her. She already knew he was an observant man. "Please thank your friend for picking out the clothes," she said, walking toward the table. "I'll pay her back."

"I already did."

"Then I'll pay you back."

"Forget it. I'm enjoying the view." He moved his right arm forward sharply in a burst of controlled power. The white cue ball thunked against a colored ball, knocking it into a corner pocket. "How are you feeling?"

"Fine, thanks. I can't believe I slept so long."

"You needed it. You have for a long time."

"But what about you?"

He shifted a few steps toward her to line up another shot and bent over the cushion. "I slept on the couch in my office after I cleaned up."

She watched him as he stretched over the cue. Yes, he had cleaned up, all right. The soot that had streaked his face was gone. His jaw was smooth from a fresh shave. His hair shone cleanly, the singed ends at the edge of his forehead hardly visible where they blended into the rest.

He was wearing a plain white T-shirt. It tightened over his biceps and his shoulders, hugging the long line of his back. His jeans pulled taut over his buttocks, outlining the subtle shift of his body as he made his shot. Another ball rattled into a pocket.

Hayley started, amazed to realize that a stab of sexual awareness had accompanied the noise. Cooper handled the pool cue with the same graceful ease that he did everything else. His sure movements, his deliberation, the strength evident in his control made the way he played almost sensual.

"Are you hungry?"

She lifted her gaze to his face. He was regarding her levelly. She had a feeling that he knew exactly where she had been looking. She also suspected there was a subtext to his question. "No, I'm fine. I made a sandwich before I came downstairs. I hope you don't mind."

"As long as you're staying with me, I expect you to help yourself to anything you want."

Yes, there was definitely an offer in that suggestion. She could feel his gaze on her mouth. Her lips tingled.

The lines beside his eyes deepened with the start of a smile. "I'd be happy to oblige," he added.

Hayley looked around the room. The space was de-
signed to hold a crowd. Being here alone with Cooper
made her more conscious of him than ever. She grasped for
a neutral topic. "You didn't open the bar tonight."

"That's right."

"I hope that wasn't because I'm here."

"I needed to wait for reinforcements." He tapped the cue
against his leg, then moved to the other side of the table.
"Pete Wyzowski, my manager, used to work with me in the
old days."

"The old days…"

"Before I went to prison, when I was still a thief. So did
Ken. They're rounding up the rest of the guys we used to
run with. Not all of them went legit like we did, but they
know the ground rules at the Long Shot, so they won't
bring their business here. They'll provide security so I can
open the place tomorrow."

"Oh. That sounds…like a good idea."

"It's the best way to handle Sproule. He's not afraid of
the law, but he's going to think twice about going up
against those men. They know how to handle trouble. No
one's going to get past them once we open."

She glanced at the shadows around them. "What
about now?"

"I had an advantage when I renovated this building. I've
broken into enough places to know what will keep people
out." He nodded toward the long, narrow windows at the
front of the room. "The Plexiglass in the windows is shat-
terproof and the doors are reinforced with steel. Everything's wired to an alarm system. Once I throw the locks,
the Long Shot's as good as a fortress."

She rubbed her hands over her arms. She'd never
thought she would be in a position to be thankful that

Cooper had been a criminal and still had his old connections, but in this case, she was. The idea of relying on men who weren't completely "legit" to guard against another criminal made practical sense, regardless of any question of right or wrong.

Besides, Cooper had warned her at the start of their partnership that once he brought her in with him, she would be all the way in. "I'm sorry that I ruined your plan to work with Oliver," she said.

"Yeah, well, I'm not sorry that my stand is out in the open." He studied the table for a while before he leaned over and hit the cue ball. It bounced off the side rail and smacked into two other balls, sending both to opposite pockets. "Now I won't have to put up with seeing scum like Izzy in this place again."

"I can understand that. The Long Shot is more than just a business to you, isn't it?"

He took a square of chalk and rubbed it over the tip of his cue. "Like I told you, it's the first decent thing I've had in my life."

"Why a bar, Cooper?"

"What?"

She leaned her hip against the pool table next to the one he was using. "When you got the loan from Tony, why did you decide to open a bar instead of some other kind of business?"

The chalk squeaked. He set it down and studied the cue. "We used to move around a lot when I was a kid. Either the landlord would kick us out for not paying the rent or we'd skip before it was due. I was always big for my age, so when I was thirteen I started hanging out in a bar down the street from one of the places and when we moved, I kept going back. It was…familiar."

Hayley had taken the stability of her family home for granted. Even though she hadn't lived there for ten years, she felt the loss of the house deeply. How much worse would it have been never to have had that security?

The image of a thirteen-year-old seeking the familiarity of a bar because his home kept changing was heartbreaking. Added to that were the details Cooper had told her the other day, of how his mother had left them and his father had had a series of girlfriends. Not only had the place he'd lived changed, so had the people he'd lived with.

Yet Cooper had spoken with no trace of self-pity in his voice. To him, the rootless childhood he had described was all he had ever known. "The bar was like a home to you," she said.

"Yeah, I guess you could say that." He twirled the cue across the tips of his fingers. "I used to earn extra money by hustling pool."

"You're very good."

He shrugged and rested the butt of the cue on the toe of his boot. "Not good enough to make a living at it. Sometimes the guy who owned the place would give me a few bucks for helping him out. That's how I got to know about running a bar, so when Tony offered me his deal, I figured I could do the same thing."

"You've done well. Have you had any business training?"

"I finished my high-school diploma when I was in the pen, then took some correspondence courses after that, but I'm still lousy with numbers. I hate the paperwork."

"If you like, I could help you with your books while I'm here. It would make me feel better if I could make a contribution to earn my keep."

He considered that for a while. "Sure. I'd like that."

"Are you going to tell Tony what happened last night?"

"I already called him. He wasn't pleased."

"He's not going to, uh, send someone from Payback to collect from you, is he?"

"Not yet. As long as I'm still working on bringing Sproule to justice, Tony's going to give me more time to repay my debt."

"Then we should be planning a new strategy."

"I know what I'm going to do next, but you might not like it." He stretched into position for a shot and braced his hand on the cloth. Instead of striking the cue ball, he gave it a gentle tap that made it nudge the next ball like a kiss. It hovered on the lip of the pocket, hanging suspended for a moment before it tipped inside.

Hayley felt another sexual jolt. She folded her hands over her stomach and tried to ignore it. "What won't I like?"

"I'm going to meet with Sproule tomorrow night."

Her mouth dropped open. "Are you crazy? He almost killed us."

"I'll take precautions."

"What could you possibly hope to accomplish?"

"For one thing, he'll know for sure you're with me." He extended his arm, preparing for his next shot.

Hayley walked around the table and snatched up the cue ball before he could hit it. "You've already made that clear. You don't have to endanger yourself."

He frowned and looked at her hand. "He also owes me money for that load of televisions."

"Surely you don't expect him to honor his word."

"No, but he'll see it as a weakness if I let it slide."

"How will this get us any closer to putting him in jail?" she asked.

"It's going to throw him off balance. He's not accustomed to anyone standing up against him."

"I did. It didn't get me anywhere."

"Uh-huh, but he thought you were alone." He took her hand, curling his fingers around hers where she held the ball. "Do you remember what I told you about Sproule when we met? I said he owns this town."

"That's right."

"He doesn't own me. He doesn't own the Long Shot or any of the people who work here. His hold over his men isn't perfect—Izzy's stealing drugs from him. I was going about it all wrong."

"I don't understand."

"I had thought the best way to nail Sproule was to join him. It isn't. I'm going to fight him, Hayley."

"How?"

"By getting in his face. By taking a stand in the open."

"I thought we had."

"It's not just Sproule who needs to know. I want everyone in town to know. Watch," he said. He eased the cue ball from her fingers and rolled it across the table. It struck the balls that remained, scattering them in a chain reaction that ended with one ball dropping into a corner pocket. "Sometimes all it takes is the right nudge to get things moving."

"By nudge, you mean…"

"Showing Latchford that Sproule doesn't own everyone. He's not as powerful as they think he is. They have an alternative."

She considered that. "I see where you're going with this. You want to make it possible for other people to come forward."

"That's the idea. We'll keep looking for hard evidence to put Sproule away ourselves. I'll find you another computer to use, and I'll get more information by calling in some favors and keeping a close eye on Sproule's activities. But we can't be the only ones who want to see his hold on the town end."

"It sounds worth a try."

Cooper set the cue stick down on the table, then rested his hand beside her hip. "Fighting Sproule in the open is going to be risky. We'll need to watch our backs every time we step out of the Long Shot."

"I realize that."

"There's no telling how long it'll take, either. It could be weeks. Maybe months. Do you think you can stick it out?"

Although he wasn't touching her, she could feel the heat from his body. She inhaled the clean scent of his soap. "Whatever is necessary, Cooper. We're partners."

"Is that all?"

"Maybe we could be...friends."

He looked at her in silence for a minute, then lifted one hand to her cheek. "Friends?"

"Is that so hard to believe?"

"When a woman looks like you do, yeah, that's a stretch."

"Cooper..."

"Then there's the way you look at me. It's more than friendly, Hayley."

It wouldn't do her any good to deny it. She felt her skin warm beneath his fingers.

"I don't know how you do it, but when you look at me, I can feel it. Everywhere." He rested his thumb on the curve of her jaw. "It's like you're touching me. It's as real as this."

She focused on the cleft in his chin. "Despite what happened upstairs earlier, I'm not looking for a personal relationship with you, Cooper."

"A personal relationship?"

She decided to be blunt. "An affair, then. I'm not going to get romantically involved with you."

"You said you had nothing to go back to in Chicago."

"I don't."

"What about a boyfriend?"

"Not anymore."

"Why not?"

"It didn't work out."

He tipped up her chin and waited until she met his gaze. "Why not, Hayley?"

"Why do you want to know, Cooper? Is it because you care, or only because you want to sleep with me?"

He regarded her in silence, just as he had the other time she had asked him the same question.

She slipped out of his grasp and turned away from the table. "Don't answer that. It doesn't make any difference."

"It's both, Hayley."

She stopped. "You don't have to say—"

"It's a hell of a thing, isn't it? If I didn't care, I wouldn't have left you alone after that kiss this morning." He moved behind her and caught her shoulders to hold her in place. "I wouldn't have walked away when every inch of my body wanted to strip you naked and have you in my bed."

She pressed her lips together. The image in her mind arose far too easily. The big bed on the platform in the far corner of the loft, Cooper moving over her, skin sliding on skin…

"If I didn't care, I would have cut you loose days ago and we wouldn't be in this situation in the first place." He stepped closer, easing her back against his chest. "You get to me, Hayley. You did from the first time I saw you. I tell myself to keep away from you, but it doesn't work."

All he had to do was touch her and her brain started to shut down. She curled her nails into her palms. "But you don't want to care about me, do you? Because I'm Adam's sister."

"It would be simpler if you weren't."

"It's more than that. You don't want to care about anyone."

There was another silence. She waited him out.

"It's not something I normally do," he said finally.

She realized that. And the more she learned about him, the better she understood his need for emotional defenses. He might be a good man underneath his tough shell, but that shell was part of who he was. Did she really want the heartache of trying to get past it? "You wanted to know why my last relationship didn't work out."

He slipped one arm across the front of her shoulders. "Why?"

"Because he didn't love me."

Cooper's arm tensed.

"That's been the pattern of my life," she said. "I always seem to fall for men who aren't able to love me."

"Hayley—"

"They say they care, and I keep hoping for more, but it doesn't happen. They keep their hearts behind their walls and I can't change them, no matter how hard I try."

"Does it have to be all or nothing?"

She took his arm and pulled it away. "It hurts too much if it isn't, Cooper. I won't go through that again."

He dropped his hand to his side. His breath stirred her hair. "Are you falling for me?"

She closed her eyes. He often told her she was no good at hiding her feelings, but she knew he couldn't see her face, so she risked the lie. "No."

It was the same gravel pit where he had met Nathan Beliveau the week before. There was no moon tonight—a cloud bank had crept in at sunset. Through the open window of his pickup, Cooper could smell the oncoming rain, but not a breath of air stirred. He waited until the headlights he'd been watching swung through the rusted gate at the entrance to the pit and fanned down the ramp, then switched on his pickup's lights. A black SUV rolled into the beams and came to a stop twenty yards away. He checked his watch. He had arrived here two hours early. Sproule was half an hour late.

It was the control thing again. He'd expected it. He hadn't expected Sproule to keep his word about coming alone, either. Another SUV followed the first and moved into position to its left. Through the dust that drifted over their tracks, a black sedan glided down the ramp and came to a stop thirty feet from the bumper of Cooper's truck.

Cooper got out and walked into the light, then halted with his arms held out at his sides.

The doors of the SUVs opened. Two of the men who had accompanied Sproule to their first meeting at the Long Shot approached Cooper to pat him down for weapons. At their nod, the driver's door of the sedan swung open. Evidently, Sproule was doing his own driving tonight. Was it a control thing, too? Or did he have personal business to tend to later, as he'd had the night he had run down Adam?

Cooper crossed his arms and waited.

In the glare of four sets of headlights, Oliver Sproule looked like a walking corpse. His face was leached of color and as expressionless as a stone. "You have five minutes," he said. "I'm a busy man."

"Busy selling the load of plasma screens I brought you?" Cooper asked.

"There was an unforeseen complication."

"Is that right?"

"Our deal was that you would receive sixty percent of the profits. There were none. Therefore, I owe you nothing."

"You might want to reconsider, Ollie."

Sproule's eyelid twitched. His lip moved into a hint of a sneer. "And you should have reconsidered your choice of women."

Cooper flicked his gaze to the men who had searched him. They had moved back a few steps, but they had been joined by two more. The drivers were still in the vehicles, so at a minimum, that made at least six, not counting Sproule.

"I had my suspicions about you all along, Mr. Webb," Oliver continued. "I'm aware of everything that happens in Latchford, and I know that you haven't done a job since you finished your sentence. I found it strange that you would want to do business with me after all that time, but a prior acquaintance of yours vouched for you so I gave you the benefit of the doubt."

He had to be talking about Izzy, Cooper thought. There was no sign of his bald head anywhere, but that didn't mean he wasn't inside one of the vehicles. Sproule likely hadn't realized yet that Izzy was stealing from him.

"It was imprudent of you to abuse my trust."

"Yeah, I can see you're a real trusting guy," Cooper said, gesturing to the men around them. At his motion, one of them slipped his hand inside his jacket, no doubt reaching for a shoulder holster. Cooper returned his gaze to Sproule. "But you still owe me money."

Sproule took a step closer, his lips compressing with irritation. "Don't push me, Webb. The only thing I'm going to give you is some advice."

"Gee, I can't wait."

"I don't tolerate opposition. You chose the wrong side

when you took in Hayley Tavistock. I advise you to correct that as soon as possible."

"I was only doing my civic duty, seeing as how you burned her house to the ground."

"An unfortunate accident."

"Yeah, seems to be a lot of that going around. First her brother, then her."

"If you're as smart as you pretend to be, you'll make sure you're not nearby when the next one happens."

"That's not a problem," Cooper said. "There isn't going to be a next one."

"You have no idea who you're talking to, Webb. I can do what I want in this town. You're a nobody, just some loser bartender who wasn't even a good thief. You're not going to stop me."

Cooper pressed his tongue to his front teeth and let out a shrill whistle.

Instantly, lights flashed on around the rim of the gravel pit. High-powered beams flooded the area, turning the night to day. Some of Sproule's men drew guns from beneath their jackets, squinting against the brightness as they pointed their weapons upward, but there was nothing to aim at. The glare was blinding.

They, on the other hand, became instant targets. The two SUVs and the sedan on the floor of the pit provided little cover. They were surrounded and completely exposed.

Cooper kept his gaze on Sproule and raised his right arm. The air echoed with the sound of weapons being cocked. "Tell your men to put their guns down," Cooper ordered.

It took a full minute before Sproule complied. He did, though. Cooper knew he would. Sproule preferred his fights to be one-sided, like running down a solitary man or trying to kill a lone woman.

That was why Cooper had come to their meeting site two hours early to even up the odds. Pete and the rest of the guys had had plenty of time to hook up the floodlights they had borrowed from a construction site near the highway and position themselves where they couldn't be seen. Cooper hadn't liked the idea of the guns—he'd never used a weapon on any of his jobs—but they were necessary when dealing with someone like Sproule.

"You didn't really think I was going to take you at your word and come alone, did you, Ollie?"

Sproule was having trouble maintaining his control. His eyelid was twitching continuously now. "What the hell do you think you're doing?"

"Giving *you* some advice. Keep away from the Long Shot. I protect what's mine."

"You fool. The woman isn't worth it, or are you so hard up for a piece of ass—"

Cooper brought his arm down fast. There was a sharp crack from his left. Dust puffed into the air ten inches from Sproule's right foot.

Sproule stumbled back. Two of his men made a motion toward the guns they had dropped but Cooper stopped them by lifting his arm again. "Don't push me, Sproule, or you'll be the first to go. Tell your men to stay where they are."

Sproule nodded and made a quick gesture with his hand. Sweat beaded his upper lip. "We don't need to do this, Webb. We could negotiate a new agreement for that load of televisions."

"I guess I forgot to tell you. They weren't mine, they were Tony Monaco's."

It didn't seem possible, but Sproule's face paled even more. "Tony Monaco?"

"I see you've heard of him."

He passed the back of his hand over his mouth. He glanced toward the lights that surrounded them. "I didn't know you were a friend of Tony's."

"We have a business arrangement."

"You should have told me that from the start. How much money do you want? Name your price."

"I already have. Keep away from the Long Shot. It's off-limits. So is anyone named Tavistock. That includes the old man."

"I'm a businessman, Webb. There's no profit in wasting my time with that invalid. My quarrel is with the woman."

"Then that makes it simpler. Hayley Tavistock is under my protection." He paused. "So is anyone else in this town who doesn't want to play your game."

Sproule regarded him flatly. "You're starting a war. Why? Because of a *woman?*"

He wasn't about to tell Sproule his real reasons.

"I'm just keeping a promise," Cooper said.

Chapter 10

Cooper leaned his back against the trunk of a lone willow, letting the memories stir at the bitter scent of the leaves. There used to be a tangled grove of willows and an old wooden boathouse along this stretch of the Latchford Lake shoreline when he'd been a kid. The area hadn't been built up then, so this used to be a popular place to party and have a few beers. When the weather was good, sometimes he would skip school and come down here in the afternoon. He could stay as long as he liked, because no one had bothered to look for him.

There was no trace of the boathouse now, or the beer cans that had once littered the weeds at the water's edge. The bank had been cleaned up and tamed with a neat cement wall topped by a railing when it had become part of Applewood Manor's manicured grounds.

Hayley stood at the railing beside her father's wheelchair, her face turned toward the breeze from the lake. Her hair streamed behind her in the sunshine in a halo of butter-blond curls. She wore the cream-colored dress again. It rippled over her breasts and thighs the way Cooper wished he could touch her. She looked good enough to eat, or maybe lick slowly....

He dropped his head against the tree trunk. Damn, why had he told her the choice would be hers?

It had been a long five days. Frustrating in every way. He didn't know how he had kept his hands off her, but he had. It helped that she slept so long and so soundly—she usually didn't stir when he got back to the loft after closing the Long Shot and she was still asleep when he got up. The rest of the time she did her best to keep busy and to limit their conversation to business, but not a second went by when he wasn't conscious of her presence.

It was a special kind of hell, and there was no end in sight.

So far, Sproule hadn't made a move against them, yet they hadn't made much progress against Sproule, either.

Ken had set up a computer for Hayley in Cooper's office, and she had been slowly rebuilding the material that had been lost in the fire, but they knew it wouldn't be enough to take to the feds. Although information was starting to trickle in from some of the Long Shot's customers, and Pete and the guys had been keeping tabs on the action at Sproule's warehouse and his estate, it wasn't enough, either. Rumors were flying that some big plan involving Sproule and Volski was in the works, yet no one was saying when or what it was.

Something had to give soon. Cooper had lost track of the number of glasses he'd broken.

Hayley brushed a strand of hair from her eyes and turned to watch a pair of seagulls swoop past. She pointed them out to her father. Cooper moved his gaze to the man in the wheelchair. It was a warm day, and the doctors agreed that fresh air and sunshine would benefit his recovery, but Ernie Tavistock was bundled in a blanket and scarf. Not surprising that he would feel chilled, considering what a cold-hearted bastard he was.

Cooper gritted his teeth. He realized Hayley would be upset if she knew what he was thinking, but it was because of her that he felt this way. She was still knocking herself out for the old man, still looking at her father with hopeless longing in her eyes. Once a day, no matter what, Cooper brought her here so she could visit him. And every day, no matter how hard she tried to please him, Ernie took her efforts for granted and only wanted to talk about Saint Adam.

It was like the lack of photographs in Ernie's study. It was too subtle to notice right away, but once Cooper knew what to look for, it was hard to ignore.

Okay, he realized the situation with Sproule had him on edge anyway so he wasn't in the best of moods. He did feel sorry for Ernie. Anyone would. The guy had lost his son and his health all at once. No one, whether he was a career cop or not, deserved to end up like that.

But Ernie's manner toward Hayley wasn't a result of his condition. From what Cooper had gathered, it had been going on for years. For some reason, Ernie was blind to what a loyal, compassionate and loving woman his daughter was. All he saw was Adam.

That's been the pattern of my life. I always seem to fall for men who aren't able to love me.

Cooper didn't have any fancy psychology degree, but it was as plain as the lines of strain on Hayley's face why she had a hangup about being loved.

She sure had gotten the short end of the stick when it came to her family.

But then, Cooper wasn't about to change any of that, was he? She had him pegged right. He didn't want to care about anyone, much less love them. Love was for other people, not for him. It was for characters on soap operas or for the kids who lived in regular houses and got grounded when they skipped school.

Why did she have to make it so complicated, anyway? What was wrong with two people simply enjoying each other?

They would be good together. Hayley was passionate about everything she did. The kisses they had shared convinced him she would be dynamite in bed. Seeing her here in the sunshine, watching the breeze flirt with her hair, made him think about how good her curls would look all tangled from his fingers, spread out on his pillow or maybe tumbled over the edge of the mattress while they made love in the middle of the patch of sunlight that fell over his bed in the afternoon....

Hayley glanced past her father and met Cooper's gaze. "We're going back inside now," she called.

Cooper took a few seconds to rein his thoughts into line, then pushed away from the tree and walked to the back of the wheelchair. He gripped the handles and turned it toward the main building. "All set, Mr. Tavistock?"

Ernie nodded. He seldom spoke to Cooper. Cooper could understand that. Even though Hayley had assured her father that their association was strictly business, it was tough for a man like Ernie to accept the fact that his daughter was living above a bar with an ex-con, a former thief his own son had arrested.

Yeah, that had been as hard to swallow for Ernie as

Cooper had found swallowing the fact that he was spending his afternoons wheeling around a former police commissioner. Who would have thought?

It was yet another consequence of bringing his partnership with Hayley into the open. He had brought her into his world, but she had brought him into hers, too.

She had worried about telling her father the truth. She had wanted to delay telling him the news about the loss of the family home, too, for fear of upsetting him. Yet he would have found out eventually, so she'd made sure a doctor was standing by and had broken it to him anyway.

Ernie's silence with Cooper during the walk back to his room wasn't because of his ongoing disapproval, though. He appeared to have forgotten who Cooper was. There was no recognition in his gaze when Cooper slipped his arms under him and carefully transferred him from the wheelchair to the bed—he probably thought he was one of the orderlies. Cooper lowered the head of the bed to the angle he had noticed Ernie preferred, then took off his slippers and drew the covers to his waist. "Anything else you need?"

Pale-blue eyes met his. They were so much like Adam's, Cooper still found it jarring. "When is my son coming?"

Cooper fixed the bed rail in place and made sure the box with the call button was within Ernie's reach. "Your daughter's here."

"No, I don't want to see her, I want to see Adam."

Cooper turned to the door.

Hayley was standing in the doorway, her expression that familiar mixture of determination and longing. She brushed past him to kiss her father's cheek, spoke softly for a few minutes, then said goodbye and moved into the hall.

Cooper slipped his arm around her shoulders as they left the building. "Are you okay?"

She nodded. She waited until they had reached his pickup and he was pulling out of the parking lot before she spoke. "Thank you," she said.

Automatically, he checked the road and his rearview mirror, but there was no sign of any suspicious vehicles that might be carrying Sproule's men, only families in mini-vans. No one was paying attention to them. "For what?"

"For helping my father into bed. It was one of his... bad days."

"No problem. I've seen how the orderlies do it."

"It was very kind of you."

"That's not why you're upset, is it?"

She rubbed her forehead with the tips of her fingers. "Cooper, every day Sproule is free is too much. We have to work faster."

"I warned you this would take time."

"You saw how Dad was. He didn't recognize you. If we take too long to bring Sproule to justice, it might be too late to do my father any good." Her voice dropped to a whisper. "I promised him, Cooper. This could be my last chance to make him—" she turned her face to the side window "—to make him happy."

That wasn't what she'd meant. The words she hadn't said hung in the air. She wanted to make her father love her.

Cooper had known something was going to give soon. He hadn't guessed how easily it was going to happen, but hell, enough was enough. He checked once more to ensure the road was empty behind him, then spun the wheel and steered the truck back toward the lake.

Hayley gripped the dashboard as they bumped over the grass. "Where are you going?"

He turned down a track that led away from the nursing-home grounds to a section of the shoreline that hadn't yet been developed. The trees were bigger, the brush on either side of the truck was thicker, but it was still recognizable. It had been another popular spot when he'd been a kid. Not for hanging out with the guys but for bringing girls. He continued down the track until it flattened out to a clearing where he could glimpse the lake through the brush, then pulled to a stop and shut off the engine.

"Why are we stopping here?" she asked.

Cooper hopped out of the truck, went around to her side and opened her door. He held out his hand. "Come with me."

"Why?"

"I need to do something."

She took his hand and climbed down. "What?"

He swung the door closed and pulled her into his arms. "This."

She held herself stiffly. "Cooper—"

He tucked her head into the crook of his neck, then crossed his arms over her back. It felt so good to simply *feel* her. He swayed from side to side, rocking her in a slow, soothing rhythm until she softened against him. "Damn," he murmured. "You don't know how long I've been wanting to do this."

Her shoulders shook. "We can't…"

"We are. Doesn't it feel good?"

She sniffed. "Yes, but—"

"I think you put way too much importance on this love thing, Hayley." He pressed his nose to her ear. "Sometimes you just have to settle for what you can get."

She stiffened again.

"I'm talking about your father."

"Cooper…"

"You're doing everything you can to please him, but

there's a point where you have to cut your losses and look out for yourself."

She sighed, then pushed her hands against his chest and shoved herself out of his embrace. She walked to the front of the pickup. "You don't understand."

"Then tell me. What's going on?"

"He's sick and he's grieving. I'm trying to comfort him."

"It's more than that." He followed her and touched her shoulder. "I've seen sickness before, Hayley. I watched cancer eat away at Donny, and I know people react in different ways when they're scared, but the way Ernie treats you isn't about his condition."

She folded her arms over her chest. Her jaw worked as if she were biting the inside of her cheek.

"Talk to me, Hayley. Why weren't there any pictures of you on your father's desk?" he asked. "It isn't only because Adam was a cop, is it?"

She kept her face averted, yet he could see the tension in her body as she considered her reply. When she finally spoke, her words came out low and fast…as if she had been saving them up for a long time and no one had asked. "No. It started long before that."

"I can't believe it's because of something you did when you were younger. You've been as straight as they come. It doesn't make sense."

"You would understand if you saw a picture of my mother."

"Your mother? What does she have to do with this?"

"I look exactly like her."

He lifted his hand to stroke her hair. The trees blocked most of the wind from the lake, but there was enough of a breeze to twine her curls around his fingers. "She must have been beautiful."

"Everyone said she was. I never knew her. She died giving birth to me."

Cooper's fingers tightened. "I didn't know."

"So you see, my father's dislike of me *is* from something I did. I took away the love of his life."

"You weren't responsible for what happened when you were born, Hayley."

"It doesn't make any difference. Every time my dad sees me, he's reminded of my mother's death. He's an intelligent man, so logically he knows it wasn't my fault. But on an emotional level, he can't help blaming me. He has very rigid ideas about crime and punishment."

Cooper wanted to argue with the unfairness of that. Hayley wasn't to blame for the circumstances of her birth, and she shouldn't be punished for them. No one should.

But life wasn't fair—that had been one of the earliest lessons he'd learned. It was right up there along with the lesson about not being a fool enough to care. "I'm sorry."

"No, don't be. I'm used to it. I've understood it for years, but I have to keep trying. I keep hoping to change his feelings."

And so she set the pattern of her life, he thought. She wanted love from men who didn't want to give it.

Go. Leave now. It's not too late… Cooper shut out the voice in his head and breathed in the scent of her skin.

"It might have been different if I'd been more like Adam," she said. "He always made Dad proud of him. I never could. I was always in Adam's shadow."

"You're not now. Adam's gone."

She met his gaze. "You're wrong about that, too. Adam's always going to be there."

"Maybe with your father but not between us."

"Cooper—"

"When I look at you, I see only you, Hayley."

"How can you? Adam put you in prison."

"That was him." Cooper stepped in front of her and took her face in his hands. "I see you."

She was silent for a while. "Cooper, I want to apologize."

"For what?"

"For the remark I made last week about your motives. I know you didn't want to sleep with me to get back at Adam. I shouldn't have said that."

He brushed his thumb over her cheek, then touched it to her lower lip. "We already got that straight, Hayley."

"Yes, but it was hurtful and you didn't deserve it."

"Fine. Give me a kiss and we'll call it even."

Her lip trembled. "I don't think that's a good idea."

"Sometimes you think too much. It makes things complicated."

"But things *are* complicated."

He stepped closer. The breeze fluttered the hem of her dress against his legs. He slid his hands to her shoulders. "Sure, but not this part."

Her gaze dropped to his mouth. "We should get back to the Long Shot."

"Later."

"Cooper, I already explained why I'm not going to have a relationship with you."

"Who said anything about a relationship? All I'm going to do is kiss you."

"But—"

"You don't have to prove anything to me. You don't need to change anything. Just enjoy."

Her breath hitched. She put her hands on his chest again, but this time she didn't shove him away. She opened her fingers. "One kiss?"

He smiled and lowered his head. He spoke against her lips. "One at a time, anyway."

Hayley knew it was a mistake. A big one. But oh, his lips felt so good. So did his arms as he wrapped them around her. So did the heat of his body and the thud of the heartbeat she felt beneath her palm.

She had tried to keep busy, to keep away from him, but he was always there in her thoughts. The loft had become more of a home to her than her apartment in Chicago had ever been. It was because of Cooper's presence, even when he wasn't there. It was because of all the little, day-to-day things she was learning about him, the way he held his fork, the way he hummed in the shower, how he made her pulse give a quick jump whenever she looked up to find him watching her.

Maybe he was right. She did think too much. Because right now, all she wanted to do was feel. And enjoy. Oh, it had been a long five days.

His kiss was rich, a blend of all the kisses they had shared before. His lips moved over hers with a sureness that silenced any more urge to protest. She could hear the trees around them rustle in the breeze, the sound of water lapping against the shore, the faint whine of a car passing along the road, but it was muffled, distant. Cooper dominated her senses, as he always did.

She couldn't get enough of his taste. She opened her mouth to him, inviting him to give her more. Her head spun with the sweep of his tongue. Oh, this man could kiss. His lips were supple yet firm, as if he savored the pleasure he gave her, as if nothing was more important than to explore every nuance of this place where their bodies joined.

Hayley slid her palm over his shirt. She could feel the breadth of his chest, hear the crisp rasp of hair against the chambray and her pulse grew heavy. She closed her eyes, reveling in the feel and the sound of him. Her fingertips brushed the edge of a button. She hesitated, but the twinge of caution was brief. She indulged herself and unfastened it. She worked upward to his collar and pushed the halves of his shirt aside, then pressed her palms over his skin.

His heat sent a tremor down her arms. His scent enveloped her. She had to break off the kiss to breathe.

Cooper moved his mouth to her cheek, to her temple, to her ear. He pulled the hem of her dress to her waist, braced his feet apart and drew her closer. The sensation of warm denim rubbing across her bare thighs made her gasp.

He ran his tongue around her earlobe. "Don't stop, Hayley. This feels too good."

She tugged his shirt from his jeans and slipped her hands beneath it. She caressed the washboard muscles of his abdomen, following the contours with her fingertips, tracing the silky line of hair that led to his navel. The need to get closer was overwhelming. She stood on her toes to slide her arms up his back, squeezing her breasts to his chest.

He reached down to clasp her thigh and guided her leg around his hip.

Hayley shuddered. The strength of her response shocked her. Blood throbbed between her legs as she hooked her ankle behind him. She could feel him swell to meet her. Their bodies fit perfectly. Intimately.

Cooper cupped her buttocks, lifted her tighter against him and turned around to lean one knee on the front bumper of the truck. Her back hit the grill. As one they brought their mouths back together.

The kiss turned wild. Hungry. She thrilled to the edge of his teeth on her lip. She caught his tongue and sucked hard. He eased her legs wider apart and slid his hand to the inside of her thigh.

Hayley gasped. "Cooper!"

He moved his fingers higher in a bold, possessive stroke. She couldn't catch her breath. Oh. *Oh!*

In the next instant, he wrenched his mouth from hers and lifted his head. His hand stilled.

Hayley shook in frustration. She grasped his wrist, wanting him to finish what he started.

He muttered a short, crude oath and withdrew his hand. "I'm sorry, Hayley. Damn, I'm sorry." He pushed her legs down, sat her against the bumper and ran to the passenger door. He threw it open and jumped onto the running board to dig through the glove compartment. "Stay down until I see who it is."

Hayley clutched the hood of the truck to steady herself and struggled to draw in air. Her entire body was vibrating with need. Her heart was pounding so hard, it took her a few seconds before she recognized the noise of the approaching engine.

Cooper leapt back to the ground from the truck, a pistol in his hand.

At the sight of the gun, the sensual fog that had enveloped her scattered. Her pulse accelerated and her brain finally clicked into gear. She whipped her gaze to the lane at the edge of the clearing.

Someone had followed them. It could be one of Sproule's men. That was why Cooper had started to carry a gun. That was why he had come with her in the first place, to make sure Sproule didn't try to hurt her again. But she hadn't given a thought to the danger of being in this isolated place. How could she have forgotten?

She tugged her skirt down to cover her thighs, her hands

trembling. How? Because Cooper had touched her, that's how. He had that effect. He shut down her brain.

Cooper sprinted toward a tree to the right of the lane. His shirt flapped loosely behind him, baring his chest, but he didn't take time to refasten his buttons. Using the trunk of the tree for cover, he levelled the weapon at the point where a vehicle would emerge.

Hayley thought fleetingly of her father's old Winchester that was still locked in the Long Shot's storeroom. She looked around quickly, picked up a fist-sized rock and took cover behind the truck. She realized it wouldn't be much use, yet it was better than nothing.

The noise of the engine increased slowly, like the low rumble of approaching thunder. Chrome glinted through the brush. A few seconds later, a large motorcycle nosed into the clearing. The rider's face was hidden behind the tinted visor of his helmet, but Cooper appeared to decide the man wasn't a threat. He lowered his gun to his side and walked forward to meet him.

"Dammit," Cooper said. "What the hell are you doing here?"

The man astride the bike shut off the engine and flipped down the kickstand, then took off his helmet and dismounted. "Looking for you. I thought I saw your pickup turn down to the lake. When you didn't come out, I figured you might have run into trouble." He glanced at Cooper's open shirt and moved his gaze directly to Hayley. He raised one eyebrow. "Did I interrupt something?"

There were too many emotions to process in too short a time. The fear that had gripped her at the sight of Cooper's gun flipped into a sudden urge to laugh. She realized it wouldn't have been difficult to figure out what she and Cooper had been doing—not only were their clothes a mess, she could feel how swollen her lips were and she knew her face was probably still flushed.

But being embarrassed was the least of her concerns. What if it hadn't been someone Cooper knew? This wasn't funny. It was dead serious. She dropped the rock on the ground and finished straightening her dress.

"Your timing stinks," Cooper muttered, tucking the gun into the waistband at the back of his jeans. He looked at Hayley and held out his hand.

She studied the new arrival as she walked forward to join them. He was dressed in black from his heavy boots and denim jeans to the leather jacket that stretched across his wide shoulders. He was as tall as Cooper, and his hair was the same raven-black, but there the similarity ended.

This man's gaze was rich amber. His eyes were deeply set in a face with chiseled cheekbones and a strong jaw. His hair was poker-straight, smoothed back from a broad forehead and trimmed neatly above his ears. He had the same aura of contained toughness that characterized the other men Cooper had brought in to help at the Long Shot, yet there was a restless intelligence to his gaze that set him apart. He wouldn't be a man who would be comfortable working for someone else.

Cooper slipped his arm around her shoulders and drew her to his side. "This is Nathan Beliveau," he said. "He's from Payback."

Hayley's stomach did a swooping dive. *Payback?* She looked at Cooper. "You said Tony would give you more time to pay your debt."

"I'm not here because of Cooper's debt," Nathan said. "I'm here because of mine."

Chapter 11

"That's some file you assembled on Sproule, Hayley," Nathan said, hitching one leg over the edge of Cooper's desk. His leather jacket was hooked on an open drawer of the filing cabinet and his helmet rested on top. What he wore beneath the jacket had surprised Hayley: it was a crisp, white cotton dress shirt that hugged his chest and shoulders with a fit that appeared custom-made and expensive. He loosened the knot of the copper-colored silk tie that hung below his open collar and thumbed through the pages in the folder. "Did you say you've only been at it five days?"

She settled into the corner of the couch and curled her legs onto the cushion. "Yes, not counting what I lost in the fire."

"You have a gift for research and data organization." He glanced at her. His amber eyes crinkled with the hint of a smile. "Ever consider working in the courier business? My head office is in Chicago. We could use someone like you."

If Nathan had been sitting behind the desk instead of on it, he would have looked like one of the polished executives Hayley had dealt with in her previous job. As the president of Pack Leader Express, he *was* an executive…yet with his snug jeans and motorcycle boots, he looked anything but polished.

The contradiction his appearance presented wasn't the reason Hayley hesitated to respond to his job offer. Nor was the fact that since Nathan was a member of Payback he must have a criminal background—over the past two weeks, her old views about right and wrong had undergone a serious overhaul. She simply hadn't thought about returning to Chicago. She hadn't thought about afterward. She would have to eventually, but not yet.

"Kind of getting ahead of yourself there, aren't you, Nathan?" Cooper asked, as if his thoughts echoed hers. He kicked the office door shut with his heel and held out one of the bottles of beer he carried.

Nathan's smile faded. "You're right." He put the file down, took a beer and twisted off the cap. "If I don't pay back Tony, I'll be looking for a job myself."

"Yeah. Tony's got a long memory."

"He's got a long reach, too. That electronics plant in Hammond closed down."

"The one where we picked up the plasma screens?"

"Uh-huh. The guy who owned it ignored the warning so Tony sent someone else back and cleaned it out right down to the paper clips."

Cooper opened his own beer. "That's too bad."

"We all knew going in what the deal was. Anyone who quits leaves with no more than they brought in."

Cooper grunted, tipped the bottle to his mouth, then sat on the arm of the couch beside Hayley. He put his free hand on her back.

Hayley's spine tingled at the contact. Even though he had focused on business since they had returned from the lake, he hadn't missed an opportunity to touch her.

Hayley suspected some of Cooper's attention toward her was for Nathan's benefit. He was staking his claim in that silent, body-language way that males liked to use, but it wasn't necessary. Although Nathan Beliveau was a strikingly handsome man, he didn't affect Hayley the way Cooper did. No man ever had.

She still couldn't quite believe what had happened by the lake. They had agreed to a kiss. One kiss. If they hadn't been interrupted, would either of them have stopped? Or would they have ended up making love on the bumper of Cooper's pickup?

No, it wouldn't have been love. He had made that clear, yet it didn't seem to make any difference to the effect he had on Hayley. Despite the time that had passed, her body hadn't cooled down completely. Whenever Cooper touched her, he stirred the embers.

"So, Nathan, are you going to tell us what we have to do with your debt?" Cooper asked.

Nathan lifted the bottle and took a long swig. "When I loaned you that semi, I heard Tony had asked you to put away Oliver Sproule."

"That's right."

"Since then, you told Tony that Sproule's connected to a Russian named Stephan Volski."

"Hayley's the one who found that out. They're smuggling heroin."

"So Tony said. With the Russian mob involved, this is

bigger than it looked at first. Tony decided that this would be a good time to stop Volski, too."

Cooper gave a low whistle. "Tony wants you to bring down Stephan Volski?"

Nathan saluted him with his beer. "You got it."

The men lapsed into silence. Hayley looked from Nathan to Cooper. "This is good. If we work together, we're bound to get enough evidence to call in the FBI and the DEA."

Cooper moved his head in a slow negative. "I don't like it. Volski's the source of the heroin Sproule's importing. The feds are going to be more interested in Volski than Sproule. He's a bigger fish. If we work this together, they'll probably end up cutting Sproule a deal and that's going to screw up my chances of paying back Tony."

"If you keep going on your own," Nathan said, "you could wind up driving Volski underground and that would screw things up for me."

"That explains your visit," Cooper said.

Nathan dipped his chin. "You said I should let you know if there was anything you could do for me. Now I am. It would be in our best interests to rig this so both Sproule and Volski are caught at the same time."

"Sproule's got to go down for the max. Otherwise, that won't be enough to settle my debt or to satisfy Hayley." Cooper rubbed his thumb along her shoulderblade. "She's out to avenge her brother's murder. A slap on the wrist won't do it."

"How close are you to putting Sproule away on your own?"

"We'll get there."

"If we team up, we'll all get there sooner," Nathan said. "How?"

"Volski's getting impatient. Your harassment of Sproule

has been cramping his style. He's got two tons of junk stockpiled and ready to move."

"Two *tons?*" Hayley exclaimed. The amount of misery that much heroin could do once it made it to the streets was chilling.

"I heard something big was in the works," Cooper said. "No one on this end is giving any details."

"Information is just as tight on the other end, but word's getting around that Volski's not a hundred-percent confident of his connection. Sproule could blow the deal if he gets jittery."

"He's too greedy to walk away from that much dope."

"He will if you keep crowding him. You need to tell your men to give him more space."

"I can give him more space but we're not going to back off completely."

"I guess that'll have to do." Nathan finished his beer and set the bottle on the desk, then stood and picked up his jacket. "I'll let you know as soon as I hear that Volski's scheduled a shipment."

"Likewise," Cooper said.

Nathan shrugged on the jacket, grabbed his helmet and moved to the office door. With one hand on the knob, he glanced back over his shoulder.

The affability he'd displayed throughout their conversation was gone. So was any resemblance to a shirt-and-tie executive. The ruthlessness that hardened his face wasn't the kind that was learned in boardrooms, it was the cold calculation of a man who had survived the streets.

"I've been waiting ten years to pay off my debt to Tony," Nathan said. "I would prefer to work with you instead of against you, but if you get in my way, I'll cut both of you loose. Whatever it takes, I intend to see this through."

* * *

Hayley nibbled on a pretzel as she watched Cooper move across the barroom. As far as she could tell, he hadn't been bothered by Nathan's parting remarks. Oddly enough, neither had she—the threat that had underlain Nathan's words was reminiscent of the way Cooper had sounded when she had met him two weeks ago.

There was a good crowd at the Long Shot tonight, so Cooper's progress was slow as he paused to talk to people he knew. The regular patrons were a rough-looking bunch, as tough as the souped-up muscle cars they parked outside, yet the respect they held for Cooper was obvious to Hayley. Although their idea of fun was often loud and bordered on rowdy, Cooper and his staff never let it get out of hand.

Judging by the daily entries she had been adding to Cooper's books, business at the Long Shot hadn't suffered from the public stand they had taken against Sproule. If anything, it was picking up. If the trend continued, by the end of the week they would be able to clear enough to pay—legitimately—the extra men Cooper had brought in for security. He had been right; there were plenty of people in Latchford who didn't like Sproule. Patronizing Cooper's bar was an easy way to show whose side they were on.

She hooked her heels on a rung of the barstool and reached for another pretzel.

A heavyset man in a brass-studded denim jacket jostled her shoulder as he pressed close to the bar. "What're you drinking, sugar?"

Hayley leaned sideways to break the contact. "I'm fine, thanks."

"Aw, come on. Pretty thing like you, sitting here all alone, you need a beer." The man smiled and put his hand on her arm. He was missing a front tooth. "I'm Bill. Where're you from, sugar? I don't remember seeing you here before."

"I'm Hayley." She tilted her head toward the other side of the room. Cooper had his back to them as he spoke with Pete and two members of the local band who were setting up their instruments on the stage. "And to answer your question, Bill," she added, "I live upstairs with the man who owns this place."

He pulled back so fast he lost his balance and bumped into the stool next to hers. He grabbed it before it could tip over. "I was just being friendly. I didn't mean no harm."

Hayley nodded. "I know. Enjoy your evening."

He moved off quickly.

Hayley hid her smile. She normally was too busy with her research or straightening out Cooper's bookkeeping to spend time in the bar, but most people seemed to have heard who she was anyway. It was another consequence of making her alliance with Cooper public. People assumed she was his girlfriend. It was easiest to let them. After all, who would believe that she and Cooper had been living together platonically for five days?

Yet after what had happened this afternoon, Hayley wasn't sure how long that could continue.

Theresa Martinez clicked her tongue as she set a tray of empty glasses on the bar. She was a compact, energetic woman with a cap of short black hair and dark eyes that missed nothing. It had taken her a few days to warm up to Hayley. Like the rest of the staff, she was fiercely loyal to Cooper. Only when she had assured herself that Hayley was truly on their side had her attitude thawed. "What on earth did you say to that man? He looked sick."

Hayley rolled a piece of pretzel in her fingers. "He

wanted to buy me a drink. I told him I'm staying with Cooper."

"Ahh, that explains it."

"The worst of it is, I think I enjoyed seeing his reaction."

Theresa laughed. "It's not very liberated to use a man's reputation for protection, but I have to admit when I started working here I enjoyed siccing Ken on overeager customers." She turned her gaze toward the slender, dark-haired man behind the bar. Her affection for her husband shone from her face. "He was something to see in the old days. Cooper didn't believe in guns, but Ken never needed one. When he couldn't talk his way out of trouble, he could knock out a man twice his size with nothing but his bare hands. If he hadn't been so good at picking locks, he could have made a fortune doing those Kung Fu movies."

Like Cooper, the people who worked for him were open about their criminal past. They made no apologies, yet they took pride in the honest business they had helped to build. If Cooper couldn't repay his debt to Tony, the loss of the Long Shot would affect everyone. "I'm glad that you and your husband stayed on to work with Cooper," Hayley said.

"After what he did for us, we owe him."

"He once told me it was hard work going straight. It must have taken a lot of courage for you to take the chance."

"It turned our lives around. Though at first, Ken and I didn't believe we could be happy being upstanding citizens." Theresa slid her a sideways glance and lifted one sleek black eyebrow. "There's nothing like that rush of adrenaline after a job to spice up your sex life."

Hayley remembered how restless she had felt when Cooper had taken her home after they had stolen the televisions. What would it have been like to feel that excitement on a regular basis? On the other hand, the anxiety during the job hadn't been something she would want to repeat.

"Too bad Cooper's such a stickler for keeping things legal," Theresa continued. "Maybe some spice is what you two need. I've never known him to break so many glasses."

No, Theresa didn't miss anything, Hayley thought, finishing her pretzel. Not everyone believed she and Cooper were sleeping together. His friends couldn't have helped noticing the tension between them. "Do you really miss the old days?" she asked.

"Truthfully, no. I don't miss the bad parts. My hair would have turned gray by now if we were still boosting trucks." She called to get Ken's attention and rattled off her order, then turned back to Hayley. "Besides, I'm so claustrophobic, I never would have been able to survive prison."

"It's lucky you weren't caught."

"Luck had nothing to do with it," Theresa said.

Ken filled her tray, arranging the glasses of whiskey and tequila around the beer bottles so they would be less likely to tip. Unlike his wife, he usually didn't say much, but this time he joined the conversation. "Theresa's right. We would have all done time if Cooper hadn't made his deal."

"I'm confused," Hayley said. "Cooper told me he made a deal to get a lighter sentence for himself but it didn't work out that way."

"That's because the arresting officer changed the deal once he had Cooper's confession," Ken said, holding her gaze. "He wanted him to give up the rest of us. Cooper refused. That's the reason he served three years."

The arresting officer. Adam. So far Ken had avoided saying his name. While he and Theresa had warmed up to

Hayley, they made it clear they held little regard for her brother.

So it hadn't been the judge or the D.A. who had reneged on the deal as Hayley had assumed. Adam must have tried to pressure Cooper into testifying against his accomplices. That would be normal police procedure, part of being a good cop, yet he would have known Cooper's father had been dying. How could the brother she idolized have broken his word and done something so cold? More than ever, Hayley could understand the resentment Cooper harbored for Adam.

She could also understand the depth of Cooper's friends' loyalty. He had not only given them honest work, he had kept them from going to prison.

Hayley mulled that over for a while. Would society really have been better off if Pete, Ken and Theresa had been punished for their crimes? They had rehabilitated themselves. They were making up for the mistakes they had made and were leading worthwhile lives now, weren't they?

On the other hand, what about the others who hadn't gone straight? Would a prison sentence have forced them to change, or would they have chosen to resume their old lives anyway as so many ex-cons did?

She rubbed her forehead. These were the kinds of issues that philosophers could debate for years. She couldn't hope to sort them out herself.

The band started up with a twanging riff of an electric guitar, then launched into a rendition of the George Thorogood classic, "Bad to the Bone." The crowd hooted their approval, making any further conversation difficult. Ken moved to serve a customer on the other side of the bar as Theresa hefted her tray and worked her way across the floor, her steps in time with the beat.

Hayley felt a hand settle on her back. She didn't pull away—she knew without looking around it was Cooper.

He leaned down to speak close to her ear. "Got a minute? I need to talk to you."

Despite the noise from the band, Cooper's deep voice sent a tremor over her skin. She struggled to concentrate. "What about?"

He straightened up, took her hand and tugged her from the stool. "Let's go somewhere quieter."

He led her toward the back of the barroom. He waited until they had reached the hallway and the door had swung shut behind them, muffling the music, before he spoke again. "It's about your house."

Her steps faltered. For a moment she had assumed he had wanted to discuss something more personal. "The fire?"

"I have some news."

They continued down the hall. Cooper paused to nod to the stocky man at the far end who was leaning against the back entrance. "Pete's in the main room, Hank," he called. "Go talk to him if something comes up. I've got some business to see to."

With his drooping outlaw mustache and perpetual scowl, Hank appeared more like someone to keep out of a place rather than to guard it, but Hayley nevertheless felt reassured to have him there. The man gave them a thumbs-up, the ends of his mustache lifting. "Sure thing, Coop."

Cooper opened the door to the staircase and waited for Hayley to step through. "I heard the guy who torched your place was a pro from St. Louis."

The official investigation into the explosion and fire that had destroyed her family home had gone nowhere. Everyone agreed that it had been arson—besides the tool marks on the gas line, there had been a disposable lighter found in the backyard near the fence—but the police hadn't come up with any suspects. "A pro?" Hayley asked. "As in a professional arsonist?"

"He goes by the name of Red, does insurance fraud mostly." Still holding her hand, Cooper started up the stairs. "If someone wants to get rid of a business that isn't paying off, he takes care of it for them. He's got a reputation for clean work. Using a pipe wrench on the gas line was sloppy. It must have been a rush job."

Hayley climbed the stairs with him. "So Sproule set it up at the last minute."

"Looks that way." They reached the landing together. He let go of her to punch in the combination for the lock on the loft door, then swung it open.

Moonlight streamed through the open blinds, bathing the room in a silver glow. Out of habit, Hayley toed off her shoes to make herself comfortable and reached for the light switch.

"Don't turn it on," Cooper said. "I want to check outside first."

Hayley padded toward the center window. "Can we tie the arsonist to Sproule?"

Cooper closed the door, set the lock and followed her. Hayley knew he was accustomed to moving around in the dark. Every night when he returned to the loft after closing the Long Shot he did a circuit of the apartment and got into bed without turning on a light.

She loved listening to him as she sank back to sleep. With each slide of his skin against the sheets her dreams filled with the image of him lying only a few steps away. He had told her he slept in the nude, but she had yet to confirm it, since he was gone each morning by the time she woke up. Besides, the back of the couch that she used blocked her view of the bed.

He stopped beside Hayley, leaned his hand on the edge of the frame and peered down at the parking lot. A pair of his men moved among the cars and disappeared around the side of the building. "We've got nothing solid, just word on the street," he replied finally.

She curled her toes. Although the music from the barroom was muted up here, she could still feel its vibrations in the hardwood floor. "Do you think it's worth pursuing?"

"Our best bet is working on the drug angle with Nathan. I just thought you'd like to know about the fire."

"I did. It's obvious the timing of the arson couldn't be a coincidence. Since it was a rush job, it looks certain that Sproule learned about our investigation because I told my father. Whether someone overheard, or my dad told one of his friends—"

"Don't start blaming yourself again."

"I can't help feeling responsible."

"Take it from me, regrets are more than useless." He pushed away from the window and caught her elbow. "Here, better step back from the glass."

She moved toward him. Cooper's men did regular circuits of the parking lot, yet the orchard beyond it was full of shadows that could conceal anything. They were all aware that simply because Sproule hadn't yet made another move against them didn't mean that he wasn't planning one. She rubbed her hands over her arms.

Cooper slipped his arm around her waist, drawing her closer to his side. "Cold?"

She shook her head, relaxing into his warmth as she looked outside. Only the tops of the apple trees were visible from here. Above them, the sky glittered with stars. The music from the bar had slowed. The soles of her feet tingled with the steady throb of the bass guitar and the rest of her was humming from the contact with Cooper's body.

She wasn't going to pretend that she didn't know where this could lead, yet she didn't consider pulling away.

Something had shifted between them this afternoon. It wasn't only because of the passion that had erupted from their kiss, it was because of the emotional closeness that had led to it. They had reached a new level of honesty. Touching him felt so natural, she no longer wanted to fight it.

"Do you have regrets, Cooper?"

"I try not to. Regrets are like a prison in your head. They lock you in one place and keep you from moving on."

"I can't imagine you in prison," she murmured. "It must have been awful."

"That's why I like windows." He moved behind her, fitting her back to his chest. Cupping her shoulders, he swayed to the beat that came through the floor. "Even when it's dark, I like being able to look outside."

"You value your freedom."

"Everyone does."

Her heart turned over as she thought about what she had learned tonight. "And yet you sacrificed your freedom for the sake of your friends."

"What are you talking about?"

"Ken told me the reason you served three years instead of a few months is because you refused to testify against the rest of them."

He muttered an oath.

"It's true, isn't it?"

"Could be."

"That was a noble thing to do."

He blew out his breath. It sounded like a huff. "I was looking out for myself, that's all. I knew I was going to do time. If word got out that I was a snitch my life wouldn't have been worth a dime in the joint."

She elbowed him in the ribs. "Oh, right. You're tough as nails. You're bad to the bone. Not one redeeming characteristic."

He caught her wrists and crossed her arms in front of her to keep her from jabbing him again. He resumed his gentle rocking. "You better believe it."

"So what's your excuse for being so considerate when you handled my father today?"

"With my record, if I bruised a former cop I'd do another three years."

"Uh-huh. And the reason you took me in when my house burned down—"

"—is because I wanted to get into your pants." He dropped his chin on her shoulder. He flexed his forearms so that his tensed muscles nudged the undersides of her breasts. "Why are you asking me all this, Hayley?"

Her nipples tingled at his subtle caress. "I thought you liked honesty."

"I'm being honest."

"Bull."

"Hayley—"

"You've got this habit about wanting people to think the worst of you. I don't know why you do it, but you don't fool me anymore."

He nipped her earlobe.

Pleasure shot through her nerves. She tipped her head as he tickled her ear with his tongue. It was difficult to concentrate through the distraction, but this was something that had to be said. "Since I met you, my entire value system has been turned upside-down. Everything that I thought was so black and white has a million shades of gray. But there's one thing I'm completely certain of."

"What?"

She turned in the circle of his arms to face him. She stabbed her index finger against his chest. "Whatever mistakes you made in your past, you, Cooper Webb, are the most honorable man I have ever met."

He fastened his hands on her hips. "I just told you I want to get into your pants. That's not honorable."

"But you haven't, have you? If you're so bad, why haven't you? You've had so many opportunities. You have to realize that I wouldn't have stopped you, but you've respected my wishes. From the very start you've shown me nothing but kindness. You're too good a man to—"

"Hayley!" He moved his grip to her waist and lifted her up so that her face was level with his. The lines beside his mouth deepened with a smile that was part bad boy...and pure dangerous man. "You know better than that."

"But—"

"Why the hell do you think I brought you upstairs?"

Her pulse jumped so fast it left her giddy. She clasped her hands behind his neck. "You said you wanted to talk about my house."

Holding her off the floor, he took a step away from the window. "I lied."

She hooked her legs around his waist to make it easier for him to carry her. "Ah. You lied."

"Yeah. If I'd only wanted to talk, I would have taken you to my office."

"Then why did you bring me here, Cooper?"

"Because I've been waiting almost six hours for the chance to get you alone and finish what we started—and I'll be damned if anyone's going to interrupt us again." He anchored her more securely to his body as he moved past the furniture in the center of the floor and started toward the platform in the far corner. "And I figured the next time I kiss you we should be near a bed."

"Mmm."

"But if you're partial to that truck bumper, let me know and we'll go out to the parking lot."

With each step he took, her breasts rubbed his chest, her thighs slid over his hips and the hard length behind the front of his jeans pressed exactly on the spot where she had been wanting to feel him since he had left her on that bumper. The sensations that pulsed through her made further speech impossible.

But what was left to say? They had both made themselves clear. She knew what he was offering. It wasn't love, but she wanted it anyway. She wanted *him*.

She pushed his collar aside with her chin and opened her mouth over the base of his neck, drawing in the taste of his skin.

He stopped moving. A tremor traveled over his body, tingling through her breasts and stomach, whispering across her thighs. He tightened his fingers on her buttocks and rotated his hips. "Hayley?"

She ran her tongue along the ridge of a tendon to his ear, then lifted her head to look at him.

Despite the shadows left by the moonlight, the desire in his gaze was unmistakable…and so powerful it stole her breath.

There was no going back, yet Hayley didn't want to. Cooper had been right—this part wasn't complicated. It was inevitable. She didn't want to wait one more second for him to kiss her. She smiled, framed his cheeks in her hands and kissed him.

Chapter 12

They never did make it to the bed.

Cooper sank to his knees on the floor with Hayley still wrapped around his body. He lowered the zipper at the back of her dress. For the second time that day, she reached for the buttons on his shirt. She heard something rip but she didn't care, didn't stop. A pair of shirt buttons bounced across the hardwood.

And still the kiss went on. She shoved his shirt over his shoulders, yanking it down his arms. As soon as he shook his hands free from the sleeves he reached behind her to unhook her bra and peeled her clothes to her waist.

She shuddered at the puff of cool air on her breasts. She moaned at the touch of his hands. She could feel his urgency in the tension that hardened his muscles, yet his caress was gentle, tender, so achingly sweet it brought tears to her eyes.

Patient, gentle, sweet. And so sexy he was making her crazy. She ran her hands over his chest, driven by the need to touch him. She traced the swells and dips of muscle with her palms, reclaiming the skin she had touched that afternoon, reveling in the freedom to explore him again.

He did the same, lavishing her with attention. He cupped her breasts, rubbing his thumbs around the tips, coming close to the center again and again but not touching until she was ready to crawl out of her skin. He caught her arms, eased her back just enough so he could curl himself forward and tongue her nipple into his mouth.

The contact was electrifying. She slapped her palms on the floor behind her, arching into his kiss. His throat rumbled with a groan of approval as he took what she offered.

She moistened her lips. She could still taste his mouth. "Cooper…"

He lowered her to her back so slowly, so smoothly, she hadn't realized she was lying down until she felt the vibrations from the floor tingle through her shoulders. He lifted her hips to pull off the rest of her clothes, got rid of his own, then knelt between her legs and kissed her thigh.

Her senses spun. She writhed impatiently, but Cooper wouldn't be hurried.

Hayley's world dissolved into a blur of skin on skin, of intimate tastes, of longing so intense it verged on the brink of pain. Yet the instant she thought she couldn't take any more, Cooper slid inside her, stretching her, filling her, sending her over the brink.

She might have screamed. She wasn't sure. His mouth was on hers, his tongue moving with the same rhythm as his hips, with the same beat as the bass throb from the barroom. He caught her hands and laced their fingers together as the strength of his thrusts pushed her across the floor.

It was what she thought it would be. Sex. Simple and straightforward. With no sweet words, no promises.

Yet it was more.

She could feel it in the tremor that shook his fingers, she could hear it in the hitch in his breathing.

She could sense it in the tenderness that glowed in his eyes as he wrapped his arms around her oh, so tightly and simply held her as the aftershocks of what they had done rippled through her heart.

Cooper rubbed the water from his hair, then draped the towel around his neck and walked naked to the bed. Hayley was curled on her side with the sheet pulled tight across her breasts. One hand was tucked under her pillow, the other stretched over the place where he had slept beside her. Not that either of them had gotten much sleep last night.

He gripped the ends of the towel, a smile of satisfaction spreading over his face. Damn, it was probably illegal to feel this good.

He had been right about the passion Hayley kept under that classy exterior. She was high-grade dynamite in bed. And on the floor. And against the wall. He couldn't get enough of her, and she had made it plain as day that the feeling was mutual.

Her face was relaxed now, but her lips were parted and still swollen. The flush that had pinkened the skin above her breasts had faded, yet a trace of red remained at the crook of her neck where he'd kissed her harder than he'd meant to. He didn't feel the least bit guilty about that. After all, she had put her mark on him—in the bathroom mirror he'd seen the lines her nails had left on his back.

Oh, yeah. He felt too smug for his own good. A guy could get used to having a woman like Hayley in his bed.

He looked around the room. He hadn't bothered to close the blinds the night before, so the place was flooded with daylight. There was no mistaking what had happened here. Their clothes were still strewn on the floor where they had tossed them, along with pieces from empty condom wrappers. The blankets and pillow Hayley had been using to make up her bed on the sofa were piled neatly on the coffee table. She wouldn't need them again. After last night, there was no way she would be sleeping alone.

Slipping the towel from his neck, he propped one foot on the platform that held the bed and returned his gaze to Hayley. She sighed in her sleep and the sheet that covered her breasts inched downward, revealing the dark pink arc of one aureole.

Cooper's pulse slammed into high gear. He dropped the towel, stepped up to the bed and gave the sheet a tug.

Hayley opened her eyes. She regarded him sleepily for a moment, then blinked hard a few times and ran her tongue over her lips. She groped for the sheet.

He saw a twinge of awkwardness on her face. Damn. He wasn't going to let her retreat now. No way were they going back to how things had been. Before she could draw the sheet into place, he knelt on the mattress, cupped her breast in his hand and bent to press a kiss to its underside.

She gasped. Her hands went to his head. "Cooper!"

He rubbed the side of his head on her chest and latched on to her nipple. "Good morning, Hayley," he mumbled, his mouth full.

Her chest heaved with a sound that was part sob, part laugh. "Cooper, you're all wet!"

"I had a shower." He pulled the sheet aside completely, rolled her to her back and swung his leg across her to straddle her hips.

Her eyes darkened. She shifted beneath him, her skin warm and sleep-soft.

Cooper gathered a lock of her hair from where it was spread out on the pillow, brought it over her shoulder and used it to wipe the moisture that he'd left on her breast. The sight of her hair sliding around her nipple made him groan. Need hardened his body, yet he did his best to keep his caress light. She was probably feeling too tender to be ready for another round. "You woke up more gorgeous than when you went to sleep."

She spread her fingers on his knees, her gaze moving slowly upward. "You're not too bad to look at yourself."

He sifted her hair through his fingers, then gathered it together again and stroked it along the side of her cheek. "I like your hair. It makes you look like an angel."

She touched her fingernail to his forearm. "I like your tattoo. It makes you look…" She paused.

"Bad?"

"Sexy. The kind of guy I might have fantasized about when I was in high school." She lifted her gaze to his briefly, then looked away. The awkwardness was back. Her cheeks pinkened. "Cooper, I…"

"Hayley, don't get shy on me now," he said quietly. He caught her chin in his hand. "I know we're different. That's one of the reasons we've got this chemistry."

"We do, don't we? Have chemistry."

"We've got a good thing going. Two people enjoying each other. It's as simple as that."

She sighed. "I know."

He rubbed his thumb over her lip. "Did I do anything that you didn't like?"

The color in her cheeks deepened. "No, Cooper. It was all good."

"I've pictured you in this bed so many times. I've thought about what it would be like to hold you while you slept, but I didn't know how good it would feel. You don't really want to go back to the couch, do you?"

She shook her head. Her hair fanned out on the pillow.

"Nothing else has to change, Hayley. We're still partners."

"Until we get Oliver Sproule."

"Right."

Silence spun out between them. Cooper had a crazy urge to say something else, but there was nothing more to say, was there? Their priorities were still the same. They both understood that.

Hayley reached up and ran her index finger along his jaw. "You know I don't have a boyfriend, but you never told me about you, Cooper."

"You want to know if I have another woman stashed away somewhere?"

She paused. "No, I guess I didn't really need to ask. I know you don't. If you did, you wouldn't have cheated on her with me."

Pleasure surged through him. It was more than sexual. Hayley's faith in his character touched him in places he hadn't known he had.

It was like the pleasure he'd felt the night before, when she had stood in front of him in the moonlight, with her gaze sparkling and that determined set to her jaw he'd seen so many times. She had told him he was an honorable man. Did she realize how much that meant to him?

He caught her hands, brushed a kiss across each palm, then twined his fingers with hers and pressed their joined hands to the pillow beside her head. "I haven't been a monk, Hayley, but it's been a while since I slept with a woman. And in case you're wondering, I've never had a woman in this bed before you."

"What?"

He stretched her arms toward the headboard and lowered himself until his chest touched her breasts. "You're the first woman who has been in this loft."

"Why?"

"Running the bar takes most of my time. Everything else comes second."

"There must be more to it than that, Cooper. What's the real reason?"

Her question made him think. It took him a minute to figure out the answer. "I guess this place is like the Long Shot. It's a chance to change the way things used to be for me."

"It's your first permanent home."

"Yeah. Aside from the three years I spent inside, this is the longest I've stayed in one place. I wanted it to be different. Decent." He gave her a gentle kiss. "When I was a kid, I remember how Donny used to bring his girlfriends home all the time, even before my mother finally split. I'm not judging him or anything, he was what he was, but I didn't want to be like him."

She smiled, her eyes glowing with an echo of the way she'd looked at him the night before. "And yet you brought me here."

"I didn't have much choice the first time."

She laughed softly. "Neither did I. You tossed me over your shoulder and carried me."

"That's how it started." He slipped his knee between her legs, easing them apart. "But I already told you the main reason I brought you home."

"I remember you said something about my pants." She

rubbed the sole of her foot along his calf. "I hope you re-member what I said."

He shifted his other knee to the inside of her thighs, spreading her legs wider as he settled his weight on top of her. Damn, he shouldn't have started to talk. It was sim-pler when they didn't talk. He had told her he wanted to sleep with her, but she had seen through that already.

And she'd been right. If sex was all that he'd wanted from Hayley, he hadn't needed to wait this long.

He knew that he cared about her, he'd told her that al-most a week ago. The hard part was accepting just how much he wanted *her* to care about *him*.

He needed more than her body, he needed to see that look in her eyes, hear the trust in her voice and feel the hon-esty in her touch. It scared him, how much he wanted from her and how little he could offer in return.

He tightened his grip on her fingers. "Hayley, I don't want to hurt you."

Her gaze was steady on his, as if she realized he wasn't only talking about the physical pain he might cause. "I know you don't, Cooper."

"But if I can't feel you around me in the next second…"

She smiled and hooked her ankle behind him, lifted her hips and drew him into her warmth.

The knock on the door made Hayley start. She blinked, realizing she had been staring at the same page on the computer screen for the past five minutes. Her mind wasn't on the financial performance of Sproule's money-launder-ing outboard-motor company, it was still reeling from what Cooper had done before he'd left this morning.

And it wasn't only her mind that was feeling the after-effects. She was tender in the most intimate places. Each time she moved, tingles stole through her body, setting off echoes of pleasure.

She pushed away from Cooper's desk and pressed the back of her hand to her cheek. She could feel it burning merely at the thought of him. "Yes?" she called.

Pete opened the door and stuck his head inside. "Have you got a minute? There's someone here who wants to talk to you."

"Sure." She glanced at the window. The spot where Cooper usually parked his truck was still empty. He was following up on his agreement with Nathan by driving to the Sproule estate to scout out the best way to ease up on the surveillance.

"Coop isn't back yet," Pete said. "Besides, if he was, he wouldn't send me and he wouldn't knock."

She returned her gaze to his. "I know. I—" She paused when she noticed Pete's teasing grin.

It was ridiculous to feel her blush deepen. She was certain Cooper wouldn't have told anyone what had happened the night before, but it must have been obvious to his friends that something had changed.

And yet, other than their sleeping arrangements, everything else was still the same, wasn't it? "Who is it?" she asked.

"A girl Cooper threw out of the place last week."

Hayley got out of the chair, automatically smoothing her skirt as she moved around the desk, but the casual flowered cotton garment didn't show many wrinkles. The clothes she had acquired to replace her lost wardrobe not only fit better, they were more comfortable. "He threw her out? What did she do?"

Pete stepped back as she approached the doorway. "Chose the wrong friend. Her name's Nina. She's just a kid, so she's probably skipping school to be here."

"Did she say why she wants to see me?"

"She says it's about Sproule."

The girl was standing just inside the front entrance of the bar. From a distance, she didn't look like a child—her snug T-shirt and hip-hugger jeans revealed the generous figure of a grown woman. Yet as soon as Hayley was close enough to see her face, the illusion of maturity faded. The girl's features were smooth and baby-soft. She couldn't be past her midteens.

Although Hayley had never seen her before, she had a sudden urge to give her a hug. The girl seemed to be trying her best to act grown up, but her dark eyes held a spark of guilty panic. "Nina?" Hayley asked. "I'm Hayley Tavistock. Pete said you wanted to talk to me."

Nina looped the strap of a tiny purse across her shoulder and glanced around the barroom. Chair legs scraped against the hardwood as Pete pulled the chairs off the tables and set them on the floor. "Can we go someplace else?" she asked.

Hayley slipped her arm around Nina's shoulder and ushered her to the back hall. "We can talk in the office. Would you like a soda?"

Nina shook her head. She didn't speak again until Hayley had closed the door of Cooper's office behind them. "I heard what you're doing here and I want to help." The words came out in a rush. "I didn't say anything before because I wasn't supposed to be there. I told my parents I was at the library just like I did when that big guy drove me home and I knew I would get grounded if I said anything."

Hayley led her to the couch and sat beside her. "Take your time, Nina. I'm not going anywhere."

The girl brought her purse to her lap and clasped her hands on top of it. "It's the only way I can get out of the house. My parents are okay, but they treat me like a kid all the time. Ever since last week they don't even want to let me out except to go to school. It's not as if I'm going to see Izzy again. He's a creep."

Izzy? The man who worked for Sproule and had brought heroin to the Long Shot? Perhaps this girl knew something about the drug shipment. Hayley leaned closer. "Nina, what happened last week?"

Nina made an erasing motion with her hand. "Izzy tried to buy me a drink but Cooper wouldn't serve me. He made that hulk who works for him take me home. My parents went ballistic."

It wasn't that difficult to put the picture together. Cooper must have realized that Nina was underage and he'd had Pete see that she got safely home. Oh, he was a good man. He couldn't help showing it in everything he did. Hayley smiled. "Your parents want what's best for you, Nina. People like Izzy will only lead to trouble."

The girl rolled her eyes. The expression made her look even younger. "I know that. I told you, he's a creep. He told me to keep quiet about this, but I'm not listening to him anymore."

"Pete told me you know something about Oliver Sproule," Hayley prompted. "Did you learn something about him from Izzy?"

"Well, sort of, but what I'm talking about happened before I met him. It was last year. Like I said, I wasn't supposed to be there, so I was afraid to say anything. I only told Izzy because I wanted to impress him."

"When last year, Nina?"

"October."

Hayley's heart gave a sudden thump. Adam had been killed in October. "Maybe it would be easier if you started at the beginning."

Nina chewed at a ragged thumbnail. "It was a school night, so my parents thought I was at the library, but I wanted to go to this place downtown that my friends had told me about. There were three of us. We were waiting for it to get busy so we could slip inside, when this tall blond man walked out. He bumped into me, so I remember his face. He was really nice about it, even though he looked kind of ticked, like he'd been stood up."

Hayley stared at her. "A tall, blond man," she said.

"There was nothing we could do. I'm sorry. The car didn't even slow down. He tried to jump out of the way but it steered right into him. It was in front of a streetlight so we knew it was on purpose. We couldn't believe it. It was like it was happening on TV or something except the noise was so awful, like a crunch—" She broke off. She looked at Hayley, her dark eyes brimming with tears.

"You're talking about my brother." Hayley tried to keep her voice controlled, despite the emotions that were surging over her. The girl was describing Adam's murder. The horror and grief that Hayley had thought she'd gotten past were once again flooding her mind. "That was who you saw get killed, isn't it? Adam Tavistock."

She nodded. "I saw his picture in the paper after. We wouldn't have guessed he was a cop. We all swore to each other we wouldn't tell because we knew we'd be grounded for life and he was dead anyway so—"

"And you never said anything because you were afraid of being *grounded?* My God. You witnessed a murder. You—" Hayley clenched her jaw and fought to rein in her temper. She reminded herself this was just a child, with a child's self-centered viewpoint. It wouldn't do any good for Hayley to vent her frustration on her. "I'm sorry, Nina. I didn't mean to shout at you. I loved my brother very much and it's upsetting to hear about his death."

"I was going to call 911, really I was. I had my cell out and everything." Nina wiped her eyes with the back of her hand, then gripped her purse again. "But when we found out who the guy in the car was, we got really scared. Everyone knows about Oliver Sproule."

"I can understand that. You must have seen his picture in the paper, too."

"No, we saw him there. He backed up and got out of his car to look at the man he hit. We thought he was going to help him. He didn't. He—" She gave a sharp sob. "He kicked him. I barfed on my phone. We ran up the alley before he could see us."

Hayley breathed hard through her nose, striving for control. Oliver had *kicked* him? Wasn't it enough that he had run Adam down in cold blood? Oh, God. No wonder the girls were so terrified. This was worse than the scene that she had imagined.

Her mind snapped back on track so fast, she had to suck in a breath. "Nina, are you positive about all of this?"

"I know what I saw. I'll never forget it."

"You said there were three of you. You and two friends."

"Uh-huh, but I'm the only one left here. Sherry and Jessica went to Springfield after Christmas when their dad got a job at a post office there."

Three girls who were in the wrong place at the wrong time and scared out of their heads.

Three eye witnesses to Adam's murder.

Hayley laid her hand over Nina's. She wanted to clutch her arm and drag her down to the courthouse right now and make her tell her story to Judge Mercer, the man who had presided at Sproule's trial, but she realized she had to use caution. The girl looked as if she was ready to bolt. "Nina, you did a very courageous thing by coming forward now. It must have been difficult for you, but you're not going to get in trouble. I promise you. Your parents will be very proud that you've told the truth."

"I haven't told them yet. I never told anyone except Izzy. The longer it went on, the harder it got, you know?"

Hayley felt a lump in her throat. She had given up on the idea of seeing Sproule sent to prison for murder. Now it looked as if it could actually happen.

It seemed too good to be true. It was definitely too much to take in.

She could get what she wanted, she could give her father closure and make him proud of her. And Cooper could pay back Tony and keep the Long Shot. She couldn't wait to see his face when he found out this ordeal was almost over.

Almost over.

Her eyes began to sting. This was what she wanted, wasn't it?

"Uh, Hayley?"

She blinked to clear her vision and looked at Nina. "Thank you. Thank you so much. You have no idea how—" Her voice broke. She tried to smile, but her chin was trembling too hard.

"I'm sorry. Really I am."

Would the FBI handle this? Maybe she should contact the state's Attorney General. As insurance against another cover-up, it might be wise to call as many law enforcement agencies as possible.

The first thing to do was to get Nina and her friends to make statements. She wasn't sure how to go about that, but she would start by approaching their parents. One way or another, the entire truth would come out. Nothing was going to stop it now. Finally, justice was going to be done.

And yet…she didn't want *everything* to end. She had only just begun to get close to Cooper. What was going to happen to them when this was over?

They hadn't had the chance to talk about afterward. She hadn't wanted to think about it, but she had better start now.

"You seem like such a nice person. Izzy must have lied about your brother."

She glanced at Nina. "What?"

The girl hesitated. "Maybe I shouldn't say anything."

At Nina's tone, Hayley had a swift jab of foreboding. She wasn't sure why. Things were going better than she could have imagined, weren't they? "Nina, if you know something else, you have to tell me. Please. What did you hear about Adam?"

"Izzy said your brother was on the take."

Chapter 13

Hayley felt oddly detached as she moved toward the glass doors at the front of the Latchford Savings and Loan. It was as if shock had disconnected her mind from her body, allowing her to put one foot in front of another with a semblance of control despite the turmoil that careened through her thoughts.

Phil McCormick, the manager of the bank and an old family friend, rested his fingertips on her elbow as he walked beside her. He smelled of clove-scented aftershave and mothballs, just as he had whenever he'd come for dinner when she'd been a child. He had been deeply upset by Adam's death, and he had been nothing but solicitous when he'd helped the family's lawyer deal with Adam's estate, yet he hadn't supported Hayley's stand against Sproule during the trial.

His lack of support had puzzled her, but she had assumed Phil had been afraid of Oliver Sproule, just like everyone else in town. That much was true, he had been afraid, yet that hadn't been the only reason he had tried to discourage her from her pursuit of Sproule.

"Is there anything else I can help you with, Hayley?"

"No, thank you, Phil."

He cleared his throat and lowered his voice. "You must understand, I had no obligation to come forward with this. The records were never subpoenaed."

"Yes. I understand." The lack of a thorough investigation had all been part of the coverup that had resulted in Sproule's acquittal, except, until now, Hayley hadn't realized the extent of what had been covered up. She took shallow breaths, focusing on the sunshine that came through the door. Only six more steps and she would be outside.

"Because your brother's will has been probated and the accounts have been closed, we'll be transferring the records to our archives. It is very unlikely that anyone will have cause to access them again. I only agreed to your request so that you'll know why you have to drop this."

Four more steps. She could feel her stomach rebel at Phil's scent of cloves and mothballs. She clenched her jaw and nodded.

"Hayley." Phil squeezed her arm and dropped his hand. "The trial's over. For Ernie's sake, let your brother rest in peace. Stirring this up now won't do any good. It won't bring Adam back."

She took her sunglasses from her purse and fitted them over her eyes. She didn't have a reply. It was going to take longer than a few hours for her brain to process this.

At first she had refused to believe what Nina had said about Adam. Her brother couldn't have been crooked. He had been killed because he had been too good a cop and he had been getting too close to arresting Oliver Sproule. That Izzy character must have lied to stir up trouble, that's all. The larger-than-life big brother Hayley had adored couldn't possibly have been dirty.

No. She knew right from wrong. She knew the good guys from the bad ones.

Everything that I thought was so black and white has a million shades of gray.

Yet the records Phil had shown her today were black and white, weren't they? Numbers didn't lie. She had seen for herself the five-figure deposits into Adam's account over the last three years, as regular as clockwork on the final business day of every quarter. According to the transfer slips she had coerced Phil into digging out, the money had come from a shell company that Hayley recognized from her research was directly connected to Latchford Marine.

There hadn't been a deposit in September, though. The last one had been in June. That's why Hayley hadn't seen anything suspicious on the final statement the bank had sent when the account had been closed.

The change in the deposit pattern had to have some bearing on why Adam had been killed. Had he been demanding his next payment? Or had he been trying to quit?

She slapped her palm against the brass plate on the door and pushed it open. After Adam's death, she had been so immersed in her father's medical crisis and in her quest for justice that she hadn't thought to scrutinize her brother's old financial records. Instead, she had entrusted that to the family lawyer who was administering the will. Like Phil, the lawyer was an old friend of Ernie's. He must have sat on this information, too.

Little had remained in the account at Adam's death because there had been withdrawals, too. Big ones. To travel agencies and to hotels in Atlantic City and in Las Vegas. She had known that Adam had liked to play cards, but it appeared as if his fondness for them had progressed to serious gambling. Is that how he had fallen in with Sproule?

Is that why there had been so little money left in her father's accounts, too? Had Adam emptied them?

No. Please, God, there must be some other explanation.

Hayley descended the steps in front of the bank, her breath coming in sharp bursts. She had spent months digging up every scrap of information on Oliver Sproule that she could, but she'd been so convinced she'd known Sproule's motive for killing Adam, she hadn't once questioned it. Why would she waste time investigating her brother?

And yet the facts she had needed were there. All she'd had to do was go and look. She was an accountant, for pity's sake. She should have thought to check something as basic as how her brother had spent his money.

But questioning that was like ripping apart the very fabric of her life. It would be betraying her brother. It was inconceivable.

Oh, God, this was a nightmare. She wished it would all just go away.

"Hello, beautiful."

At the sound of Cooper's voice, her mind blanked. She looked around. Cooper's pickup was parked at the curb a few spots down from the bank. He was leaning against the passenger door, his arms folded over a plain black T-shirt that stretched over his chest. Faded blue jeans hugged his long legs as he stood with one booted foot crossed over the other. A corner of his mouth tilted upward in a crooked smile.

Hayley instinctively started toward him. He looked so

solid, so real, she wanted to run to him and fling herself against him, beg him to wrap her in his arms and carry her someplace safe, as he had done so many times before.

Cooper pushed away from the door and walked to meet her. "Good thing you came outside when you did. I'm pretty sure the people in the bank were starting to get nervous."

"What?"

He grinned. "I've been standing beside my truck, watching the place for twenty minutes."

"I'm sorry. I didn't realize you were here."

"It's a joke, Hayley. Bank? Truck parked in front? Getaway driver?"

A car honked somewhere down the street. The breeze rolled a paper coffee cup across the sidewalk. Hayley blinked and forced a smile. "I get it now. Sorry to keep you waiting. Where's Pete?"

"I sent him back to the Long Shot. He said you came here after you met with Nina." He pinched the arm of her sunglasses and lifted them up so he could look into her eyes. His grin faded. "What's wrong? Did that kid do something to upset you?"

Her mind clicked back into gear. Cooper! She had to tell him about what Nina had said, and she needed to tell him what she had learned at the bank. This additional information would break the murder case against Sproule wide open.

Yet she couldn't bring herself to say the words. Once the truth about her brother was made public, there would be no going back. The shock of learning about Adam's death had triggered her father's stroke. In his weakened condition, there was a strong possibility that discovering the truth about the payoffs his son had taken could kill him.

Oh, God. She had lived all her life knowing she had

caused her mother's death. If she revealed what she knew, she could cause her father's, too.

"Hayley?" Cooper ran his fingertip along her eyebrow. "Are you okay?"

No, she was not okay. She would never be the same again. There was a huge rip in the fabric of her life and it was getting bigger by the minute.

She took her sunglasses from Cooper and fitted them back into place on her nose. How could she get justice for her brother if it meant exposing his corruption?

How could she endanger her father's health and destroy his illusions about the son he idolized?

Yet by remaining silent, she was betraying Cooper. She was denying him access to the evidence that would allow him to fulfill his bargain with Tony.

Whatever she did, she would end up hurting someone. How could she choose between the people she loved?

The people she loved?

There was no question about it. She loved all three of them. Adam. Her father.

And Cooper.

Oh, yes, she loved this man from his too-long hair to the dimple in his chin, from his bad-boy tattoo to his cowboy boots. She loved him from his tough shell to the tender soul he tried so hard to hide.

She wanted to scream, and she wanted to weep. When had it happened? How? She had fought so hard against it, yet she had been helpless to stop the feelings that had been growing in her heart. How could she not love a man who had shown her time and again the goodness he kept inside and yet could make a joke about being mistaken for a bank robber?

Oh, God.

Now what?

* * *

A twisted heap of blackened debris surrounded by yellow police tape was all that was left of the stately old two-story Victorian. The acre of lawn that had surrounded the Tavistock house was blackened with drifts of cinders and gouged in places with ruts from the fire trucks. The maple that had stood at the side of the house had been reduced to a charred trunk and stubby limbs. The ones at the back fence had been far enough away to escape the flames, but their leaves had been seared brown by the heat. The breeze from the park beyond rattled through what was left of them and swirled past the debris pile, bringing with it the lingering taint of smoke.

Hayley stood on the front walk at the edge of the police tape, her sunglasses firmly in place even though the sun was already going down. She lifted her hand toward a point above the right corner of the foundation. "Adam's room was over there above the veranda when we were growing up. Mine was in the back."

Cooper looped his arm around her shoulders. She was so tense, she felt brittle.

He hadn't wanted to bring her here. For one thing, the neighborhood was too close to Sproule's estate, and Cooper had just asked the guys who had been keeping an eye on the place to pull back. For another, this was the first time Hayley had returned to the house since the fire, and it had to be upsetting. Yet she had been so insistent, he hadn't been able to refuse. He could see she was working something through in her head.

She had been this way since he had picked her up at the bank today. It worried him, but he hadn't yet figured out what was going on. There were so many emotions flickering over her face she was difficult to read.

"I used to be scared of thunder when I was young," she said. "So whenever there was a storm at night, Adam would take me down to the kitchen and make us these huge banana splits. After a while, I forgot about being afraid. Did I tell you that?"

"No." He rubbed his fingers gently along her upper arm. "You never mentioned it."

"By the time I was in high school, Adam had moved out of the house because he liked his privacy, but he used to visit regularly. He always brought me presents that my dad used to say were too extravagant, but I adored Adam. I thought he was the best brother in the world." She inhaled unsteadily. "We drifted apart after I moved away to college."

"That happens."

"I didn't come home as often as I should have. When I did, I spent most of the time with my father. I was always trying to please him, but it never happened."

Hayley had visited her father at the nursing home this afternoon, as she always did, yet her manner toward him had been different. Ernie had been fully lucid today, his subtle slights toward his daughter as hurtful as ever, yet Hayley hadn't looked at him with longing. She had appeared more guarded than usual, as if she had been working something through in her head then, too.

"It wasn't fair, Cooper."

"No, it wasn't."

She stepped away from his touch. Her shoes gritted against some cinders that lay on the sidewalk. She bent down to pick up a piece of broken glass. "I think part of me was jealous of Adam because he was Dad's favorite. That's the main reason we drifted apart."

"That's understandable."

"But I didn't want to admit it." She straightened up,

holding the glass fragment gingerly between her index finger and thumb. "In my mind, Adam could do no wrong. I believed he was the best, just like my father did. You were the first person who made me see that he might not have been that perfect after all."

Cooper raked his fingers through his hair. "I'm sorry for spouting off about him, Hayley. Is that what's bothering you?"

She twisted to look at him over her shoulder. Her eyes were hidden by her sunglasses but her eyebrows were arched in surprise. "What are you talking about?"

"I've known all along how strongly you feel about your brother. I shouldn't have criticized him."

"You were only being honest, Cooper. You described what he did. A man's character comes through in his actions. Adam's did. So does yours. But just because my brother wasn't perfect doesn't mean that I don't love him." She glanced at the piece of glass she still held, then lobbed it past the police tape. It struck a blackened beam and bounced out of sight in a tangle of pipes. "I promised my father that I would get justice for Adam, but putting Oliver Sproule in prison isn't going to change anything."

"What do you mean?"

She waved her hand at the wreckage. "It's not going to rebuild my mother's family home or restore my grandfather's books and my grandmother's china. It won't bring Adam back. It's not going to make my father love me."

"Hayley—"

"It's true. I can't make my father love me if he doesn't want to. I've been clinging to this idea that if only I manage to do this one last thing to please him, I'll finally make amends for what happened when I was born and everything's magically going to change. But I don't have any control over the way I feel, so how could I hope to change him?"

He could see how much the admission was costing her, and part of him wanted to argue just to comfort her, but she was right. It was unlikely that Ernie was going to change, not after so many years. Cooper was glad Hayley had finally recognized that.

She turned to face him squarely. "I've been thinking a lot about what you said to me yesterday, Cooper. It's time to cut my losses. I want to get on with my life." She clasped her hands together. "That's why I've decided to quit."

A sudden gust rattled the trees at the back of the yard. Cooper started. He couldn't have heard her right. "Did you say you're quitting?"

"I want to let Sproule go."

"You *what?*"

"I don't want to go through with this. I don't care if he goes to jail."

"But we're getting close, Hayley. That drug shipment Nathan told us about is bound to happen soon."

"There's no guarantee of that. It might not happen at all. Even if it does, you realized yourself that Sproule might end up getting a deal so that the authorities can stop Stephan Volski."

He took her sunglasses from her nose and tipped up her chin. He tried to read her expression, but her emotions were still too confused. "I wouldn't have gotten this close to Sproule without you, but if you want me to take it from here, it's okay, I will."

"That's not enough. I want you to quit, too, Cooper."

He stared at her. She couldn't have meant…

"You have to let him go," she said. "Please."

He dropped his hand. "You're not really asking me to

give up, are you? Even with everything I've got riding on bringing Sproule to justice?"

She nodded. "It's too dangerous, Cooper. If we keep chasing Sproule, we're going to stir up more trouble than we bargained for. People are going to get hurt."

"I know there's a risk, especially with Volski and the Russian mob involved, but we'll be careful. That's why I brought in the guys for extra security."

"People are going to get hurt," she repeated, her tone verging on desperate. "You don't need to do this. You can walk away."

"The hell I can. If I walk, I lose everything. You know that."

"Not everything."

"I'll lose my bar, my home and my business. That's all I have."

"It's only a place, Cooper. You'll be the same person wherever you go. You made it once, you can do it again. Please, you have to give this up."

He still couldn't believe what he was hearing. He'd thought she understood how important the Long Shot was to him. After the intimacy they had shared the night before, she knew him better than that, didn't she?

Or was the sudden worry of hers due to the change in their relationship? She was such a passionate woman, maybe the days of living under the threat of more trouble from Sproule had finally gotten to her and that was why she wanted him to quit. He knew he would do anything in his power to keep her from harm.

He took her hand and led her to where he had parked his pickup beside the curb. "If you're concerned about the danger, we should go back to the bar. It would be safer than standing out here."

She retrieved her sunglasses from him and climbed into

the truck. Instead of putting them back on, she held them in her lap, opening and closing the arms. She didn't look back once as they pulled away from the wreckage of her house. She waited until they were most of the way across town before she spoke again. "Could you at least think about it?"

He tried to keep his tone reasonable. "I'm not going to let anything happen to you, Hayley, but I can't quit. I have to keep my promise to Tony."

"No, you don't. If he takes the Long Shot, we can start again. We can open another place somewhere else." She stored her sunglasses in her purse and tucked her fingertips beneath her thighs. Cooper recognized the pose—she always sat like that when she was anxious. She spoke quickly. "I'm positive that Pete, Ken and Theresa would come with us. They're terrific workers and they think the world of you."

"I'm not going to run scared."

"Hear me out. I've seen your books. Your business plan is solid and your cash flow is steadily improving. You've proven that you can succeed. You don't need Tony. With my connections to regular bankers I can find conventional financing for your new bar."

He glanced at her. The streetlights had come on while they'd been driving. In the sliding squares of light that moved across her face, her eyes had a sheen of tears. He could see that she was sincere. "You're saying 'we' and 'us.'"

"I'll help you, Cooper. I'll do whatever it takes to rebuild your business."

"I won't need to rebuild because I'm not going to lose it."

"I'm sorry. You have no idea how sorry I am. I know how proud you are of the place, but we'll manage somehow. I've thought this all through and it's the only way out."

"You're not making sense." He turned onto the road that would take them to the city limits. "If you want to bail, that's fine. Go ahead and bail, but that's no reason to ask me to do the same."

"Yes, it is. We're partners."

"Right. To get Sproule."

She was silent for a while as she chewed her lip. Finally, she took a deep breath and spoke. "I want us to give up on Oliver Sproule, but I don't want our partnership to end."

At first, Cooper didn't want to acknowledge the hope that flashed through him. He knew better than that, didn't he? His knuckles whitened on the wheel. "Do you mean you want to be business partners?"

"No, that's not what I mean. I want more than that. I realize we haven't known each other that long, and neither of us made any promises last night, but I don't want to leave you, Cooper. I want to stay."

He hit the brakes so fast the tires squealed. He yanked the wheel and pulled the truck to a stop at the side of the road.

The lights of the Long Shot glowed just around the bend up ahead. A car honked as it went past. A billboard advertising the local hospital fund-raising drive rose from a vacant lot beside them. Cooper was aware of everything, the whiff of exhaust that rolled in the open window, the rumble of the engine, the sound of a freight train in the distance. Part of his mind remained alert to his surroundings.

Yet the rest of him heard nothing but the echo of Hayley's words.

She didn't want to leave him. She wanted to stay.

No, people came and went and only a fool let himself care.

Cooper was finding it hard to breathe. He thought of how Hayley had felt in his arms that morning, and how her presence had filled his life since the night they had met.

And he couldn't imagine not having her there.

He flexed his fingers and lifted his hands from the wheel to shut off the ignition, then draped his arm over the seat and turned to face her. "You want to stay with me?"

She nodded.

He touched his thumb to her cheek. Her skin was wet. His voice roughened. "I want that too, Hayley. Like I said before, we're good together."

"What we have between us isn't just chemistry." The confusion that had been swirling through her expression cleared. She brushed her lips across his palm and smiled. "I love you, Cooper."

Joy, sudden and fierce, slammed through him without warning. It was hard to believe he was really hearing this. It was more than he'd asked for, way more than they had agreed on and a hell of a lot more than he deserved.

But it was what he wanted. Deep down inside him where he knew better than to look, it was what he'd craved since the first time he'd touched her. He'd wanted it so much, he hadn't dared to put the thought into words.

And yet this woman with the face of an angel and pure honesty shining from her eyes had just spoken the words no one had ever said to him before.

"I know that I told you before it had to be all or nothing," Hayley said. "But I'm through thinking that way. I'm changing the pattern. I'll be happy with whatever you're willing to give as long as we can build a future together."

He stroked the hair from her temple, his fingers unsteady. "Unless I pay back Tony, I won't have a future."

"No, you're wrong. We'll be fine. Once we quit we can leave all the ugliness of Sproule and his crimes behind us and get on with our lives."

"We can't do that by walking away."

"Yes, we can! It's the best solution."

"Keeping the Long Shot isn't about the building or the money, it's what you talked about yesterday. It's about honor."

"You *are* honorable, Cooper. The way you've turned your life around is amazing."

"I haven't turned it around yet. I've told you where I came from and what I did. I've worked at getting clean for seven years, but I won't be able to wash off the last of the dirt until I fulfill my bargain with Tony."

"Cooper—"

"If I break my word, I won't be the man you say I am."

She tipped her face into his hand. "You don't have to prove anything to me."

"But I have to prove it to myself." He felt a pressure in the back of his throat. He didn't know where the words were coming from. It was as if a wall inside him was starting to crumble and feelings he'd done his best to contain were pouring out.

He had to swallow hard before he could go on. "You once said that I want people to think the worst of me. It's not deliberate, Hayley. It's because in my heart I'm still Donny's brat, just a troublemaking thief who got suckered into doing time. Don't you see? That kid would have walked. And that's why I have to see this through."

She closed her eyes. Her lashes gleamed with tears. "Oh, Cooper," she whispered. "You don't realize what a good man you are."

He brushed his fingertip beneath her eyes. "Don't ask me to give up now, Hayley. I can't."

She kissed his palm, her breath hitching on a sob.

He leaned toward her and pressed his forehead to hers. "More than anything, I want to feel that I've earned the right to your faith in me. And I want to earn the right to say those words back to you—"

The distant crack of a gunshot split the air. It was followed by three more shots in quick succession. Headlights appeared at the bend in the road.

Even as his mind struggled to switch tracks, his body was reacting. Cooper yanked Hayley down on the seat, threw himself on top of her and reached into the glove compartment for his gun.

Chapter 14

The door of the Long Shot stood wide open as people streamed from the barroom. Some joined the circle that had formed in the parking lot, but most were heading for their vehicles. There were so many leaving that Cooper couldn't pull in. He drove over the curb, bumped along the border of the lot and stopped in the long grass at the edge of the overgrown orchard.

Pete spotted him immediately and jogged over to meet him. He spoke through the driver's window. "One shooter," he said. "No one saw who it was."

"Where is he now?"

"Gone. Took off heading south. He was alone."

"Must have been him that passed by us," Cooper said. "We were just around the bend and heard the shots. Anyone hurt?"

"Only one. The cue ball."

"Bad?"

"Yeah. Theresa's giving him first aid, but it doesn't look good."

Cooper tucked his gun into the back of his waistband and tugged his T-shirt out of his jeans to cover it. He glanced at Hayley.

Her face was pale and her cheeks still damp. Her hair was a wild tangle around her head from the way he had shoved her beneath him. The seconds that had passed before Cooper had realized that no one was shooting at them had been the longest seconds of his life, but in those instants he'd known he would gladly have given his life to save hers.

Damn, the feelings kept pouring out. This wasn't the time or the place, but now that they had started, he couldn't stop them. *She'd said that she loved him.*

He grasped Hayley's wrist and returned his gaze to Pete. "Take Hayley upstairs. Check the place out to make sure it's clear, then—"

"No!" Hayley wrenched her wrist free, grabbed her purse from the floor and pushed open her door. "I want to know what happened."

Cooper threw his door open and jumped to the ground. He caught her arm as she rounded the hood. He would prefer to have her safely out of sight, but he didn't have time to argue. He looked around the parking lot for the rest of his men, but it was hard to make out faces in the commotion of the departing vehicles.

The exodus didn't surprise him. Out of habit, most of the bar's patrons wouldn't want to stick around to get interrogated as eyewitnesses. "Where's Hank?" he asked Pete.

"He's the one who saw it go down." Pete gestured toward the road. "He took a few shots at the car but he missed. He's picking up his casings before the cops get here so he doesn't get busted for breaking his parole."

"Damn, I told him not to shoot unless he had to."

"Yeah, that's Hank. He hasn't changed. Ken's calling it in now."

"Good." Cooper pulled Hayley securely to his side and surveyed the area once more. "If Hank's busy picking up shell casings, who's watching the back door?" Cooper demanded.

"Aw, hell." Pete pivoted and ran toward the rear of the building.

Cooper whistled to get the attention of the men who were supposed to be keeping track of the front entrance. He pointed to the open door emphatically, waited until the men had returned to their posts, then started for the circle where the remaining crowd was the thickest.

The floodlight that was fixed to the side wall bathed the scene in a stark glare. Cooper saw the gleam of Izzy's shaved head first. The man was lying on his back on the pavement at the side of the building about halfway between the front and rear entrances. Theresa was on her knees beside him, a stack of towels from the bar on her lap. She was holding one to his chest with the heel of her hand. As Cooper moved closer, he could see the towel was soaked with crimson.

Hayley gasped and made a choking noise in her throat.

Cooper turned and stepped in front of her to block her view. "You don't need to see this," he said.

She kept her gaze on Cooper's chest. "Who is it?"

"Izzy Pressman."

"The man who brought those drugs to the bar?"

"Yeah."

She breathed hard a few times. "Who do you think did this?"

"My money would be on Sproule. Izzy was stealing from him." Cooper continued to scan the crowd, watching for anyone who looked as if they didn't belong or might cause trouble. "Sproule would take it personally if he thought someone on his payroll was cheating him. He's a control freak and would want to do the job himself."

"The way he killed my brother."

He felt another tremor go through her shoulders. He looked at her face. Her skin was turning a sickly shade of white. There was a sheen of perspiration on her upper lip. "Hayley?"

"I don't do that well with blood. I threw up the last time my father took me hunting." She pushed her hair from her forehead, her hand unsteady. "I'm sorry. I—"

"It's all right." He drew her away from the crowd. A siren sounded in the distance just as he saw Pete returning. Cooper waved him over.

"Sorry, Coop," Pete said. He braced his hands on his knees and inhaled noisily to catch his breath before he continued. "The guys didn't think before they took off. Everything's secure now."

Cooper gave Hayley a quick, closed-mouth kiss and guided her toward Pete. "Wait for me upstairs," he told her. "Lock the door behind you. I'll be there as soon as I can."

She didn't argue this time. Cooper watched until Pete got her safely inside, then pushed through the circle of bystanders and knelt beside Theresa. "Want me to take over?" he asked.

Theresa nodded. Her hands and wrists were streaked with blood, her arms trembling from the strain. "There's nothing we can do except keep pressure on it."

Cooper took a fresh towel from her lap and placed it over the soaked one as she withdrew her hands and got to her feet. It was impossible to see the extent of the damage, but judging by all the blood, Pete was right. It was bad. Izzy's chest was hardly moving. Cooper shifted his gaze to Izzy's face.

His eyes were open and he was staring right at Cooper. His lips moved.

Cooper leaned closer. "You want to tell me something, Izzy?"

"Sproule," he grated out. "Sproule did this."

"That's what I figured. He found out you were dipping into the merchandise."

"Didn't take…that much. No cause…t' shoot me."

"Hang on. The ambulance should be here any minute."

Izzy's eyelids fluttered. He coughed on a bubble of blood. "'S she here?"

Careful to maintain a steady pressure on Izzy's chest, Cooper took another towel from Theresa with his free hand and gently wiped Izzy's chin. "Who?"

"Th' hot li'l bitch. Nina."

Cooper had never liked Izzy. The man was a pig. He had wanted to give heroin to an underage girl.

Yet it still moved him to see how gravely the man had been wounded. Whatever Izzy's mistakes, he was still human. He didn't deserve to end up like this. How much more blood was going to be on Sproule's hands before he was finally stopped?

"No, she's not here," Cooper replied. "Save your strength, Izzy."

"Sh—" He wheezed in a breath. "She tell you?"

"Tell me what?"

"'Bout th' cop. She…said…sh' would."

Izzy's speech was no more than a whisper, his words slurring. The siren grew louder. Cooper saw more of the people who circled them melt away. "What cop?" he asked.

"Sproule's pet cop." Izzy coughed again. This time the blood that came up was thicker. He blinked as Cooper cleaned it off his mouth. "Am I...gonna die, Webb?"

"Probably, Izzy. Feel like confessing your sins?"

His upper lip curled back from his teeth. "Screw...you. Wheresnina. Gotta see'r."

"She isn't here."

"Tell'er...keep'r mouth shut...'bout Adam Tavistock."

Cooper stiffened. "What do you know about Adam Tavistock?"

"He was dirtier th'n us, Webb." His eyelids lowered. "Ain't that...somethin'?" His head rolled to the side and he slipped into unconsciousness.

There was a loud whoop of siren from the road. Red lights flashed across the people who remained as the ambulance pulled into the parking lot. Cooper stayed where he was until the paramedics took over, his mind still trying to register what he had learned. He straightened up, wiping his hands on the last clean towel, then dropped it with the others on the foot of the stretcher as Izzy was loaded into the ambulance.

Theresa moved beside him. "What was he telling you? I couldn't hear."

Cooper looked around quickly. Theresa had been standing the closest to him. If she hadn't heard, no one else would have, either. "He said Sproule was the one who shot him."

"That figures, but what was he doing here?"

"Izzy was looking for his girlfriend and he thought she was at the Long Shot again," Cooper said. "Pete told me she was here this morning."

Cooper watched as a pair of police cars entered the parking lot. All except a handful of the customers had departed. Several cops started to question the ones who were left. Evidently Hank had managed to dispose of his gun and his casings—he voluntarily walked over to speak with a tall uniformed woman.

"Mr. Webb?" A short balding man strode toward him. He was wearing a suit, so he was probably the one in charge. "I have some questions. Are you the owner of this place?"

"Yes," Cooper said. "The Long Shot is mine."

And the stakes for keeping it had just gone up. One way or another he was going to nail Sproule. The bastard was getting bolder to do a hit on Cooper's turf. It had been a mistake to ease back on the harassment. Sproule must have viewed it as a weakness. The hell with what Nathan wanted, Cooper was going to tell his men to get back in Sproule's face.

"I'm Detective Ford," the cop said. He flipped open a spiral-bound notebook and clicked his pen. "Did you see what happened?"

"No, I was on my way here. I heard the shots and saw a black sedan go by but I didn't get a licence number or see who was in it."

Ford scribbled something in his notebook. "I understand the victim is a man by the name of Isaac Pressman. Do you know him?"

Cooper answered the cop's questions honestly, but he didn't offer any extra information. There was no way he was going to repeat what Izzy had said, not until he'd had the chance to think this through.

Yet it wasn't that big a leap in reasoning. As a matter of fact, it fit. Cooper knew first hand that Adam Tavistock wasn't a man of his word. He hadn't had a high opinion of Adam's character or his ability as a cop. If Adam had been dirty, it put a whole different spin on his murder. It could be why Sproule had been brazen enough to do the job himself. It also might have been why even the honest cops hadn't wanted to help Hayley nail his killer.

It was lucky that Hayley had gone inside when she did and hadn't heard any of this. She had already been upset. She would be devastated if she learned…

A thought floated through Cooper's consciousness. He didn't want to look at it. He tried to keep his attention on Ford, but he couldn't stop the facts from clicking in his head.

Nina had come here this morning to talk about Adam. She had spoken with Hayley. Hayley had been upset, and she never had given him a straight answer when he'd asked her what Nina had said.

Was *this* what had triggered Hayley's talk about quitting?

By the time Ford and his colleagues had finished taking statements and photographing the scene, it was too late for Cooper to consider reopening the bar. He sent Ken and Theresa home, dimmed the lights and walked behind the bar to pour himself a shot of whiskey. He downed it in one swallow and wrapped his fist around the glass.

Pete came through the swinging door at the back of the room and walked over to join him. "The back end's locked up tight so the guys left. They're going to cruise around Sproule's turf for a while and make sure everyone's behaving."

"Okay."

"Hell of a night, eh boss?"

"Yeah." Cooper took the gun from his belt and secured it in the strong box under the bar. "How's Hayley?"

"I don't know. I haven't seen her since I took her upstairs."

"How was she when you brought her inside?"

"She didn't say much. Just watched me check the loft and then locked the door behind me like you told her to."

Pete sat on a stool across from Cooper and propped his elbow on the bar. "She looked upset. Man, I thought she might pass out when she saw the blood."

"How was she this morning after Nina left?"

"She looked kind of sick then, too. It was some turnaround from before the kid got here. Hayley had been going around all morning with this sappy smile on her face. Whatever you two did last night—"

"Did she tell you what Nina talked about?" Cooper interrupted.

"No. She was in a big hurry to get to the bank."

Cooper set the glass down and poured another shot. Some of the liquid splashed onto the bar. Moving mechanically, he reached for a towel, but there weren't any left. He swiped at the drops with his hand, doing his best to anchor his mind on the small task while reality continued to shift around him.

It all made sense now. Nina must have told Hayley that Adam had been on Sproule's payroll. That was why Hayley had gone to the bank. She was a forensic accountant and would want to verify the information by following the money trail. She had power of attorney for her father and was the executor of her brother's will, so she wouldn't need a warrant to look at her family's accounts.

What had she found?

If we keep chasing Sproule, we're going to stir up more trouble than we bargained for. People are going to get hurt.

That was what she had said. He had assumed she had meant the two of them. She had obviously been talking about someone else.

"What's going on, Coop?" Pete asked. "You don't look so good."

People are going to get hurt.

Cooper concentrated on keeping his hands steady as he

replaced the cap and put away the bottle. He left his drink on the bar and moved to the front door. "I'm fine. Go home, Pete. I'll finish locking up."

As soon as Pete left, Cooper set the bolt, activated the alarm and returned to the bar. Instead of moving behind it, he sank down on a stool, dropped his head in his hands and stared at the whiskey in his glass. It was good stuff, triple malt. He didn't pad his profits by watering it down or pouring cheap brands into good bottles. He ran a clean place. He was proud of what he'd built here.

Hayley wanted him to give up the Long Shot because that would be the price of letting Sproule go. It was obvious now why she had been so desperate to convince him. If Sproule was arrested by authorities who weren't part of a coverup, and if there was a genuine investigation into Sproule's criminal dealings, then the truth about *all* of those dealings was bound to come out.

Cooper remembered how frail her father had seemed when he'd lifted him into bed. Hayley would think she had no choice—learning the truth about Saint Adam would set back Ernie's recovery. It might even kill him.

Just because my brother wasn't perfect doesn't mean that I don't love him.

Hayley's feelings for her brother and her father ran deep. Her loyalty was only one of the things Cooper admired about her. This must be tearing her apart. No wonder she had been so close to tears all day. She would do anything for her family.

Anything. Even if it meant saying that she loved him?

Could she have lied?

Cooper refused to believe she had. Not Hayley. She might be able to keep things inside, but she'd never been able to lie worth a damn.

She had said that she loved him, and he'd seen the truth in her eyes. He'd felt it in her touch. The woman who had lived in his home, who had slept in his bed and had come apart in his arms again and again would be incapable of lying about love.

And what he felt was real. Despite knowing what he did now, his feelings for Hayley hadn't changed. He couldn't push them back inside. Whatever it cost, he still wanted her.

Whatever it cost…

He moved his gaze around the room, looking at the place that had been more than a home to him for four years. He was so close to fulfilling his dream. He didn't want to lose it now.

But he didn't want to lose Hayley, either. He would do anything to make her happy.

Anything.

He snatched up his drink, gulped the whiskey down and pitched the glass across the room. It shattered against the wall, sending fragments of glass skidding over the hardwood floor. Before the noise could fade, Cooper had moved to the corner of the bar, picked up the phone and punched in Tony Monaco's number.

After four rings, there was a series of clicks as the call was transferred and the ringing started again. It was answered on the seventh ring by Tony himself. The velvet baritone voice that came through the line sounded annoyed. "This better be important."

Cooper could hear music in the background, some quiet, classical stuff, along with the clink of crystal. He had no way of knowing which of Tony's houses he'd reached, so he couldn't guess what time zone the man was in. "Yeah, it's important."

"Cooper. I hope you're calling to tell me you're finished."

"Not in the way you think. Our deal is off, Tony. I'm dropping out of Payback."

"Do you need more time?"

"Time isn't going to change my decision. I'm giving up on Sproule."

"What about the Long Shot?"

Cooper took one last look around, a hollow ache settling in his gut. "Take it. It's yours."

There was a pause, followed by the sound of footsteps on marble. The music faded. "What's going on, Cooper? I heard you were making progress."

"Yeah, well, something came up."

"Tell me."

"Look, Tony, if I could pay you back, I would. I know I still owe you. You gave me a break when no one else would."

"I wasn't giving you a break. We had a bargain. Now I'd like to know why you're reneging on it."

He put his free hand on the edge of the bar, splaying his fingers over the varnished pine. He had done the action so many times, the feel of the wood was imprinted in his memory. "It was good while it lasted but it's time to move on."

"This is about the woman, isn't it? Hayley Tavistock."

There was no point denying this. If Tony wanted to know something, he had a way of finding out. "Yes."

"Why?"

"If I get Sproule like you wanted, it's going to destroy what's left of her family. I don't want to hurt her."

"So that's it? You're walking away from something you've sweated toward for four years because of a woman?"

"That's the way it has to be."

"I hope she's worth it."

Cooper didn't even have to think about his reply. "Oh, yeah," he said. "She's worth it."

Through the phone line came the chink of glass against crystal. The volume of the music increased. "All right," Tony said briskly. "I'll give you twenty-four hours to clear out before I send someone over. You know the deal. Make sure you leave with no more than you brought."

"Understood."

"The number you dialed will be disconnected as soon as you hang up."

"Right."

"Good luck."

Cooper replaced the receiver. Now that things had been set into motion, there was no stopping them.

He was officially out of Payback. He wouldn't be talking to Tony Monaco again because he would have no way to reach him. The twenty-four hours Tony had given him had been only a courtesy—it wouldn't take that long to pack the two sets of clothes and the $532.00 that Cooper had arrived here with four years ago.

He didn't waste time with regrets. They were useless. He still had one more call to make. He pulled the phone closer and dialed another number.

"Sproule residence."

The voice of the man who answered had the trace of an English accent. No doubt one of the servants at the estate, Cooper thought. The rest of Sproule's men must be busy. "It's Webb. Let me talk to him."

"I'm sorry, Mr. Webb, but Mr. Sproule is out for the evening."

"Yeah, establishing an alibi."

"I assure you, I don't know what you mean. Do you wish to leave a message?"

"Tell him to call me."

"And may I inquire to what this pertains?"

"Sure. I—" Cooper paused and tilted his head to listen. He thought he'd heard a noise from the back hall. Had Hayley come downstairs to look for him?

"Sir?"

He turned his attention back to the phone. He wanted to have this settled before he saw her. They were going to have little enough time as it was before they would have to clear out, and he wanted their last night here to be—

The noise came again. It was a clunk of metal on metal, a heavy, full sound, like two large cans knocking together.

Cooper dropped the phone and vaulted over the bar to reach for the strongbox.

Before he could work the lock, the back door of the barroom flew open and slammed against the wall. A familiar gaunt, silver-haired man was framed in the opening, a gun gleaming in his hand.

Cooper had a moment of disbelief. How could Sproule be here? How could anyone have gotten inside without tripping the alarm?

The answers burst across his mind: the open front door, the confusion in the parking lot after the shooting. Izzy had served as a distraction while someone must have disabled the alarm. If they'd had enough time, they could have sabotaged the locks, too, to make it easier to get inside. Sproule hadn't gone far, he'd only been waiting for his opportunity. His primary target hadn't been Izzy, it had been the Long Shot.

And the people who were in it.

Hayley! Oh, God no!

"Sproule, don't!" Cooper said. "It's over. You win."

"Of course, I win, Webb. The outcome of this little war

you started was never in doubt." Sproule gestured with the barrel of his gun as he walked past the pool tables. "Hands where I can see them."

A red-haired man moved into the barroom behind Sproule. He didn't look familiar to Cooper; he couldn't be one of Sproule's regular men. He was wearing coveralls and gloves, and he was carrying a pair of square metal containers. Cooper caught a whiff of gasoline.

The lock of the strongbox finally clicked. Cooper slipped his hand inside. "Listen to me, Sproule! I'm backing off. The war's over. You don't have to do this."

"On the contrary. If I want something done right, I need to do it myself. Hands up. Now!"

"I swear. We were pulling out tomorrow. Just let us walk out of here and no one has to get hurt."

"You're wasting my time." Sproule glanced at the redhaired man. "Bring in the rest of the gas cans. You'd better use enough to make sure there won't be any survivors this time."

The instant the man moved off, Cooper closed his hand around the butt of his pistol and swung it toward Sproule.

Pain exploded in his left shoulder. The impact of the bullet knocked him backward into a row of beer mugs, sending them crashing to the floor. He fought to keep his grip on his weapon, but before he could aim it, Sproule levelled his gun at Cooper's head.

"Drop your weapon and come out from behind the bar, Webb," Sproule ordered. "I'd prefer to have you alive to see this, but if I have to shoot you again, I will."

Cooper staggered through the opening of the bar, his boots crunching on glass shards. He let the gun slide from his fingers so that it dropped to the floor at his feet.

"Very good. Now kick it over here."

With Sproule's gun pointed at his head, Cooper decided it wasn't the time to try anything. He hung on to the bar for balance and drew back his foot to send his pistol skidding to the opposite side of the pool tables from Sproule. "Leave Hayley alone, Sproule. Let her go. I started this, not her."

"She's been a thorn in my side for seven months. Don't insult my intelligence by expecting me to let her go." He kept his gaze on Cooper, his gun never wavering. "I watched your friends leave. They're busy chasing my men all over town, so I know you won't be pulling any surprises on me this time. There are only the two of you left here. This is my night for tying up loose ends."

"Then let Hayley walk. That's what she wants." He could feel blood pulsing from his shoulder to run down his arm. He pressed his palm over the wound and whitehot agony knifed to his bones. The room spun for a minute before he was able to speak again. "She's had enough."

"So have I, Webb. You and your girlfriend and this dump you run are all finished. It will serve as an example of what happens to people who oppose me."

The coveralled man returned with more cans, set them down with the others, then opened one and moved around the room, methodically pouring gasoline along the base of the walls, on the wooden tables and upended chairs and on the hardwood floor. He picked up another container and disappeared down the back hall.

Cooper shook with helpless rage. Not because Sproule meant to destroy the Long Shot, but because he was going to hurt Hayley. More than hurt. He planned to have her burned alive, just as he'd tried a week ago.

Gritting his teeth, Cooper ground his palm against his

wound, using the pain to keep his temper in check and focus his thoughts. He wouldn't be any good to Hayley if he got himself killed before he could help her.

"Go ahead and torch the place, if that's what it takes," Cooper said. Careful to keep out of the puddles of gasoline, he managed to take a few steps in the direction of the pool tables. "But leave Hayley out of this. She's no threat to you now. She found out that her brother was on your payroll, so she doesn't want to see you in prison."

"Ah, so she already knows." Sproule's mouth twisted in an expression that was too tight to call a smile. "What a shame. After the slanderous comments she made to the press about me, I would have enjoyed seeing her face when she found that out."

"She's no threat," Cooper repeated. Feigning more weakness than he felt, he wavered on his feet, then stumbled backward and fell on a dry patch of the floor.

Sproule fired a round at the pool table to Cooper's left. The bullet ricocheted from the slate top and struck the rack of pool cues. "Don't even think about going for the gun you dropped," Sproule said. "I'm in control now, Webb. Get back on your feet. I don't want you to miss the main event."

Cooper got to his knees, pausing to catch his breath. Damn, if he didn't make his move soon, the weakness wouldn't be faked. He needed to get closer if he was going to have any hope of reaching that weapon, but it was good to know the table would provide cover...

His thoughts lurched to a stop. He glimpsed a movement in the doorway behind Sproule. It wasn't the red-haired arsonist. It was a blond woman.

No, Hayley! Cooper thought. *Leave now! Run!*

Hayley stepped over the threshold as silently as a

shadow. Her face was drained of color, her eyes were clouded with horror…and in her hands she carried her father's old Winchester.

Chapter 15

No nightmare could have been worse. There was so much blood. It glistened from Cooper's sleeve, it ran down his arm and it was dripping on the floor where he knelt.

But his ice-blue gaze was more intense, more beautiful and more vital than Hayley had ever seen it. She could feel his presence reach across the distance between them, strengthening her as it always did.

Somehow, she managed to swallow the bile that rose in her throat and took three quick sideways steps that would place the wall at her back. She had slipped out of the storeroom just as the man with the gas cans had gone into the stairwell to the loft, but she knew he could return at any time.

"Put the gun down, Oliver," she said.

Sproule jerked. He lowered the gun to his side but he didn't drop it. Instead, he turned slowly toward her. "I'm glad you could join us, Hayley. I was concerned you would miss the party."

At the sight of his face, Hayley trembled with an echo of the fury that had propelled her through the last seven months. This was the same way he had looked at her in the courtroom whenever their eyes had met. His gaze was chilled with arrogance, his mouth twisted with disdain.

This was her brother's killer, the monster who had gone back to kick the man he had run down.

But it wasn't hate for Sproule that had brought her here. Her urge for revenge wasn't what had made her pick up her father's rifle. She was here because she was in love with Cooper.

"Hayley," Cooper said. "For God's sake, get out of here while you can."

She tightened her grip on the rifle, pressing the butt snug against her shoulder. "I'm not leaving you, Cooper."

"What do you expect to do with that relic?" Sproule asked, tipping his head dismissively at her rifle. "You don't even have the strength to hold it."

She ignored Sproule's taunt as she used her right hand to work the bolt, then curled her index finger around the trigger. "I called the police. They're on their way."

Sproule sneered. "The police won't touch me. You don't think your brother was the only one in my pocket, do you?"

At Sproule's remark she reflexively flicked her gaze to Cooper. She didn't see surprise on his face, she saw... sympathy.

The truth flashed through her mind. *He knew about Adam.*

Hayley wanted to explain, to apologize and to beg his forgiveness for what she had kept from him. It had been madness to ask him to quit. She'd known it even before the words had left her mouth, but then Cooper had repaid her selfishness by opening his heart. He had shown her his vulnerability, he had let her see the goodness in his soul.

Oh, how was it possible to love him more?

Yet what he thought of her, or whether he could ever forgive her, was of no importance right now. Cooper's life was seeping out of him as she watched. She wanted to stall Sproule until the police got here, but how much time had passed since she had heard the shot? She prayed Cooper could hang on until the ambulance arrived.

It couldn't be over. Dear, God, it couldn't end like this.

"It will all come out at your trial," Hayley said. "You're going to pay for what you did to Adam. You're going to be charged with murder this time."

"It's all right, Hayley," Cooper said. "He knows we're giving up. I told him we're quitting."

Was Cooper trying to bluff? She didn't want to risk taking her gaze off Sproule to look at him again. "It's too late, Cooper. I've already put it into motion."

"Hayley…" Cooper began.

"That's what I was doing when I saw you and your friend arrive, Oliver," she continued. Was that a siren? Her pulse was hammering so loudly in her ears she couldn't be sure. "I was on the phone with the state police. I've told them where to find the evidence against Adam. The trail of bribes leads right back to you."

"Don't expect me to believe that," Sproule said. "The high and mighty Tavistocks wouldn't want their dirty little secrets aired in public."

"Nothing can stop it now," Hayley said. "Killing Cooper and me won't do you any good. I e-mailed the files I've collected on your businesses to the FBI. The truth is going to come out."

"You don't have anything."

"But the investigation into my brother's death is sure to justify warrants that will expose everyone else who is on your payroll," she said. "Drop your gun. You're finished."

Sproule laughed. It was a sharp, grating sound. "I still don't believe you, Hayley. And you're not going to pull that trigger. That gun probably isn't even loaded. You're as spineless as Adam." His hand twitched. Light glinted from the barrel of his gun. "Do you want to know why I killed him?"

"It doesn't matter," Cooper said. From the corner of her eye, Hayley saw him push himself backward along the floor. "Hayley, you don't need to do this. Just leave."

"Your brother wanted to leave, too," Sproule said. "He didn't approve of my new business partner. He was going to foul up the whole deal, and this after I had invested so much in him."

Hayley's arms were beginning to tire from the weight of the rifle. Her palms were sweating so badly that the stock slipped. Were those footsteps in the hall or her own heartbeat? "My brother made mistakes, but that doesn't change how I feel about him. Real love doesn't come with conditions."

"Oh, spare me the sentiment. You're wasting my time."

"But even though I love Adam, I'm not going to live in his shadow. I won't let him stand between me and—"

"This has gone on long enough," Sproule snapped. "Let's get on with business." He lifted his hand with a flourish. The barrel of his gun pointed not at Hayley, but at Cooper.

Hayley's mind froze on a silent scream. No, *no!*

Time slowed to a crawl. It had been more than two weeks since Hayley had held this rifle, over sixteen years since she had fired it, yet as she saw Sproule take aim at Cooper, all her father's lessons came back to her.

Keep your eye on your target. Breathe slow and easy. Concentrate and squeeze.

She hadn't been able to do it to avenge her brother.

But to save the man she loved, she would do anything.

Hayley's shaking hands suddenly became rock-steady and her grip firmed. She focused on Sproule, exhaled slowly and pulled the trigger.

Time clicked back on track. The recoil from the powerful rifle knocked Hayley against the wall, her ears ringing from the noise of the shot.

Sproule's shot went wide and hit one of the light fixtures, touching off a shower of sparks. He dropped his gun and crumpled to his knees. His mouth rounding in shock, he stared at the crimson circle blossoming on his chest.

Hayley gagged, bent over and fought to keep her stomach from heaving.

Cooper launched himself in a skidding dive across the floor between the pool tables, came up with a gun and fired toward the doorway.

Hayley glanced behind her just as the coveralled man fell over the threshold, his forehead cracking hard against the edge of a discarded gas can. A small black pistol fell from his hand as he slumped to the floor and didn't move.

She whipped her gaze back to Cooper. He was leaning heavily against the edge of the pool table as he worked his way around it toward her, his face pale with pain. He pressed the heel of his hand to his shoulder.

Sproule moaned and toppled sideways. His eyes unfocused, he squirmed on the floor as his blood mixed with a puddle of gasoline.

"Hayley!" Cooper's voice was raw with urgency. It snapped her out of her daze. "We've got to get out of here now!"

Hayley slung the strap of the Winchester over her shoulder and ran to Cooper. His condition looked worse the closer she got. "I called the ambulance when I heard the shot," she said. She touched her fingers to his forehead and found it was clammy. "It might be better if you don't move."

He put his arm around her and pushed away from the table. "We don't have any choice. The whole place is going to go up!"

Only then did she smell the smoke. She looked past Cooper and saw flames racing across a puddle of gas beneath the sparking light fixture that Sproule's stray bullet had hit. Fire licked up the legs of a table, igniting with a *whoosh*. It was a sound she would never forget, a noise from another nightmare.

It still wasn't over.

There was no time to help the two men on the floor. Hayley dropped her rifle and anchored her arms around Cooper's waist as she fitted herself to his side. Locked together, they wove through the flames that were spreading across the room. Hayley could feel Cooper's muscles tremble from the effort it took for him to stay upright, but somehow they reached the front door without falling.

They made it to the parking lot just as the first police car pulled in. The police raced for the men who were left inside but were met with a wall of flame. The red-haired arsonist had done his job too well. The interior of the building had become an inferno.

Cooper sat on the hood of the police cruiser as more emergency vehicles arrived, his expression strangely calm while he watched the Long Shot burn.

But Hayley was frantic. This couldn't be happening. Not *now!*

Someone draped a blanket around her shoulders. She

clutched it tight, despite the heat from the blaze, her body shaking from the force of her sobs. It wasn't fair, dear God, this wasn't right. The place that meant so much to Cooper, the symbol of the life he'd so painstakingly built, was disappearing before her eyes and there was nothing she could do to save it.

The paramedics tended to Cooper where he sat, preparing him for the ride to the hospital by packing his wound to stop the bleeding and hooking him up with an IV drip that hung from a wheeled pole. They draped a blanket like Hayley's around his back and deemed him stable enough to wait while they saw to the burns of the first policemen who had tried to enter the building. As soon as they had moved off, Cooper held out his hand to Hayley.

She clasped his fingers and moved to stand between his knees. The night was filled with sirens and flashing lights as fire trucks continued to converge on the scene, yet Hayley felt a pocket of stillness settle around them. There were so many things she wanted to say, but none of them could get past the lump in her throat. She lifted his hand and pressed her mouth to his knuckles.

"Don't cry, Hayley."

She shook her head against a fresh wave of tears. "I'm sorry, Cooper. I'm so sorry. I should have told you about Adam sooner."

"It's okay. I understand why you didn't."

How could he sound so calm, so…forgiving? She rubbed her cheek against his fingers. "I was wrong. I should have realized how much your promise meant to you."

"No, Hayley, you were right. I didn't need the Long Shot."

He was already talking about it in the past tense. She hiccupped on a sob.

"It's like what you told me," he said. "I thought that if

I did this one last thing, everything was going to magically change, but I was wrong. What I've built here, no one can take away from me."

She lifted her head and met his gaze. Incredibly, he was smiling.

"I already called Tony and told him I'm quitting Payback. I was going to let Sproule go, just like you wanted."

She stared. "You *what?*"

"I wasn't bluffing when I told Sproule we were giving up."

It took a moment for what he had said to sink in. "Oh, my God, Cooper. You didn't have to do that. I wasn't bluffing, either. I really did call the FBI. I told them about Adam. They're going to hold off until Dr. Byers and I can break the news to my father, but she said the risk was manageable and she'd get him counseling so—" She broke off as a sudden flare of light bathed the parking lot. She twisted to look behind her.

The roof of the Long Shot collapsed. A fountain of smoke and embers streamed into the sky, filling the night with a glow as red as blood.

She gave a strangled cry. "No!"

Cooper squeezed her hand and pulled her to face him. "Hayley, it's okay. It's only a place."

"But—"

"We'll be fine. We can rebuild." His smile grew. "I was right about you."

"What?"

"You can't lie worth a damn."

She used her free hand to wipe her cheeks. "Cooper—"

"I knew what you told Sproule was the truth, just like I knew you were telling the truth when you said that you loved me." He used his thumb to blot a tear that she'd missed. "You never needed to prove anything to me, but you did."

"I meant everything I said, Cooper. I do love you. I never want to leave you."

"Good, because I'm not planning on letting you go." He leaned toward her, pure emotion sparkling in his gaze. "I love you, Hayley Tavistock."

Another fire truck rolled over the curb. Shouts went up as hoses were unrolled to add more streams of water to the billowing flames. The crackle of the police radio came through the open window of the cruiser where Cooper sat.

Yet Hayley heard nothing but the sound of walls crumbling as Cooper laid bare his heart.

She grasped his cheeks in her hands. "And I love you, Cooper Webb."

Neither of them knew who moved first. All Hayley remembered afterward was that even with a bullet in his shoulder and an IV drip in his arm, his business in flames and the entire Latchford fire department milling around them, oh, this man could kiss.

Epilogue

"Rise and shine, you two! You have a visitor."

Hayley folded her arms on Cooper's chest and glanced at the bedroom door. "Maybe if we're really quiet she'll go away," she whispered.

Cooper stretched his arm over the edge of the mattress, picked up one of his boots and heaved it at the door. It hit the panels with a resounding thud. "Go away, Theresa," he shouted.

Hayley pressed her mouth against Cooper's good shoulder to muffle her giggle.

Theresa laughed and knocked at the door again. "Ten minutes, then I'm sending him up."

"You do and you're fired!" Cooper said.

"You'd have to hire me first," Theresa retorted.

Hayley rolled off Cooper and got to her feet. She reached for the silk kimono their current landlady had lent her. They had been staying in the Martinez's spare bedroom since the fire. "Thanks, Theresa. We'll be right down."

Cooper caught the end of the sash before she could tie it and tugged her back to the bed. "What's your hurry? We've got ten minutes."

"It's probably Detective Ford or one of those FBI agents again. I need a shower before I get dressed."

Cooper sat up against the headboard and patted the spot beside him. He smiled. "Okay, five minutes. I'll work fast."

She couldn't resist him when he smiled like that. Actually, she was coming to realize that he was impossible to resist no matter what he did. There was just something about the way his hair fell across his forehead and those lines framed his mouth and that bad boy sparkle lit his eyes…

She sighed and got back into bed. She snuggled against his side, laid her head on his chest and opened her robe so she could slide her leg over his.

She cherished these quiet times with Cooper. The past three days had been some of the busiest of her life. As soon as Cooper had been released from the hospital, they'd been swept into what seemed like endless rounds of questioning by every law-enforcement agency that wanted a piece of the Sproule organization, even though Sproule himself had already paid the ultimate price for his crimes.

Ironically, Izzy Pressman was turning out to be the star witness. Against all odds, he'd survived Sproule's attempt on his life and had started talking the minute he'd come out of surgery. Sproule's accomplices were falling like dominoes.

As Hayley had predicted, the warrants that had arisen from the information she had revealed about Adam had uncovered the full extent of the police corruption. At the top was Jim Johnson, the man who had replaced Hayley's father as the Latchford police commissioner. Ernie had told him about Hayley's plan to investigate Sproule's smuggling, and he'd been the one to alert Sproule.

Ernie hadn't taken the news of his friend's betrayal any better than the news about Adam. He'd suffered a major setback, but the doctors were optimistic that he would eventually regain the ground he'd lost and continue his recovery, especially now that the nursing home had brought in a specialist in geriatric psychology.

Cooper picked up a lock of her hair and stroked it along her wrist. "I've got a lead on an apartment. It's not fancy, but we can move in by the end of the week."

"That's great."

"We won't have much to move in."

She turned her head to brush her lips over his nipple. "We don't need much, Cooper. We already have the most important thing."

"A bed?"

"Love."

"Well, yeah. That kind of goes along with the whole bed theme, doesn't it?"

"Mmm. We don't do so bad on the floor, either."

He gave her a one-armed hug. Although his wound was healing with amazing swiftness, his left shoulder would be tender for a while yet. "Have you heard back from that banker?"

"Yes." She lifted her head to look at him. "Sorry, Cooper. He won't give us the amount we'll need. But it's still early. I've got feelers out everywhere. We'll find an investor somewhere to rebuild the Long Shot."

He picked up her hair again and twined it around his fingers. "I've been thinking about that. Maybe we should call it something else."

"Such as?"

"What would you say to the Sure Thing?"

"I like the sound of that."

He looked at her in silence for a while, his gaze brimming with the love he didn't even think to hide. "Hayley, what would you say if we made us a sure thing, too?"

"I thought we already were."

"I mean legally. I know I'm a long way from being able to offer you the kind of home I wish I could, but like you said, we've already got the most important thing."

She smiled. "Oh, we've got plenty of that."

He took her hand. "The love I feel for you isn't going to change. Today, tomorrow, until I draw my last breath, I'll be loving you. So…" He pressed her hand over his heart. "Hayley, will you marry me?"

Her gaze misted. Despite all the obstacles they'd had to overcome, and despite all the problems that awaited them, this part really was simple, wasn't it?

She rose to her knees and cradled his face in her palms. "Cooper, I would be honored to have you for my husband."

Their kiss started out as solemn as the pledge they had just made, yet it didn't take long for the passion to spark again. Cooper slipped his hands into her robe, then grasped her waist and guided her to straddle his lap.

It was a good hour, a very good hour, before they finally went downstairs.

The person waiting for them in the Martinez's kitchen wasn't a cop. No, Nathan Beliveau wouldn't be mistaken for the law any more than Cooper would. He was wearing his riding leathers, his long legs stretched out and crossed at the ankles as he drummed his fingers against a large white envelope that lay on the kitchen table beside his helmet.

He rose to his feet when they entered. "I heard about your trouble," he said. "How are you doing?"

Cooper slipped his right arm around Hayley's waist and pulled her back against his chest. "Never been better," he replied. "Sorry about Volski. I heard he went underground when the business with Sproule hit the fan."

Nathan nodded. "Like a rat to his hole. I'll smoke him out."

Hayley pressed into Cooper's embrace. There was a hint of ruthlessness in Nathan's tone that chilled. "I wish you luck."

"Thanks." Nathan glanced at the way they stood together before his amber gaze met hers. "I don't suppose you'll be taking me up on that job offer."

She shook her head and covered Cooper's hand with hers. "No. I'm sticking with a sure thing."

Cooper chuckled. "Hayley's one hell of a bookkeeper. She's got a job with me for life."

"That's what Tony figured." Nathan reached for the white envelope and held it out to Cooper. "He sends his regards."

Cooper's expression sobered. He let go of Hayley and took the envelope. "Tony? What does he want?"

"Seems there was a problem with the transfer of the Long Shot when you terminated your deal. Tony never received his property."

Hayley frowned. "Sproule was the one who burned it down, not us. Tony isn't holding Cooper liable for that, is he?"

"I'm afraid so," Nathan replied. "Tony had given him twenty-four hours to clear out. The place burned down on his watch, so Tony wants recompense."

"But that's not fair," Hayley said.

"Take that up with Tony," Nathan said. "I don't know the details, I only delivered the package." He picked up his helmet and walked to the door. "But as far as I'm concerned, you still owe me a favor, too."

Cooper waited until Nathan was gone, then swore under his breath and ripped open the envelope. He withdrew a sheaf of papers and scowled at them for a few minutes before handing the papers to Hayley. "Here. They've got numbers. You'll be able to make more sense of them than I can."

Hayley skimmed them quickly. She gasped, then went back over them more carefully to make sure she hadn't missed something. When she was done, she held them out to Cooper, her pulse racing. "This has nothing to do with Payback. It's a legitimate partnership agreement."

"What?"

"Tony wants to be a silent partner in your next bar. He'll provide the start-up capital in exchange for a fixed share of the profits."

Cooper retrieved the papers from her, his big hands suddenly unsteady. He went through them again, then swallowed hard and looked at Hayley. His frown was gone. In its place was a dawning sense of wonder. "He was wrong."

"No, it's a smart idea, and it's a fair deal for both of you. Your new place will be even better than the last one."

"Our new place, Hayley. Not mine. Ours." He laid the papers on the table and caught her hands in his. "I meant Tony was wrong about Payback."

"How?"

"He had told me I would leave with no more than I brought in." His voice roughened. He inhaled deeply and curled her hands to his chest. "But he was wrong. My life is richer than I dared to dream it could be."

"You earned it, Cooper. You earned every bit of it."

He drew her closer, his smile as warm as his touch. "I'm not talking about the money, Hayley."

"I know, my love. Neither am I."

* * * * *

Coming in June 2005 from Intimate Moments,
watch for LOVING THE LONE WOLF
by Ingrid Weaver.
In this provocative second installment
in the PAYBACK series,
it's renegade millionaire Nathan Beliveau's turn
to repay his debt to his mysterious benefactor…
but will it come at the ultimate *price?*

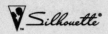

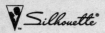

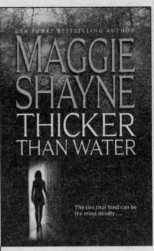

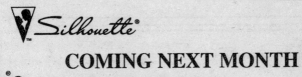

COMING NEXT MONTH

#1357 SWEPT AWAY—Karen Templeton
The Men of Mayes County
Oklahoma farmer Sam Franzier and Carly Stewart weren't likely to get along: he was a single father of six, and she wasn't one for children. But when the two unexpectedly became neighbors, Carly found herself charmed by his kids and falling for this handsome family man. Problem was, love simply wasn't in Sam's plans—or was it?

#1358 RECONCILABLE DIFFERENCES—Ana Leigh
Bishop's Heroes
When Tricia Manning and Dave Cassidy were accused of murdering her husband, they did all they could to clear their names. Working closely, the passion from their past began to flare. But Dave wasn't willing to risk his heart and Tricia was afraid to trust another man. Could a twist of fate reconcile their differences?

#1359 MIDNIGHT HERO—Diana Duncan
Forever in a Day
As time ticked down to an explosive detonation, SWAT team agent Conall O'Rourke and bookstore manager Bailey Chambers worked to save innocent hostages and themselves. The siege occurred just hours after Bailey had broken Con's heart, and he was determined to get her back. This ordeal would either cement their bond or end their love—and possibly their lives.

#1360 COLE DEMPSEY'S BACK IN TOWN—
Suzanne McMinn
Now a successful lawyer, Cole Dempsey was back in town and there would be hell to pay. Years ago his father had been accused of a crime he didn't commit and Cole was out to clear his name—even if it meant involving long-lost love Bryn Louvel. Cole and Bryn were determined to fight the demons of the past while emerging secrets threatened their future.

#1361 BLUE JEANS AND A BADGE—Nina Bruhns
Bounty hunter Luce Montgomery and chief of police Philip O'Donnaugh were on the prowl for a fugitive. As the stakes rose, so did their mutual attraction. Philip was desperate to break through the wall between them but Luce was still reeling from revelations about her past that even blue jeans and a badge might not cure....

#1362 TO LOVE, HONOR AND DEFEND—Beth Cornelison
Someone was after attorney Libby Hopkins and she would do anything for extra protection. So when firefighter Cal Walters proposed a marriage of convenience to help him win custody of his daughter, she agreed. Close quarters caused old feelings to resurface but Libby had always put her career first. Could Cal show Libby how to honor, defend *and* love?

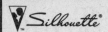